D0019024

Previously published Worldwide Suspense titles by
MEGHAN HOLLOWAY

HUNTING GROUND

HIDING PLACE

MEGHAN HOLLOWAY

W RLDWIDE

TORONTO • NEW YORK • LONDON
AMSTERDAM • PARIS • SYDNEY • HAMBURG
STOCKHOLM • ATHENS • TOKYO • MILAN
MADRID • WARSAW • BUDAPEST • AUCKLAND

If you purchased this book without a cover you should be aware that this book is stolen property. It was reported as "unsold and destroyed" to the publisher, and neither the author nor the publisher has received any payment for this "stripped book."

WORLDWIDE™

ISBN-13: 978-1-335-47506-0

Hiding Place

First published in 2021 by Polis Books, LLC.
This edition published in 2022 with revised text.

Recycling programs
for this product may
not exist in your area.

Copyright © 2021 by A. Meghan Holloway
Copyright © 2022 by A. Meghan Holloway, revised text edition

All rights reserved. No part of this book may be reproduced or transmitted in any form or by any means, electronic or mechanical, including photocopying, recording or by any information storage and retrieval system, without permission in writing from the publisher.

This is a work of fiction. Names, characters, places and incidents are either the product of the author's imagination or are used fictitiously. Any resemblance to actual persons, living or dead, businesses, companies, events or locales is entirely coincidental.

For questions and comments about the quality of this book, please contact us at CustomerService@Harlequin.com.

Harlequin Enterprises ULC
22 Adelaide St. West, 41st Floor
Toronto, Ontario M5H 4E3, Canada
www.ReaderService.com

Printed in U.S.A.

HIDING PLACE

For Rickie.

Every woman should be lucky enough to have a friend so ready to say "I'll bring a shovel" when you tell her there's a body.

PART ONE

ONE

HECTOR

She was sitting on the cinder block that served as my front stoop when I arrived home.

I parked my truck in front of the Airstream trailer. The days were beginning to lengthen as spring struggled to loosen winter's grip on the land. A slant of dying sunlight gleamed on her hair and glinted off the side of the tin can I called home. I had scrubbed and scraped, but the red MURDERER scrawled across the aluminum exterior had never fully disappeared.

Frank's ears pricked when he noticed our visitor, and he let out a low whine. When I opened the door, the standard poodle leapt down and loped over to greet her. I leaned against the front bumper to wait.

She called herself Faye Anders. She had a driver's license that backed it up. I studied it two months after she moved to town when I pulled her over for having a broken tail light. She was compliant with my request for license and registration. She was unfailingly polite. And she was terrified.

She arrived in Raven's Gap, Montana four years ago with her young son, Sam. She had purchased an old property on an oxbow of the Yellowstone River at the east end of town. The inn was decrepit when she purchased it, but it was a prime location. After she finished remodeling the interior and opened it to visitors, The River Inn remained full from March until October.

Despite the business the inn brought to town, its proprietor remained aloof. As far as I had ever seen or heard, people knew her name and that her huckleberry pancakes were so good a man would sell his mother for a stack of them. But that was it. Only this year had she put her son in the public elementary school in Gardiner.

I knew a woman in hiding when I saw her.

She ran her fingers through Frank's topknot, and the poodle leaned against her bent knees. Faye's son, Sam, was not with her, I realized, and I glanced around to see if he was playing in the surrounding meadow. Nothing moved through the new growth of alpine wildflowers except for the wind.

When I turned back to the woman on my doorstep, she was watching me. I folded my arms across my chest and waited for her to break the silence.

It only took her a few moments.

"I need your help." Her voice was quiet and held the educated, upper crust clip of the East Coast. She paused, and I could see she was waiting for me to respond. When I did not, she continued. "Sam didn't come home from a school field trip today."

"What did the school say?"

Her fingers tapped a nervous rhythm on her thigh. "His teacher said she counted him with the class just as they were loading onto the bus, but when they got back to school, he wasn't with his class."

"Did you go to the station?" There was a time when family and friends had to wait a specified amount of hours after someone was missing before reporting the individual to the police. Those days were gone.

She dropped her gaze to Frank's topknot as she parsed his curls. "No," she said. "I came to you."

I studied her. She was a young woman, in her early to mid-thirties, but there was a wariness about her that made her seem older. Her face had a stillness to it, an alert and careful watchfulness that reminded me of a prey animal. "I'm off duty for the day. Go to the station and report him as missing."

Her eyes met mine, and for an instant, I saw the terror I had seen when I pulled her over before that composed, still mask fell in place. "I can't do that. Missing persons reports are available nationwide through NCIC."

It was a quiet acknowledgement of what I had already guessed about her. She was in this remote western outpost of civilization to avoid being found.

I had no desire to become entangled in someone else's issues. I had my own to deal with.

"Like I said, I'm off duty. You need help finding your boy, go to the police."

"You're still wearing your badge," she said, a hard edge creeping into her voice. "And Frank is a search and rescue dog." She withdrew a neatly folded t-shirt from the pocket of her jacket and held it out to me. "I brought this so Frank would have something of Sam's to smell. I just need—"

"Go through the process of reporting him missing." I whistled for Frank, and he reluctantly left Faye and came to my side. "When the call comes from the SAR team, Frank and I will look for him."

She drew a small Glock from a concealed holster at her side and placed it across her knee. I stiffened and straightened.

"I'm afraid I can't take no for an answer," she said softly. "I know where Sam is. I just need you to help me bring him home."

"You're going to threaten a police officer?" I did not reach for my own weapon.

She arched an eyebrow. "I'm not threatening you. I'm asking you, and I need you to know the only answer I will accept from you is a yes. And like you said, you're off duty."

She was either stupid or desperate. I stared at her for a long moment. Though her gaze was straightforward and the pistol balanced on her knee was compact and deadly, there was tension around her eyes and a tremor in her fingers. My bet was on desperate, but desperation made people do stupid things.

I sighed. "Put the gun away before I have to arrest you."

She stood as I approached, the Glock disappearing under her jacket. My gaze swept over her and took in the slight difference in the shape of her jeans at her right ankle. Another concealed holster. The woman was bristling with weapons, but she did not pull any more on me.

She moved aside to let me enter the Airstream. I opened the door, and Frank darted within. Faye followed close on my heels and stood in the open doorway.

"You said you know where he is?" I asked.

"The school field trip was to Broken Arrow Ranch to see the new foals."

"Grant Larson's ranch?" I took the department-issued holster belt off and sighed at the immediate relief to my lower back. I knelt to place it and my badge in the safe under the sink.

"I've heard that you and Senator Larson are friends."

"I wouldn't go that far," I said. The department's standard issue was a Sig Sauer P226, but I only carried it when on duty. I grabbed my CZ P-10 C before I closed and locked the safe. "Let me change and get my bag."

I avoided looking at the ceiling in my cramped bedroom as I changed out of uniform. I had hung most of the material there within the first year of my wife and daughter's disappearance. Maps with Winona's usual route in and out of town highlighted, memories of things she said that might be a link scrawled on Post-it notes, receipts, photos printed from the CCTV camera footage around town in the weeks leading up to that one day. Tacks were shoved into the map at the locations she visited regularly. At the center of the web, I pinned a photograph of Jeff Roosevelt. That space was blank now.

I knew the man was a predator. I had watched him for fifteen years. But until a woman moved to town four months ago, I had not realized he was a serial killer. He was dead now, at the hands of that same woman, but not before killing three others. The phone call from the coroner last month killed my hopes of finally laying my girls to rest.

The remains of fifty-six women were found in the greenhouse in the woods. DNA testing was ongoing, and the FBI were still working to identify the women. But Winona and Emma had not been found in Jeff Roosevelt's thorny, rose-filled mausoleum.

Anger burned bitter and dark in my gut.

I checked the magazine in the CZ and chambered a round before I tucked it into my concealed holster. The backpack in the corner was always ready for call outs from the local Search and Rescue team. I left the bedroom and filled two canteens at the sink, water for Frank and for me.

"Larson and his men will help us look for your boy."

She remained silent, and when I turned from the sink, screwing the caps on the canteens before tucking them into my pack, I found her leaning in the doorway, gilded by the dying sun. She was a small woman, slightly built with a chin-length cap of dark, wavy hair. Her gaze had been on the surrounding hills, but now she turned to me.

"What is the likelihood of us being able to search for Sam without anyone knowing we're there?"

"On Larson's land?" I chuckled, and her brows drew together. "Slim to none. Unlike you, he and his men don't bluff with their guns." She had the presence of mind to flush and look away. "You got a history with Larson I need to know about beforehand?"

She took a long moment to answer. "Not with Senator Larson, no."

I wondered if I was going to get shot tonight. "Let's go, then."

She climbed into the passenger's seat of my truck. The winter had left my drive rutted and rough, and I needed to haul dirt and gravel in to smooth the furrows before the snowmelt turned them into gullies. When I reached the state road, I turned west toward Gardiner.

Faye remained quiet as I drove. I glanced at her from the corner of my eye. I had dealt with a number of missing child cases. Almost all of them were an instance of a child going to a friend's house without telling his parents, or a kid innocently enjoying the thrill of hiding from her parents when they called for her, not realizing the genuine panic.

The more dire cases were not ones I worked as a police officer, but the ones I worked as a member of the local search and rescue team. In this area of the country, the wilderness was mere steps away. Yellowstone was as dangerous as it was beautiful, and a child wandering away could be gone in seconds.

Frank and I had been on eight rescue operations that ended not with relief but with a call to the coroner. Three of those operations involved children.

Regardless of whether I worked a missing child case as a police officer or a member of the search and rescue team, one thing always remained the same: the agony of the mother. I had dealt with more tears, panic, and terror on missing children cases than on any other.

But the woman sitting next to me was composed. She stared straight ahead, face blank, eyes dry. She was not frantic. Had I not seen her terror when she pulled her gun on me, I never would have guessed at her desperation. Now, the only thing that gave away her tension were her hands clenched in her lap.

The drive passed in silence, and I was content not to break it. Grant Larson's ranch sprawled over four hundred fifty thousand acres. The valley floor stretched into rolling hills before the terrain became more rugged and wild. The Absaroka Range flanked the lowlands in the east, the Gallatin Range in the west. Larson was known the world over for his horses, both the ones he bred and trained and the wild herds that roamed his backcountry after he rescued them from the Bureau of Land Management's slaughter pens.

When I turned off the interstate north of Gardiner and passed between the brick gates that marked the entrance of Larson's ranch, it was fully dark.

Faye finally spoke as we approached the guard house. "Don't mention Sam's name, please."

I glanced at her as I slowed to a stop as the guard stepped out and held up a hand to halt my progress. I could not see her face in the shadows. "And your name?"

"Using my name won't be an issue."

I buzzed down the window as the guard approached. Frank tried to stick his head out the window but I ordered him to stay in the backseat. Larson hired his own security detail, and I knew what type of man he preferred to watch his back and secure his land. I kept my hands visible as the guard arrived at the window.

"I'm Hector Lewis. My friend's son got left behind at a school field trip today," I said. "I'm with the Raven's Gap Police Department and a member of the search and rescue team. I brought my dog with me to help find him."

The man stepped back and spoke quietly into the radio clipped to his shoulder. He came back a moment later. "The boy is with the senator at the east barn. You have permission to drive on. Do you need a map?"

"No," I said. "I know where it is."

I thought the news of Sam being with Larson and not lost in the wild Montana spring night would bring Faye some relief, but, if anything, she was even more tense as we traversed the mile-long drive to the sprawling compound of Broken Arrow Ranch.

The house was a massive structure of glass, stone, and timber. Each of the surrounding outbuildings and the three barns shared the same stone and timber construction. It was a beautiful estate, the grounds immaculately kept, wealth and prestige on full display.

I turned and followed the drive that branched around to the east barn. The way was well lit, and a number of vehicles were parked beside the barn. I parked near the wide entrance and left Frank in the truck as we entered the barn.

The interior was even more impressive than the exterior. The stalls were larger than my Airstream. When my wife first took the job here eighteen years ago, she joked that she wished a stall had been given to her as housing. It certainly did not look like any barn I had ever mucked stalls in, but the smell of hay, horseflesh, and shit was still present. I breathed in that old familiar perfume and felt a pang of longing.

Faye did not pause to admire the barn or the horses that watched us from their stalls with large, limpid eyes and inquiring whickers. She headed straight toward the cluster of people standing before a stall at the far end of the barn. A palomino stretched her neck toward me over her stall door. I stopped to let her sniff me before I followed Faye.

Kneeling in the hay next to the newborn foal, his jeans stained and his sleeves rolled up past his elbows, Grant Larson looked like a ranch hand, a man who spent more time in the saddle than out of it, an expert in horseflesh. He did not look like the wealthiest man in Montana or the senior senator of the state.

Sam looked to be both too old and too young for his age. He had to be eight or nine years old, but he was small for his age and appeared even slighter crouched beside the tall, broad-shouldered figure of Larson. He could have easily passed for a boy closer to five than ten. Even though his eyes were wide with wonder as he gently stroked the damp neck of the newborn, his face held the same still wariness his mother's did.

"You're not the vet," one of the hands leaning against the side of the stall said as we approached.

"No," I agreed.

Our voices drew Larson's and Sam's attention, and the boy started to stand when he caught sight of his mother. Larson's hand on his shoulder held him in place. I could not see Faye's face, but she stiffened.

"Slowly," Larson said, voice low and calm. "Remember what I said. Once you've earned an animal's trust, it's a matter of honor that you not break it. Any fast movements will startle Boadicea, and she'll think she needs to defend her colt from us."

Sam nodded and moved with conscientious slowness as he touched the little foal's forelock and then stood and exited the stall. The mare watched him with only a flicker of her ears.

The boy walked straight to his mother and held her gaze for a long moment before she pulled him into her arms. "I was worried," Faye said quietly.

"No need to be." Larson followed Sam from the stall and gave her the smile that charmed Washington. "I apologize for not calling earlier to let you know your boy was safe." When she said nothing, he glanced back and forth between us. The mare stamped a hoof in the stall. "Boadicea went into labor sooner than expected. We've been a bit preoccupied this evening." His gaze turned to me, and he extended a hand. "Hector. It's been too long."

I shook his hand. "Handsome colt."

His grin held all the pride of a new father, but his

expression sobered as he met my gaze. "I wish Winona were still here to train him."

The words slipped like a knife between my ribs. My wife had lived and breathed horses. My exit from the circuit was involuntary, but Winona willingly gave up chasing the cans after my right knee, hip, and shoulder were crushed by a bull. Barrel racing was not the extent of her talent, and as soon as I finished rehabilitation and we moved to her hometown of Raven's Gap, the job offers came rolling in for her. She had worked at a number of local ranches for years. Working at the Broken Arrow was a dream come true for her, and I could still remember her excitement when Larson approached her about training his Thoroughbreds.

"The Friesians are new," I said.

He turned back to the stall. "Beautiful, aren't they?" He offered his hand to Faye, who hesitated before accepting. "Grant Larson."

Her pause was almost imperceptible. "Faye Anders. It's a pleasure to meet you, Senator Larson." While her words may have been charming, her tone was flat. "I apologize for any inconvenience."

He stared at her for a long moment, expression considering. "Not at all. Your boy stepped right up to help me with the foaling."

She forced a smile, and Sam remained silent at her side, his gaze on the colt struggling to his feet. "It's late. We'll be leaving now. Thank you for looking out for him."

I could see the curiosity in Larson's eyes, but before he could respond, a grizzled man carrying a medical bag approached. The vet had arrived. I nodded to Larson when he caught my eye.

"Don't be a stranger," he said, before turning to the vet.

"Slowly," I reminded Faye under my breath when it looked like she would bolt.

She nodded and set an unhurried pace through the barn, but I could see the tension in the set of her shoulders. Once we were outside, I thought she would reprimand the boy, who kept glancing at me curiously. But all she said to him in a low voice was, "Did they hurt you in any way?"

He drew his gaze from me and looked up at her. He shook his head, and some of the stiffness eased from her shoulders.

I moved ahead of them and opened the back door of the truck for the boy. The floodlights on the exterior of the barn highlighted the excitement that lit his face when he saw the poodle in the backseat. "This is Frank," I told him.

He clambered into the backseat, greeted by tail wagging and inquisitive sniffing, and I shut the door behind him.

I turned to Faye and found her staring at the entrance of the barn, brow furrowed. "Too easy?" I asked.

She met my gaze. "Let's leave now."

If she thought anyone would try to halt our departure, she was wrong. No one attempted to delay us, and the guard at the gate merely lifted a hand as we passed. Mother and child were equally silent as the dark miles rolled passed until Faye said, "Thank you for coming with me. I'm sorry for…earlier."

"I could have arrested you tonight." I glanced in the rearview mirror and saw the boy's head come up, even though I had kept my voice low. Frank was sprawled across the backseat with his head on Sam's knee.

"You could have," she agreed, tone unaffected. "But you didn't. I was willing to take that risk."

I did not respond. Miles later, I turned off of the state road and drove along the rough stretch of lane leading home. The moonlight was a pearled gleam on the curved roof of my Airstream.

I glanced at Faye as I parked, but she stared straight ahead. When I opened the back door, Sam's gaze flew to mine, his fingers clenching around something in his palm.

He hurriedly secreted away whatever he held deep into his pocket before he clambered down from the truck. His gaze darted to mine again before he ducked his head as his mother rounded the truck and placed a hand on his shoulder.

Frank wanted to follow the boy as Faye and Sam moved to their own vehicle, but I called him back to my side. My gaze trailed the boy and noted the way he slipped his hand into his pocket and angled a quick glance over his shoulder toward me as he climbed into the backseat of Faye's battered SUV.

"Thank you again," she said.

Her desperation, I realized, had not been over the fact that her boy was missing. Not solely. Her fear came from the encounter with Larson. I studied her face carefully as I said, "Now that he's safe, you don't have to worry any longer."

The twist to her lips was too pained and bitter to be considered a smile. "I wish that were true."

I did not consider myself a curious man, but could not refrain from asking, "Why did you come to me tonight?"

Faye remained silent for a long moment. She studied me in the moonlight, but I could not interpret her expression. "Because I don't think law and order are high on your list of priorities. But justice is."

TWO

FAYE

"HE ISN'T HERE," Laurel Kennedy said when I arrived to pick Sam up from school.

My mind could not process her words. "What do you mean he isn't here?"

She twisted her hands together, anxiety written into every line of her body. "He slipped away today at the senator's ranch."

My stomach twisted itself into a tight, hard knot. "What senator?"

She explained and reminded me that I signed the approval slip for Sam to go. The teacher had done everything I asked when I pulled her aside shortly after I put Sam in the school. If something happened with him, do not draw attention; do not call the police. She had been skeptical, but I knew a battered woman when I saw her. When I explained how dangerous his father was and how far reaching his connections were, Laurel readily agreed.

We had been here too long. I had grown too comfortable and did not even think to look up who owned the Broken Arrow Ranch before signing the release form. And I had been complacent for so long that I had forgotten how it felt when fear grabbed me by the throat, how it gripped my heart and clenched tighter every time I tried to inhale.

It had not loosened its grasp even now as I drove home from Hector's with Sam buckled into the seat behind me. I had seen the curiosity on the senator's face, the befuddled look of a sense of familiarity he was trying to place. I wanted to rail at Sam, to reprimand him both for frightening me and for drawing attention to us. Guilt pierced me immediately, and I loosened my death grip on the steering wheel and adjusted the rearview mirror so I could see the shadow of his face.

He was just a little boy, I reminded myself. A little boy whose world was upended and who retreated into silence five years ago but who still smiled at me every day and gave the tightest hugs.

"I'm glad you're okay," I said. Being a mother had never come easily to me. It was not a role I ever felt suited for. I struggled with what to say and do, when to be firm and when to be soft. I lay awake at night eaten by doubt. "I was frightened when Miss Kennedy told me you left the group you were supposed to be in and didn't get on the bus." I glanced at the mirror, and the dusk to dawn light at the corner lit his face as we passed under it. He was watching me in the mirror. I pulled into the inn's drive and parked the car before flipping on the overhead light and turning in my seat to face him. "Please don't do something like that again. You could have gotten lost or hurt, and I couldn't bear either of those. Okay?"

He had ancient eyes in a child's face, eyes that had seen far too much. His gaze searched my face for a long moment before he nodded.

He did not speak. He had not spoken in five years.

Silence, I learned, was akin to a cancer left undiagnosed until it was too late to be anything but terminal. In the beginning, I threw my entire existence into treating it. I talked until my voice ran hoarse. I filled the quiet with song and laughter, even if both rang false. But there came a point when I knew all efforts were futile, and I gave up and drowned in the silence.

It did not come all at once. Resignation was a gradual process. At first, it was simply not telling a story over breakfast. Then I did not bother to ask how his day was because I knew he would not respond. Finally, I went to bed at night and realized I had not uttered a word throughout the entire course of the day.

Silence spread malignantly until it fully permeated my life. I learned to bear it, and the pain of it became ingrained in my every breath, and the loneliness of it was so constant I was not certain I recalled what it felt like to not exist in its presence. It was a fatality that I gave into eventually, and after years of it, even hope was cast aside. I simply carried on in its wake and forgot that a time existed when the silence did not reign.

And then someone came into our lives and reminded me that the silence had not always been so pressing.

The light on the front porch was on. Evelyn Hutto stood illuminated at the wide windows watching for us. She had shown up on the inn's doorstep several months ago asking to rent a room. She became a friend, reminding me that communication was more than words, and I realized that my silence perhaps only encouraged Sam's.

"Let's get inside," I said. "I'll make us some dinner."

Evelyn met us at the door. The relief on her face when she saw Sam was evident. "He was able to help you."

Approaching Hector Lewis was her idea. I knew the man only by his reputation around town. The rumors I had heard over the last years stated his wife and child had not been found after they went missing fifteen years ago because he murdered them.

I knew about men who would kill to make someone disappear from their lives. While his face was cold and hard, I didn't see cruelty in it or the kind of rage that lashed out with words and fists until a woman was curled bleeding in a corner. I didn't believe the rumors, but I still avoided him. Cops were the same the world over: loyal to one another and to whoever wrote the largest checks.

But Evelyn was certain Hector would help me find Sam, and I was desperate enough to be unswayed by his indifference.

"He was," I said, and left it at that. "Did anyone need anything while I was gone?"

"The older couple in room three asked for an extra pillow, but aside from that, it's been quiet."

When I bought the inn, the place was a dump, but the location on an oxbow of the Yellowstone River was stunning. It took me the first three years we lived here before I finished renovating the six rooms, den, dining area, sun room, kitchen, and the rooms Sam and I lived in. The exterior still needed work, and a lot of it. But the cash I took when we fled New York had dwindled dangerously low after those three years of sinking money into the inn.

Now, I was finally starting to turn a profit, and I was researching contractors for the work. YouTube tutorials went a long way when I was laying plank flooring and installing sinks and showers, but the carpentry work needed to restore the inn to its former glory on the exterior was something I would leave to the professionals.

I was beginning to think of Evelyn as a roommate more than a boarder, and three of the six available rooms were currently occupied. The season already promised to be a busy one with reservations made through the end of October.

Raven's Gap was our sanctuary, and I loved being able to add to each visitor's experience of Yellowstone with a quiet, comfortable, rustic place to lay their heads. Now my stomach twisted with the knowledge that it could come to an end.

"Thanks for keeping an eye on things for me."

"Of course," Evelyn said, and limped after us into the kitchens.

"Do you need a pain killer?" I asked when I caught her grimace as she eased into a chair.

In January, she killed a man, a serial killer who had lived among us as a neighbor. It still made my skin crawl to think about it. She survived Jeff Roosevelt only to nearly lose her life in a blizzard. Hector and his poodle, Frank, found her before the cold could take her, but not before it had stolen pieces of her.

She confessed to me that she could bear losing fingers and toes and part of her ear when faced with the knowledge that she could have lost much more. She seemed to be coping well, emotionally and physically, but I knew the two missing toes on her right foot were still something she was learning to deal with. The missing toes caused her more physical discomfort than the two and a half fingers on her left hand, she told me.

"Yes, please," she said. I knew she was hurting when she stayed seated and let me grab a bottle of pain reliever and a glass of water for her. "I made spaghetti for us. It's in the fridge and just needs to be heated up." She turned to Sam, who took the chair next to her. "Are you okay? What happened?"

She addressed her question to Sam. She never talked through him or did not acknowledge him because he did not offer anything verbal in response. I answered her and told her what I knew as I heated three plates of spaghetti in the microwave. So much could have happened to him, and I would never know, because he could not tell me. The thought staggered me.

"Were you frightened?" Evelyn asked softly, and shame washed through me. Not because he nodded. Of course an eight-year-old little boy would be frightened in such a situation. Because I had not thought to ask him that myself. Evelyn smiled at him. "You didn't need to be. You know your mom would move heaven and earth for you."

His eyes sliced to me, and I forced a smile as I slid a plate before him.

Evelyn and Sam cleaned their plates. I found myself pushing the noodles and sauce around my plate until they were finished.

Later, when I crawled into bed, I pressed my hand to my chest and stared up at the shadowed ceiling. The hard thrum of my heart knocked at my palm. I loved it here. The chaos of New York City was like a cocaine high. I loved it once, even needed it. Now that I was sober, though, I needed the quiet, the peace that enveloped this small town in its wilderness embrace. I never realized I could not breathe until I moved here, where the air was so crisp and clean it sometimes hurt to inhale.

This inn was the first thing that had not been given to me. I loved the bakery, but I had not known hard work until the inn. Mary would have loved the inn. She would have thrown herself into the renovations right alongside me, chattering to me endlessly about plans and dreams for the place. Perhaps that was why the silence sometimes felt so oppressive. Life felt so cavernous without the echo of Mary's laughter to fill it.

The inn was the first thing I actually worked for and invested blood, sweat, tears, and money in. I had calluses on my palms now, and pride that filled me every time I glanced around and took in what I created with my own two hands.

Now, our days were numbered. It would only be a matter of time, and I wondered if we should leave this very night, slipping away in the dark before we were discovered, or if I should wait. Maybe the senator would forget about us. Maybe he would never make the connection.

But I learned five years ago that if I relied on *maybes*, I would end up dead and Sam would pay the price for my hesitation.

I closed my eyes and pondered how swiftly fear shattered the joys I chipped out for us and how often motherhood felt synonymous with failure.

THREE

GRANT

"You're certain the boy didn't see anything?" I asked the man who slipped from the shadows and joined me. I stared after the tail lights as the vet's truck disappeared into the darkness and considered my earlier guests.

"Not one hundred percent, no. We didn't even know the kid was here until Rogers caught sight of him on the cameras outside the north barn."

"Shit." I raked a hand through my hair.

"Do you need me to contain the situation?"

The man beside me had come highly recommended, with good reason. John Smith had worked for me for years now. The anonymity of his name was appropriate. He was damn good at what he did. So good that sometimes it chilled me, and the thought crossed my mind that one day I would end up being the situation he needed to contain.

"Not until we know if it is going to turn into a situation. But find out everything you can about the woman and boy. I want to be prepared." A sense of familiarity nagged at me with both of them.

"And the man?"

The irony was not lost on me. "You don't need to do a background check on Hector Lewis. He told the guard at the gate the woman was his friend, though. Keep an eye on him, but discreetly."

John smiled, teeth gleaming in the darkness. It was not a pleasant expression. "Discreet is my middle name."

I retreated into the barn to check on Boadicea and her foal. The Friesian watched me as her gangly son nursed. "How about Caligula?" I asked. She blinked those wide, warrior eyes at me.

I offered to name the foal after the boy, trying to draw him out and get him to talk to me. When he was first brought into my office, I thought he was deaf, but it was clear the boy could hear. He wrote out his mother's phone number when I asked for it, but my curiosity piqued when he refused to write his name. He remained silent, not speaking even when his mother arrived. Again, the sense that I knew the boy or had seen him before tugged at my subconscious.

Hector Lewis could be a problem. His wife had been, in the end. Winona was, after all, the reason I hired John Smith fifteen years ago.

FOUR

HECTOR

NOTHING CAME BACK in the system on Faye Anders aside from her driver's license and her vehicle registration. It was not unusual. For most law-abiding citizens, that was the extent of the records kept in the state and national crime database.

I pulled up Coplink, a crime analytics software that shared data between agencies, and performed a hunt and peck across the keys with my index fingers. A query brought back no results, so I attempted searches with various spellings of her name and her birthday as it was listed on her driver's license. Nothing came back on the searches.

I snagged the phone on my desk.

"It's Hector," I said when he answered on the third ring.

"Is my ma okay?" the gruff voice at the other end of the line asked. William Silva was retired Special Forces. He had done a short stint in the FBI and decided he preferred shades of gray to black and white. The man had a sixth sense for finding people. In addition to that uncanny ability, he had a wealth of resources and connections. It was why the sign on the door on his office in Denver read FUGITIVE RECOVERY AGENT.

"Maggie's fine." I rubbed the back of my neck. "I need to ask a favor of you."

"Name it," he said immediately.

He had been a solid kid, raised by strong, hard-working parents until his father dropped dead of a heart attack at the age of forty-three. Then he became a strong, hard-working son who helped his mother at the diner every day before and after school. He only joined the military after he asked me to promise to look after his mother. He had been a good kid, but he was an even better man.

"I need you to see what you can dig up on someone. A woman here in town."

He chuckled. "Another one?" I called him months ago asking him to look into Evelyn Hutto.

I gave him Faye's name and birthday and the rundown on everything I had gleaned about her, which was little to nothing. "And find out what her connection is to Grant Larson."

"The senator?"

"The very one."

He made a noncommittal noise. "Powerful man, there. Wealthy. Connected."

"Not telling me anything I don't know," I said. "You'll see what you can find out about her?"

"I'm on the road right now. A high bond skip is headed down to Mexico. Not much to go on with your girl, but as soon as I get him taken care of, I'll do some digging for you."

It might not be much to go on, but the man might as well have been a bloodhound. The only time his skills let me down was when I asked him to help me look for my girls. "Much appreciated, William."

I leaned back in the chair as I hung up the phone and rubbed my jaw before pulling my reading glasses from my pocket. They looked ridiculous, but they helped with the strain of reading on the computer screen and deciphering my own scrawled paperwork. A finger-print smudged the right lens, and I breathed a ghost of fog across the glass and polished them with the tail of my shirt.

I paused, struck by an idea. I tossed my glasses on the desk and strode down the hall. Ted Peters, the de-partment's evidence technician, was at his computer.

"I need you to lift some prints for me and run them, see if there's a match in the system."

"Sure. What kind of surface am I working with?"

"The handle on the passenger's side door of my truck."

The radio cued with a call from dispatch as soon as Peters finished lifting a thumb print from the door han-dle. The rest of the afternoon was spent dealing with a local rancher's herd that broke a fence and wandered onto the interstate.

The sun glinted off the Airstream when I arrived home. Frank hopped down from the truck and raced straight to a tennis ball left lying against the cinderblock stoop. I tossed the ball for him, and he took off after it.

Frank caught sight of the white wolf at the edge of the woods before I did.

She had appeared like a ghost in the darkness al-most every night over the last two months. One eve-ning when I was throwing a ball for Frank, she loped out of the forest. I automatically reached for my gun, leery as she approached my dog. They stood shoulder to shoulder for a moment, tails erect but no hackles raised or snarls. Frank broke the tension by dropping into a playful stance, and soon they were racing back and forth through the meadow.

I had never seen anything like it. She never approached me, and I knew better than to leave food out for her. But she kept returning, and I kept looking for her.

Keen to be chased, Frank snagged the ball and ran in a wide loop around and around the Airstream. The white wolf watched him for a moment and then trotted after him, her expression bemused by the barking poodle.

They were an oddly matched pair. Both white, one playful and carefree, the other larger, rangier, and possessing that untamed edginess of a wild creature.

Shaking my head at their antics, I turned and opened the front door. The smell caught at the back of my throat, choking me and freezing me in place for a moment.

Vandalism had been commonplace in the first few years after Winona and Emma disappeared. At first, everyone speculated that Winona had grown tired of me and finally moved on to find someone who was more deserving of her.

But my wife was not one for elaborate gestures or manipulation. She was blunt and straightforward. She would have told me she was leaving me. She loved this town, and she would never have put her friends or family through the agony of thinking something had happened to her. She would have packed her bags, made no secret of the fact, and gone to Maggie's to sleep on her couch.

I knew something was terribly wrong from the beginning. And by the second day she and Emma were missing, so did everyone else.

I had been a shit husband and an even worse father. Everyone knew that. But soon, everyone also thought I killed my wife and daughter. I knew many still thought that.

In the months following their disappearance, more often than not I came home to a ransacked trailer. The worst instance was walking in to find the blood of some slaughtered creature smeared on the floors and walls and poured across my bed. Even now, years later, after the warm spring sun had spent the day curled around the Airstream, I could smell that sickly sweet metallic odor.

I went straight to the cabinets underneath the sink. I knocked a bottle of cleaner over when I reached for the air freshener, and it rolled on its side to the back of the cabinets. "Fucking hell," I muttered, lowering myself to a knee to lean under the sink.

I never would have spotted it had I not been stooped low to reach into the depths of the cabinet. The envelope was taped to the back side of the cabinet, close to the underside of the counter, behind the sink. The tape had been in place for so long that in pulling it free, a strip of the finish on the inside of the cabinets peeled off with it.

There was no writing on the envelope, but my fingers shook as I peeled it open. There was no note within. I upended the envelope, and a USB flash drive fell into my palm.

Frank's alerting bark startled me. I dropped the flash drive back into the envelope and tucked it into my pocket before moving to the threshold. I was not surprised to see Maggie Silva's old station wagon parking beside my truck. A glance around showed the white wolf was gone.

"Come grab the crockpot," she said as she climbed out of her vehicle. "I brought chili."

I hauled the oversized cookery inside and placed it on the counter, nudging the cabinet door shut as I plugged it into the outlet. I slipped my hand into my pocket, rubbing my thumb along the edge of the envelope containing the flash drive.

The soft sound of Maggie's voice as she spoke to Frank jarred me into action, and I grabbed two bottles of beer on the way outside. Maggie was kneeling next to the fire pit, building a fire. Louie, the Bichon Frise I had taken in several months ago, was at her side. The fluffy little dog's owner was viciously murdered in January by the serial killer stalking Raven's Gap. The loss had been difficult for the sensitive dog. I had no doubt dogs mourned. Grief was not an emotion confined to humanity. I thought I would keep him myself, but he was wary around men. He needed a lap to lie in and a gentle female presence in his life to match what he had before.

When I broached the subject with her, Maggie had plucked the little dog from my arms so quickly I'd been left holding air before I realized she was already stroking his head and murmuring softly to him. It was the right decision. He looked happier than I had seen him since coaxing him out of hiding when I found him after his owner was reported missing.

I collected the camp chair Maggie kept in her car and planted it beside my Adirondack.

I took a seat, and Frank dropped the worn, soggy tennis ball at my feet, prancing back and forth until I lobbed it across the meadow for him. While I threw the ball, I watched Maggie out of the corner of my eye as she meticulously laid the kindling.

"I wasn't sure if Joan would be here," she said, voice carefully casual. Her tone was blank, but she had an expressive face. I knew exactly how she felt about my long-term affair with the police chief's wife.

"Not tonight," I said. She only showed up on my doorstep when her husband began using his fists. There was no set schedule. Sometimes she was in my bed several nights a week; other times it was a month before I saw her outside of the police department, where she worked the front desk. It always perplexed me that she came to me, of all men, for gentleness, but I gave it to her as best I could.

When the fire was blazing against the darkening sky, Maggie straightened and dusted her hands off, sighing as she sank into the chair and stretched her feet toward the fire pit.

I popped the top on a bottle and offered it to her, unable to resist returning the sweet smile she directed my way. She accepted it and leaned over to pick up Louie and deposit him on her lap.

Panting and gnawing on his tennis ball, Frank settled under her outstretched legs. I leaned forward to stir the fire with a stick, waiting her out.

I did not have to wait long.

"William called me. He said he spoke with you today."

I glanced over my shoulder and watched the firelight play over her face but remained silent.

"I'm sure it has not been lost on you that Faye and

her boy are on the run from something, someone, and seeking shelter here."

"She tell you that?" I asked.

"No, I don't know the girl, though I would like to get her pancake recipe. She doesn't need to tell me. I can see it on her face. What's more, I can see it on her child's face. Unless you were born and raised here, people only come to Raven's Gap to forget." She was staring into the fire, the flames dancing in her dark eyes. She turned her head and met my gaze. "Or to be forgotten."

I looked away and took a long pull of beer.

"Don't ruin that for her," Maggie said softly. "You start digging around into a woman's past when she's finally found a hiding place she feels she's safe in, you're going to ruin things for her and for that little boy."

It was my turn to stare into the fire for a long moment. "We had a serial killer walking our streets for fifteen years. Three women had their lives snuffed out by him in a matter of weeks. Almost four. I want to know who is in this town and why. Especially if she is going to bring trouble here."

"Oh, bullshit. You're not an altruistic man, Hector." Maggie leaned into me and rested her head on my shoulder to soften her words. "And you've never given a rat's ass about being a cop."

I hid a smile and worked the peeling edge of the bottle label with my thumb. She was not wrong. She had always seen me clearly, and even though she was my wife's best friend and had likely heard the intimate details of our unhappy marriage, she never judged me.

"Do you want to know what I think?"

"I think you're going to tell me whether I want you to or not," I said.

She chuckled. "I am." She leaned away and waited until I turned my head and met her gaze. "I think you are a man who needs an obsession. The rodeo, your bitterness over losing that." She paused and said on a whisper, "Jeff Roosevelt." I stiffened, and she forged ahead. "Finding Winona and Emma has been what's driven you for fifteen years."

"I'm still trying to find them," I bit out. Frank stood at my tone, and Maggie leaned back into me, wrapping her arm around my shoulders.

"I know you are. But that search went off course when they didn't find Winona or Emma's bodies with his other victims."

"There may be other victims buried elsewhere."

"There may be," she said quietly. Then she voiced what had been swirling in my mind since I received the phone call from the coroner. "But now you have no way of finding them with that monster dead, and he may not be the one who..." Her voice trailed off. "What I'm saying is, now you're lost. Floundering. You need something to latch onto." She rested her head back on my shoulder. "I want you to be safe. I want you to be happy. I've spent a lot of years watching you not be. But... I want you to not get that girl and her little boy hurt just because they crossed your path when you needed something to focus on."

Had she been anyone else, I would have shrugged off her embrace and told her to fuck off. But she was Maggie. She had a big heart and a blunt, forthright manner that soothed me even when she pissed me off.

I drained my beer, and we sat in silence. Frank lay back down and shifted so his chin was propped on my boot. Louie started to snore in Maggie's lap. The fire ate at the wood, crackling and releasing sparks into the sky. Full night encroached beyond the gleam of the fire. The stars overhead were dense and brilliant.

Finally, I said, "You done?"

I felt her cheek move with a smile against my shoulder. "For now."

"You think that chili is ready? I'm starving."

"I'll check on it and see." She straightened. "No cheese, extra Fritos?"

"You got it."

Her hand slid over my shoulder and squeezed the back of my neck before she placed Louie in my lap and stood. She opened the door to the Airstream, and the smell of the chili rolled out, fragrant and spicy. I hoped it covered the rank odor of old blood. I rubbed my thumb along the edges of the thumb drive in my pocket and stared into the darkness beyond the fire.

FIVE

GRANT

IAGO EYED ME suspiciously as I entered the small corral. The wild horse had come to me as part of a trainer incentive program after a roundup of mustangs from the Three Fingers Herd Management Area in Oregon.

Winona Lewis was the first to encourage me to reach out to the BLM and rescue entire herds from the cramped pens they were contained in before slaughter. If ever someone was owed the title *horse whisperer*, that woman was. The first time I met her, one of my ranch hands had radioed in about a break in the fence along the state road.

When I made it out to the state road, heart in my throat at the thought of an idiot tourist killing one of my Thoroughbreds in an accident because they were not paying attention, I saw her.

She stood in the center of the road, long blue-black hair caught in a whirlwind around her. Her voice, low and soft, reached me on the wind as she spoke to Patton. He was my most unpredictable and cantankerous horse. He was too dangerous for anyone to handle but me. He would sooner kill a person than look at them. Truth was, I should have put him down years ago, but I had a soft spot for the mean brute. He pawed the pavement now.

I knew better to call out and warn her. All I could do was watch.

But instead of trampling the woman, he lowered his head and approached her slowly. A flick of his tail could have knocked me over when he nuzzled her hair.

Looking back, I had probably fallen in love with her at the exact moment as my bastard of a horse.

Shaking off memories, I focused on Iago. The mustang had been gathered and gelded last year. Once I gentled him, I would find him a home or keep him myself. Most of the wild horses I worked with ended up as ranch horses throughout the west. But I liked Iago's spirit and had half a mind to keep him. He reminded me of Patton.

It was our first day in the pen. He eyed me from across the corral, snorting and bobbing his head, hooves stamping the dirt. I did not bother with a halter or lead. I wanted him to judge his movements based on mine, and I wanted him to move freely around the pen.

I walked slowly around the perimeter, and he sidestepped nervously, keeping the narrow expanse of trampled dirt between us. He was vocal the entire time, nervous and watchful. With a gust of air blown through his nostrils and a kick of his heels, he broke into a canter around the perimeter of the pen. I moved to the center, turning to keep pace with him. When he finally stopped, I adjusted my stance so I was not facing him but was instead turned sideways to him.

I could see my visitor out of the corner of my eye as he approached the corral and draped his arms over the railing.

"What have you found out?" I asked. Iago's head went up at the sound of my voice.

"Very little," John Smith said. "Which intrigues me. She has a clean record, no run-ins with the law, not even a traffic ticket. Owns and operates The River Inn in Raven's Gap, and very interestingly paid cash for the property."

"How much cash?"

"Almost a neat million. Nine hundred ninety-eight thousand."

I began to walk slowly around the perimeter of the corral once more. With a huff, Iago echoed my movement, this time at a more sedate pace. "That is interesting."

"You'll find this even more so. Faye Anders only began to exist five years ago."

SIX

FAYE

I RINSED THE dye from my hair until the water in the sink ran clear and squeezed the excess moisture from the ends before I straightened. I grabbed the hand towel from the counter and rubbed it over my head.

I had been using the cheap boxed dye for so long now I no longer grimaced when I caught my reflection in the mirror. The black was stark, and it did not suit my pale, freckled coloring. My eyebrows and eyelashes were too pale, highlighting the unnatural tint of the black. I only attempted to dye my eyebrows once. The result was so appalling and ludicrous I never bothered again. The color struck me as garish, but I was no longer startled when I caught sight of it. The black hid the very memorable deep red of my natural hair color. That was all that mattered.

I turned and started when I found Sam standing in the doorway watching me. "Good morning," I said, offering him a smile.

He did not return my smile. His brow was pinched, and the set of his mouth was troubled. He glanced over his shoulder at my bed. I followed his gaze, taking in the two suitcases I packed in the early morning hours after finally giving up on sleep.

Sometimes I wondered how much he remembered.

He had only been three years old. I doubted he could recall how many cheap motels with paper-thin walls we stayed at that year. I doubted he could recall the numerous cities and towns we sought shelter in or the nights we slept in the stolen car in a rest area parking lot. Every wail of a police siren, every CCTV camera had me clenching in fear, certain we would be found.

At first, I thought we could stay on the East Coast, but Sam's father had too many connections. As soon as I saw the TV special that twisted the story and cast everything in a far different light than reality, I knew we needed to get as far from New York City as we could. I left the stolen car in a Walmart parking lot in Maine and wiped it clean before stealing another one with a child's car seat in the back and heading west.

I did not think Sam remembered any of that, not in any clear detail. But I had no doubt the terror and uncertainty and anxiousness were imprinted in his memory. Just as I was certain my hand tight over his mouth as we hid under the bed listening to the screams in the other room and my tearful whisper that he must be quiet and not make a sound had fostered these ensuing years of silence.

He turned back to me, and when he met my gaze, he was shaking his head. He knew what the packed bags meant.

"This is not your fault," I told him quietly. "But the man you met yesterday at the ranch…" He did not need to hear my fears. He had already been having trouble sleeping the last few months, and a number of nights he crawled into my bed still trembling from a nightmare. I would not add to that. "It would be best for us if we left."

He shook his head harder and thrust a folded piece

of paper toward me. I accepted it. Sam knew how to read and write, but he rarely communicated even in written form.

I unfolded the piece of paper, and my throat tightened. He had no particular artistic talent, but there was no mistaking the culmination of the details on page. He had drawn the inn, complete with the swing on the front porch, the woods on either side, and the river flowing around the oxbow. In big block letters across the top of the page was the word HOME.

He stabbed his finger to the paper, pointing at the word. He jabbed his finger at it again and again, until he tore a hole in the paper. I caught his hand in mine and stilled the frantic movement.

Motherhood was so damn hard. Despite my best efforts, I could never shield him entirely from hurt or fear. I weighed my decisions and balanced the odds and thought carefully of the repercussions, but I still questioned whether my choices were the right ones.

I stared into Sam's wide, damp gaze. My decision to run, based solely on fear, was the rational choice. I had long ago learned to trust my gut, and my gut said our interaction with Senator Larson would lead Sam's father straight to our doorstep. If we were here when he arrived, he would kill me. He might not kill Sam, but he would destroy him. Every choice I made over the last five years was to ensure Sam's safety, to make certain he never again knew a life of fear. He had known too much of it already.

He had also known heartache and loss and loneliness. If I could do one thing that made him happy, that earned me a genuine smile, that drew us closer to the moment when he would finally break his silence, I would do it. I would walk through fire for this wounded child who stood before me. And at the moment, what he wanted most was to stay in the place he loved and knew as home.

Staring into those eyes that had seen too much at such a tender age, I decided I would give him that for as long as I could. I would likely regret it. But in this moment, that did not matter.

"Let me make you some breakfast," I said, "and then I'll take you to school."

He studied my face for a long moment, and then the tension slowly leaked out of him and he leaned forward to press his forehead into the center of my chest. His thin arms came around my waist.

I might regret my decision later, but right now, I hugged him back even as I started planning.

SEVEN

HECTOR

ALL OF THE files on the flash drive were encrypted save one. I double-clicked on the file and a document with a single line of text on it opened onscreen.

Hector, if something happens to me, use this. You know the password. —Win.

The words struck me like a blow, and I leaned back in my chair in an attempt to absorb it. I stared at the letters until they morphed into an indistinct blur. *If something happens to me.* The file dates were listed as September 7, 2003. A little over a month before she and our daughter disappeared in October that year.

I cast my mind back, trying to recall any hint of unease Winona might have given in those months before she went missing. But fifteen years was a long time, and now it was hard for me to even remember the sound of her voice. I kept a photo of my girls on the table beside my bed, the same picture that was used for the missing persons banners that went up on billboards across the state. I traced the lines of their faces every day to keep them firmly etched in my mind.

I remembered the dimple in Winona's left cheek, the swing of her hips as she walked, the stretch of her body as she sat on the edge of the bed every night and brushed her hair to gleaming. I remembered my daughter's fondness for huckleberries, how she loved to sit on her grandfather's knee as he played the banjo, how her shadow made her laugh and laugh.

I stared at my name typed by my wife's hands. I could remember all of that. I could remember my coldness toward them and the twin deflated expressions on their faces before I turned away. But I could not remember the sound of their voices, the lilt of Emma's squeals and giggles, the cadence of Winona's singing and laughter.

Hector. I read my name over and over, wishing I could remember what it sounded like on my wife's lips. She had loved me, far more than I deserved, and there had always been a softness in her voice when she said my name.

A noise in the hall startled me. I had come into the police department well before my shift started. Frank looked up at me as I stood and moved to close the door, but he did not move from the dog bed in the corner. I locked the door and returned to my desk.

My throat was tight as I clicked on the other files. She was right, I did know the password, though it took me three attempts to input it before I realized she set it for *Emma* with a lowercase *e* and included her birthdate.

I braced myself before accessing the first file. *If something happens to me.* I was at a loss. Had I missed something going on in her life? Had she attempted to tell me something, and I ignored her? Had I overlooked a threat? Had I forgotten something in my fixation on Jeff Roosevelt?

The file I opened did not enlighten me. I donned my reading glasses and leaned closer to the screen. The two files were spreadsheets. The first contained a list of what appeared to be surnames in one column, date ranges in the next, and a string of numbers in the third column. Over three hundred fifty names were on the list, and the dates were for roughly week-long periods. The list was ordered by date. The first entry was for a week in April 1998, the last was for a week in September 2003. I glanced back at the file date and realized the file had been uploaded to the flash drive three days after the final date in the spreadsheet.

The second spreadsheet was similar to the first, with one column a list of dates. Each listed a single date, not a range of dates like the first spreadsheet. The other column simply contained a letter. I skimmed over the file. The letters were either W, G, E, C, or WV. There was no set pattern to the letters that I could see, although there was only one E and WV in the list. There were several Cs, but most of the entries bore either a W or a G.

I brought up the first spreadsheet and resized both until I could look at them side by side on the screen. The same number of entries had been made in both spreadsheets, and the dates listed in the second sheet always fell within a date range listed on the first.

I clicked on the first spreadsheet again and resized it to full screen to study the third column. They were latitude and longitude coordinates, I realized, and as I studied the list, I saw the same six coordinates were repeated.

I pulled up a web browser and plugged in one of the coordinates into the search bar. A map popped up, and I clicked on it. I moved the cursor to zoom out from the pinpoint on the map. I stared at the brown and green screen and then plugged in another set of coordinates. I repeated the search for all six sets.

I rubbed my jaw and leaned back in my chair. Each set of coordinates landed right long the delineation of the national park in the upper northwest corner of Yellowstone that abutted Shooting Star Mountain, Sheep Mountain, Big Horn Peak, and Crown Butte. The lines of the park were not neatly drawn. There were no fences marking the edges of Yellowstone territory. These were the wild borderlands.

I studied the spreadsheets again, trying to make sense of the letters and names. I toggled back to text document. *Hector, if something happens to me, use this.*

"What the hell are you trying to tell me, Winona?" I whispered.

I FOLLOWED THE worn dirt track that branched off of the Old Yellowstone Trail. The road had no name. It undulated through the swells and hollows of the wild borderlands of Yellowstone. I drove slowly. Ed Decker, the local mechanic, tow truck driver, and Winona's father, had been out here a number of times to haul out the city slickers who had blown a tire driving too quickly on the rough, rocky terrain.

Hoppe Creek and Deaf Jim Creek were flowing high with snowmelt over the dirt track. At the final branch in the trail, I turned left and followed the road to its dead end. The road was little more than an indention in the dirt, and in a meadow, the track disappeared completely.

I parked and glanced at Frank where he sat in the passenger's seat. A personal matter had come up was my excuse to the sergeant when I left work early for the day. "You coming or staying?"

He tilted his head and yawned before hopping into the driver's seat and leaping to the ground. He waited patiently as I tied a bell to the loop on his collar. The more noise we made, the less likely we were to surprise a bear. When I finished, Frank stretched and roamed a circle around the meadow, investigating.

I pulled the handheld GPS unit from my pocket and plugged in the easternmost coordinates on Winona's list. The pin on the map dropped roughly two miles to the southwest, near Mulherin Creek.

I shouldered my pack and grabbed my rifle from the hooks in the back window. The brass frame of the Henry Lever Action .45-70 had a rich patina from years of use, and I preferred the octagon barrel over the round. I removed the tubular magazine, ensured the chamber was empty, and closed the lever. I thumbed the hammer down and dropped four rounds into the magazine before I inserted the tube and cycled the action to chamber a round. I pocketed eight more rounds of ammo.

The Henry was a classic rifle. The .45-70 kicked like a son of a bitch and packed a mother of a one-shot drop on most game. I had never had the opportunity to test it, and hoped I never would, but I thought it would at least slow a grizzly's charge.

I carried it over my shoulder and whistled for Frank as I set off into the woods. Winter still clung to the land in the depths of the forest. The snow was hard and icy in the shadow of the trees. Frank raced back and forth ahead of me, startling a snowshoe hare from beneath a lodgepole pine. When it darted away and Frank started to give chase, I called him back to me.

"Stay close," I told him.

Spring was the season of birth, but in this wilderness stretch of the country, death often followed close on the heels of new life. It was brutal and gritty, nature at its most grim and bloody. The bear woke up hungry and cantankerous. Spindly-legged newborn calves, be it moose, elk, or bison, made for the easiest meals for newly awakened grizzlies and for winter-starved wolf packs.

I kept my eyes peeled as we hiked. The terrain was rugged. The mountains were craggy and steep, the footing precarious and uneven. We hiked due west around the northern edge of a spiny ridge and then followed the curve of a valley south. The quiet was absolute. There was no sound of civilization here, merely a vast quiet broken only by the wind and the occasional cry or cackle of a bird.

Some men found peace in the stillness and silence. I had found it soothing once. But now I could not venture into the wilderness without searching for the gleam of sunlight on the bleached-white surface of bone. I could not help but ponder if this valley had once echoed with screams. I could not cease wondering if some shallow grave in this godforsaken country held the remnants of my girls. I could not find peace any longer when ghosts dogged my steps. I could not see the landscape's beauty without also seeing its danger and the ease with which a paradise could turn to a hell.

The wilderness was no longer a place of respite for me. Instead, tension coursed through me, and I scanned every shadow for a threat. I brought the rifle for any human we might encounter as much as I did for the bear.

We were alone, though. Any animals in the vicinity stayed hidden, and I saw no signs of human presence. Frank stayed close at my side, the bell tied to his collar chiming with every step. When we reached the end of the valley, we ventured west again, and within half a mile, we reached the coordinates listed on Winona's spreadsheet.

I expected to find something. The remnants of a ghost town, a mine shaft, anything that might give a hint as to why this location was significant to Winona. I found nothing as I searched the area. I looped back, glancing at the handheld GPS tracker until I stood in the exact place she listed.

I turned in a slow circle, studying my surroundings. The lodgepole pine were dense. The green of spring beginning to take over the bleakness of winter. The forest floor was thick with underbrush, with saplings and with aged, fallen pines weathered and bleached like old bones. The wind still held the bite of winter even as it was rich with the fragrance of spring, but the sun was bright overhead, the swath of blue sky uninterrupted.

The bell on Frank's collar jingled. When I caught sight of the poodle backtracking between the same cluster of trees with his nose alternately on the ground and in the air, I saw it.

The camera trap was secured low on a tree, the camouflage case almost blending in with the bark. I stood staring at it for a long moment. If it were still recording, Frank and I were certain to be caught on film. I turned my gaze away but kept the camera in the corner of my eye as I moved out of the lens's field of vision. I circled to it, careful to stay clear of the viewfinder, and knelt beside it.

The Park Service often tracked wildlife with camera traps such as these, but we were not quite on park land and there were no emblems for the National Park Service on the camera case. A small padlock secured the case.

I rubbed my jaw and glanced at the GPS handheld tracker. The next coordinate on the list was a little over two miles to the northwest in the foothills of Shooting Star Mountain. The following coordinate was another two miles to the northwest in the foothills of Sheep Mountain. Both locations were within the park boundaries.

"Frank, let's go," I called, and headed out.

Our trek was uphill, the way steep. The poodle was in better shape than I was, but when I stopped for water, Frank drank thirstily from the bowl I poured for him. We crossed the Sportsman Lake Trail, a hiking trail that stretched from Mammoth Hot Springs sixteen miles across the Gallatin Range. From a glance at the map, I knew we were right along the Gallatin Bear Management Area.

My senses were on high alert. From May through November, travel in this section of the park was allowed only on designated trails, and visitors were encouraged to travel in groups of no less than four individuals. This was grizzly country.

I spotted the humped back across a meadow in the treeline about a hundred yards away the same time Frank did. A growl rumbled in his throat.

"Heel," I said, and he reluctantly fell into step close at my side as I slowly moved along the trail.

The rifle was a welcome weight on my shoulder as I kept an eye on the grizzly in the distance. His head lifted as soon as we were upwind of him, and I turned around, walking several slow, careful steps backward to watch the big bastard. He did not lumber any closer, though, so we continued.

We followed the Sportsman Lake Trail between

ridges and then branched off into the deeper backcountry. We reached the second location within an hour, and this time, I knew what I was looking for. The camera trap was mounted low on the trunk of a lodgepole pine. Like the other, it was unmarked, and the case was padlocked.

With the park restricting access in this area because of the concentration of bear, it would not be unheard of for biologists to set up camera traps to monitor the wildlife in the area. But I could not think of any reason for Winona to have kept track of the camera traps used by the national park in this area. She loved the park, and she was passionate about conservation. As far as I knew, though, her involvement never amounted to more than being a regular visitor, hiking in the summer, cross country skiing and snowmobiling in the winter.

I hiked on with Frank at my side, venturing farther west and north. We met up with the trail again and followed it for some distance before leaving the trail to cut through dense forest. I carried my rifle in both hands and cast a watchful gaze around us, but I did not spot another grizzly between the second camera trap and the third.

The third was the same as the others. This time, I slammed the butt of my gun against the edge of the lock and broke it off. With the lock busted, it was merely a matter of popping the two latches on the side and opening the case. I felt along the base of the camera system within and found the slim edge of the memory card. It was a spring-load system, and when I pushed against the card, it ejected. I slipped it free and tucked it into my pocket.

The pungent, musky odor reached me as I straightened and thumbed down the hammer on the Henry, tucking the brass plated butt into my shoulder. I turned in a slow circle. I could smell the bear but could not spot it. That made me more uneasy than if the beast were standing five feet from me.

Frank could smell the bear as well, for his lips drew back in a soundless snarl.

"At my side," I reminded him, speaking loudly. I moved cautiously, scanning the area constantly. Frank stayed close at my knee. "*A long, long time ago, I can still remember how that music used to make me smile.*" Frank glanced at me askance, but I sang at the top of my lungs as we retraced our steps.

Soon, it was only the fresh scent of snow melt and new growth I was inhaling. I could no longer smell the musky odor and Frank relaxed at my side. I kept up the concert, though, and kept my rifle at the ready. I could not sing my way out of a wet paper bag, and hoped my tunelessness frightened the bears as much as my volume did.

When I finished all of the stanzas of Don McLean's *American Pie*, I sang the ABB classic *Ramblin' Man*, which led to Lynyrd Skynyrd's *Simple Man*. My voice had grown hoarse, and I was halfway through the Eagle's *Hotel California* when we made it to my truck. I relaxed only when we were both locked in the cab.

Evening was descending over Raven's Gap when I drove into town, and the library was already closed for the day. I knew the computer on my desk at the police department did not have a memory card port. I drove to the diner.

Maggie was taking someone's order when Frank and I walked in, and when she shot a smile my direction, I pointed toward her office. She nodded, and I retreated down the hallway. Louie was curled up on the couch in her office. He yapped a greeting to Frank, who ran over to the smaller dog and leapt onto the couch beside him.

I moved to Maggie's desk and powered up her computer. I purchased the iMac for her last year for Christmas after seeing the state of the desktop she used to keep her records. I slipped the memory card from my pocket as I logged in and inserted the card into the port at the side.

It took several long moments to load. When it finally did, I clicked on the folder that showed up on the desktop. All of the files were jpegs, and I started at the top and worked my way down.

I was engrossed in studying the photos and did not hear the door open until Maggie slid a plate across the desk to me. I sat back in my chair and watched as she placed two bowls of scrambled eggs with ham on the floor for the dogs.

"Did Winona ever mention anything to you in the months before she disappeared?"

Maggie straightened from leaning against the desk and her gaze swung to mine. Her brow wrinkled. "How do you mean?"

"Did she ever say anything that made you think she was uneasy about something?" I asked. "That she didn't feel safe or that she felt threatened by someone?"

"No, she never said anything like that. But…" Her gaze took on a faraway look, and I leaned forward. "I remember thinking she seemed worried about something. She never told me, and I never asked. At the time…" She sent me an apologetic glance. "I thought it was just something going on between the two of you."

I rubbed the back of my head and scrolled through more of the images on the screen.

"Have you found something?" Maggie asked, leaning over the desk to peer at the computer.

"I don't know," I told her truthfully.

There were hundreds of photographs on the memory card. The cameras must operate via motion sensor, because each still had captured an animal's movement across the camera's field of vision—porcupine, coyotes, foxes, a bobcat, moose, elk, and several grizzlies. Aside from the last photos of Frank and me, the stills contained only animals.

Chuck, one of Maggie's cooks, called for her, and when she left, I pulled up a map in the web browser. I typed in the coordinates of the first camera trap again and expanded the viewfinder after the pin dropped.

Grant Larson's land ran directly adjacent to Yellowstone along the corner of the park, curving down and around the northwestern border, crossing US Highway 191, and hugging the park's border almost all the way south to West Yellowstone. I pulled the scrap of paper from my pocket where I had scrawled all of Winona's coordinates. I plugged each one into the map, and the pressure in my chest tightened.

Each coordinate lay within the wild, hotly contested borderlands between Yellowstone National Park and Larson's land.

EIGHT

GRANT

"THE BOY TALKED," John Smith said as he approached the corral.

The wild horse bolted away from me and put the width of the pen between us. Iago had let me approach him to within five feet before John startled him. I gave the horse a moment to relax before I moved toward him again. "You're positive?"

He held up a file. "See for yourself."

Iago's head bobbed up and down at John's swift movement. "Whoa, boy. Whoa," I murmured. He blew out a breath and lowered his head to investigate the hay I scattered in the pen.

I moved to where John stood and accepted the file from him, flipping open the folder. "Shit," I breathed. The pictures were grainy, but there was no mistaking Hector Lewis and his dog in the grayscale images.

I hated the man as soon as I saw the ring on Winona's finger.

That day on the state road, watching her stroke the neck of a horse that barely tolerated my own touch, I offered her a job on the spot.

"Name your price," I told her. "I'll pay you whatever you want if you'll come work for me."

She agreed, and when I saw the excitement in her

eyes, I hoped some of it was for me as well, not just for the opportunity to help train my horses.

I banked on that hope a month later when I invited her to the house after a long, grueling day for dinner. I couched it as an invitation to all of the hands, but when the men met my gaze and nodded, I knew they understood their appearance would not be welcome.

She missed the undertone of the exchange with the other men, but she understood when she walked in, saw the candlelight, and heard the low strains of jazz music. Her face had tightened with apprehension.

"I hope this isn't what it looks like," she said, and I knew from the cautious tone of her voice I would not be able to win her. "Grant, I am willing to be your friend and your employee, but no more than that."

"Why not?" I asked.

She laughed, and the sweet sound slipped right between my ribs. "Well, first of all, I'm married."

"Happily?"

Her laughter cut off abruptly at my question, and she looked away. She stared at the carefully prepared table for a long moment. I memorized the strong, proud lines of her profile.

I thought her hesitation might mean capitulation, but when she met my gaze, I could see the resolve in her eyes.

"I love my husband," she said, voice firm.

I studied the grainy images of that husband now. He had no idea how close I had come to destroying him. The only thing that kept me from doing so all those years ago was the knowledge that Winona was proud and stubborn, and she would never turn to me knowing how I felt about her.

"I suppose it's too much to hope that he was just out for a hike and stumbled across the site," I said.

John grunted. "Those photos are from two different camera traps, miles apart. After the first one, he knew what he was looking for. He found the next almost immediately after he walked into range. Nothing random about it. We think he found a third one as well, but he busted the lock and took the memory card."

I stared at the photos, but out of the corner of my eye, I saw Iago slowly approaching me. "How did he know where to find the cameras?"

"I don't know. I grilled Jones and Rogers about what the kid could have overheard. Both could only remember talking about the menu for our upcoming guests."

Iago stopped a few feet away and stretched his neck toward me. I felt the velvet texture of his nose brush my arm, but I remained still and did not turn toward him. My voice was low when I finally spoke. "When you take care of this, I want it done quietly. Neatly." I looked up and met his gaze. "Make it look like accidents."

This could not leak. I had taken measures to ensure it did not leak fifteen years ago, and I would do so again.

NINE

HECTOR

I COULD HAVE waited on the porch of his cabin, but I jimmied the lock on his front door and took a seat in his recliner for the sheer pleasure of messing with him.

Jack Decker was the main culprit for the repeated ransacking and vandalism of my Airstream after Winona and Emma disappeared. After seven years, the man eventually developed hobbies that did not involve desecrating my home on a regular basis.

I crossed to Jack's refrigerator, grabbed a beer, and returned to his recliner. I made myself comfortable while I waited for him.

His reaction when he opened his front door an hour later was exactly what I expected. He froze, and he flinched in fear before a cold mask of anger settled over his face.

"The fuck are you doing in my home?" he said, voice sharp as a blade.

I tipped the bottle back and drained the last of my beer before responding. "I want to know if Grant Larson was doing something fifteen years ago that made Winona suspicious."

He took a quick step back as if I had physically shoved him. "I don't know what you're talking about."

I kicked the footrest down on his recliner but stayed

seated. "I think you do. She helped get you that job at Larson's ranch when you got out of the Army. If something had happened, she would have told you about it." I met his gaze. "I want to know what it was."

He stayed in the doorway. His smile was completely devoid of humor. "Always trying to pin the blame on someone else. One day you'll run out of men to accuse. Maybe then you'll admit to what you did to my sister and Emma."

It was nothing he had not said to me countless times before. His voice was as hard as ever, but I thought I saw something in his eyes I never noticed before. I thought it looked a lot like guilt.

I stood and moved into the kitchen as if I owned the place. I opened his cabinet doors until I found where he collected his bottles for recycling and tossed the empty beer bottle into the box before turning to him. "If you've been hiding something for fifteen years that would have helped me find Winona and Emma, I'll see you six feet under, you little shit."

Fury swept across his face. "Get out of my house."

I kept my stride unhurried as I crossed to the doorway and paused when I reached him. We stood toe to toe for a tense moment before he backed out of the threshold to allow me to pass. "You know where to find me when you decide to tell me the truth."

I TORE THE Airstream apart when I returned home. I searched every nook, overturned the cushions and the mattress and boxspring, explored each cranny. I found it when I pulled one of the drawers in the kitchenette completely free of its track. A key was taped to the back of the drawer.

I tore the tape free and studied the key. It was shaped and cut for a safe deposit box.

She did not have a safe deposit box at the bank in town. Our finances had been picked over with a fine-toothed comb in the aftermath of her disappearance, first to see if she was still spending from our accounts and then to see if I had made any suspicious withdrawals or deposits around the time she went missing. We did not have a safe deposit box, and the investigation would have uncovered if she opened a box in town without my knowing.

A good portion of the town, including the bank manager, had come forward with information they thought would be helpful to the investigation. Most of Raven's Gap was eager to share their stories of witnessing my apathy and Winona's unhappiness.

I turned the key over in my hands. There were no markings to indicate which bank it was from or what the safe deposit box number might be. I moved through the Airstream to the small shelf beside my bed and placed the key beside the memory card from the camera trap and the flash drive.

I picked up the framed photograph and studied the faces staring back at me. My wife's American Indian heritage was evident in the structure of her facial features, her skin tone, and the lustrous fall of dark hair around her shoulders. She stared directly into the camera with that slight smile on her lips that so easily spread into a quicksilver grin that made her eyes light up like a beacon. Laugh lines fanned out around her eyes, and I could tell that when the photo was snapped, she had been moments away from laughing.

Emma was two years old in the picture. She was

perched on Winona's hip with her head resting against her mother's shoulder. She had Winona's dark hair, though Emma's was fine and curly. Her skin was lighter, and her eyes were mine. She grinned at the camera, one hand stretched out toward whoever was on the other side of the lens.

I thought it was Betty or Ed, Winona's parents. As much as I committed this image to memory, I had to acknowledge the light, affectionate expressions on my girls' faces were not for me.

Hector, if something happens to me, use this.

"What did you find?" I whispered. Frank lifted his head at the sound of my voice.

I needed air. I strode outside and leaned my head back, studying the dense sprawl of stars as I sucked in deep breaths. "What did you find, Winona?" I asked again, voice directed at the sky.

The sensation of being watched brought my head down, and I forced myself not to react when I found the white wolf standing a mere ten feet away from me.

Unlike a dog, her tail did not start wagging when I looked at her. She stood still and watchful, the keen predator gaze fixed on me unwaveringly. I was careful not to stare into her eyes.

"Do you have answers for me?" I asked quietly. "My wife was Lakota, but she told me of a Diné legend. Skin-walkers. A human disguising themselves as an animal."

The white wolf's head tilted, and it was such a dog-like behavior that I almost stretched my hand out toward her.

"Is that what you are? The Diné believe skin-walkers are evil witches, though. Perverting the good of the medicine people. They see them as malevolent forces. I don't think that's you."

She neither confirmed nor denied it.

I studied her. She was gorgeous. Powerfully and leanly built, at the top of the food chain, but elegant and majestic to behold. "Did my wife send you to me?" I whispered, finally voicing the idea that plagued me when the white wolf kept returning.

It was a trick of the moonlight, but I thought the wolf smiled at me before she turned, loped across the meadow, and disappeared into the forest.

My sleep was restless, filled with half memory and half nightmare of hearing my girls cry out for me in the dark forest and not being able to find them.

I woke suddenly, disoriented, and it took me a moment to realize what prodded me from sleep. Frank stood over me whining. And then I smelled it.

Acrid and sharp, the smoke stung the back of my throat when I inhaled. I rolled out of bed, yanked a pair of jeans on, and stuffed my feet into my boots without bothering to scrounge for socks. The safe deposit box key, memory card, and flash drive went into one pocket, and I pulled the photograph of Winona and Emma from the frame and slipped it into another pocket. I tucked the CZ into the waistband of my jeans.

Frank was nervous, the whites of his eyes gleaming in the flickering light of the fire. The flames licked the window over my bed. The fire was outside, for now, but it would soon eat through the metal and be within.

"Let's go." I strode to the door and twisted the handle. It turned under hand, but the door did not open. I threw my shoulder against the door, but it was jammed.

I moved to a window and shoved it open. I bent to

wrap an arm around Frank's chest to lift him. The bullet punched through the side of the Airstream just above my head. I ducked, swearing.

Frank barked, high pitched and frantic, and I pushed him flat to the floor. He was panting hard.

I moved across the narrow expanse of the trailer to open a window on the back side of the Airstream. As soon as I shoved the window open, gunfire erupted again. I dropped into a crouch, realization as bitter as the growing haze of smoke. This was not an accident. This was an execution.

And fuck if I was going to sit on my goddamn laurels and wait for my dog and me to roast.

I kept my head down and crawled back into the bedroom. My rifle was in the narrow closet. I grabbed the Henry, a bag of full bore .45-70 ammo, and the two extra magazines for the CZ.

Heat seared my skin, and I struggled to keep my horror at bay as fire ate through the exterior wall of the Airstream over my bed. Frank was trembling and whining when I reached him.

The rifle was still loaded from our trek into the Yellowstone borderlands. I snatched a cushion from the dining nook and pulled the pistol from the waistband of my jeans. Bullets punched through the cushion as soon as I lifted it into view. Five bullets, five angles. At least five shooters spread out around the front of the Airstream.

I rolled to my knees and swept a line of bullets from left to right across the night. Shouts pierced the dark, and while they were scrambling for cover, I snatched up the Henry.

What the fuckers of Raven's Gap did not realize was

that I had been preparing for someone to take vengeance for fifteen years. The Airstream sat in a meadow, and though the treeline was thirty yards away, the stickers gleamed in the light of the blaze. I thumbed the hammer down, aimed at one of the green glints of reflection, and pulled the trigger.

The explosion rent the night, a bright flair of light followed by a massive, concussive blow of sound. Dirt and debris rained down, thumping on the roof of the Airstream. I cycled the lever to eject the spent shell and chamber the next round, aimed at the next reflection, and pulled the trigger. A choking cough sent my shot wide. I clenched my teeth against the noose of smoke, and my next shot found its mark. The dynamite exploded, sending trees lurching up from the ground, and rattling the trailer like an earthquake. I heard screams and running. I cycled the lever and put a round in the next.

To the casual observer, I looked like a bird enthusiast with birdhouses attached to the trees around the meadow. But those birdhouses were secure, weatherproof, and packed with five pounds of dynamite.

It was a war zone outside as I picked off the next homemade bomb, but it was hell inside. Frank was crouched on the floor pressed against my legs, and the flames howled as the fire ate its way through the bedroom. The heat was blistering my skin, and thick black smoke was clustered in the ceiling of the Airstream.

I was out of ammo in the rifle. I grabbed another round from the bag, handloaded it, and fired at the fourth birdhouse. While debris was still falling from the sky, I grabbed the CZ from where I had dropped it to the floor, tucked it into my waistband, and tossed the rifle and bag of ammo out the back window.

I picked up Frank and ran, turning and leaping into the window, busting it all the way out of the frame as I hit it with my shoulder. I twisted as we fell and took the full brunt of the impact with the ground. The shock of it jolted through me and stole my breath. I pushed Frank off my chest and rolled to my knees. The poodle hunched beside me in fear.

I crouched and swept up the rifle. I handloaded another round, tucking three more rounds between my fingers.

"Frank," I said, putting the firmness of a command in my words even though my voice was a croak. I pointed to the treeline behind the Airstream. "*Go.*"

He bolted for the safety of the woods. The report of a bullet was followed by a yelp. Frank went down, and my heart stopped for an instant. The poodle scrambled to his feet, a swath of red streaming over his white hair, and kept running. Dirt kicked up in front of him with another bark of a bullet. Fury as hot and wild as the flames at my back filled me, and I shouldered the rifle as I stepped into the open.

The man was at the edge of the trees immediately to my right. He aimed again at my dog, but before he could fire, I drilled him with my own bullet. There was a reason big game hunters favored the .45-70. The man's head disappeared when the round found its mark.

I spun, loading the rifle as I strode to the side of the engulfed Airstream, and lit up the fifth birdhouse full of dynamite. The blast punched me back a step. I turned and ran for the woods where Frank disappeared. Pain flared hot and sharp across my left arm.

I broke into the cover of the trees and paused to catch my breath, bending double as a wracking, smoke-laden cough scorched through my lungs. When I straightened, Frank was by my side.

I leaned my rifle against a tree and dropped to my knees beside him. He shivered against me as I carefully ran my hands over him. The wound was black in the low light, angled across the back of his neck. It bled freely, but it was a shallow graze. I wrapped my arms around him and rested my chin on his head as I turned back to peer through the trees.

The Airstream was engulfed, the fire roaring and cracking as it ate through my home. Shadows moved against the firelight, but none appeared to follow us. They were in retreat. Debris was still drifting to earth from the explosions. Sirens wailed in the distance.

I straightened and picked up the rifle. "Let's go," I said softly to Frank. I had no desire to linger and watch my world burn.

TEN

FAYE

I LURCHED AWAKE. The sound came again once my breathing and heart slowed, and I realized it was what startled me from the depths of a nightmare.

The deep, percussive sound was not thunder. It was a more abrupt, violent blow of sound. I rolled over and closed my eyes, but it came again. I lay still, ears pricked. I did not have to wait too long to hear the fourth and fifth shockwave of sound. Those were explosions.

I rolled out of bed and moved through our private rooms, punching in the security code to turn the alarm system off before I left our apartment and wandered through the inn. It was dark. A glance at the glowing clock on the microwave in the kitchen showed the time to be four in the morning.

In the den, I went straight to the wall of glass that faced northeast toward town. I searched the darkness but saw no glow of light indicating a fire anywhere.

I heard a shuffle of footfall behind me and then Evelyn's voice. "You heard it, too."

I turned from the windows to see her crossing to the southwestern side of the room to search the darkness that lay beyond the river. "Do you see anything?"

"Nothing," she said after a moment.

But then the sudden, sharp wail of sirens pierced the

night, and she joined me at the windows facing town. The sounds faded, indicating they were headed out of town toward Gardiner, the only direction one could go from this last stop in the road.

"This town is nowhere near as peaceful as I thought it would be," Evelyn said, voice wry.

I had to chuckle at that. "It was pretty quiet until you arrived," I told her teasingly.

I expected her to laugh, but we stood in silence together at the window for long moments.

"Sometimes I think I draw it to me," she whispered suddenly.

My stomach clenched at my thoughtlessness as I turned to her. Her eyes were unseeing as she stared out the window, face pale, the moonlight bathing her pale hair in a shimmer of silver.

"I shouldn't have said that. I'm sorry."

She waved away my apology. "You were joking."

I had been, but now I was kicking myself at the look on her face. "What happened was not your fault," I said, voice gentle. "What happened to those women, what happened to you. That falls squarely on *his* shoulders. Don't take it on. That is not your burden to bear." The words were familiar, an echo from the past, and I shivered to say them now.

Her eyes were haunted and hunted, but she nodded. "Sometimes it's hard to remember that in the dark."

That was why we reached for the light in the darkness. "Come into the kitchen," I invited. "I'll make you breakfast."

I was better with food than I was with people. I had lingered too long in the silence over the last years, when I always had a tendency toward shyness. Donning a mask of professional friendliness for guests was one thing. It left me exhausted, but it was my job, and based on my repeat visitors, it was one I did well. But being a friend was a role I had not filled in years now.

I was born with the proverbial silver spoon in my mouth. Everything I ever wanted was handed to me. My childhood was the typical "poor rich girl" story. My parents were happy to spoil me but completely uninterested in raising me. That task was left to nannies when I was young. There had been no cruelty, no abuse, but the loneliness was crushing, and the emotional toll of being raised by adults who were paid to do so was crippling.

By the time I was sent to boarding school at twelve, I had no clue how to talk to girls my own age, let alone any knowledge of how to be their friend. And friendship with teenage girls was no casual feat. There were tests and sly challenges and thorny nuances I did not understand.

Boarding school was where I first learned what cruelty was. It was where I first realized someone could smile into my face even as they slipped an emotional knife between my ribs. It was where I realized I did not have to be alone to be lonely. It was where I first felt the high of cocaine and the sudden rush of confidence and composure that came with it.

It was also where I met Mary. Her father was a groundskeeper at the boarding school, her mother a cook. Mary attended the school on a scholarship. Teenage girls were cruel, petty creatures. The rules of their carefully orchestrated society dictated that Mary was an individual to be looked down upon and shunned. But Mary had other ideas, and she was notorious for her ideas. It was impossible not to be drawn to her. She was like the sun. Too bright to be looked at, but everyone revolved around her anyway.

We did not become friends until I was sixteen. She burned bright and hot, and while I admired her, I never dared to draw too close. My parents forgot to send for me that Christmas, and I had nowhere to go for the holiday break. The prospect of staying in the dormitories alone was bleak, but Mary's parents invited me into their home. For the first time in my life, I found myself enfolded in a family in all its chaos and loudness and open displays of affection. It was beautiful and painful all at once, and I cried when I unwrapped the matching set of mittens, scarf, and hat Mary's mother had swiftly knit for me. Mary crawled across the scattered wrapping paper and hugged me as I struggled with my emotions.

Of course I fell in love with her.

Mary's mother was the one who taught me how to make pancakes and shared with me the secret ingredients: seltzer substituted for milk and a few tablespoons of mayonnaise added to the batter.

I combined the ingredients now as the griddle heated. Evelyn stood at the sink washing huckleberries. It was dark outside the window, the early morning quiet companionable. It made me remember the mornings Mary and I spent in the bakery in the hours before opening. Though unlike Evelyn, Mary had always been humming or singing or telling a story.

The Institute of Culinary Education was Mary's idea. We sat down together in the months before we were to finish our last term at boarding school and made a list of what we could do together. She was wonderful with people and had a keen mind for business, and I discovered at her mother's side that I loved being in the kitchen. *Bakery* made the top of our list.

My parents readily paid for me to attend, happy to toss money my way. It was, I realized, the only way they knew how to show me they cared. While Mary worked on a business and marketing degree, I excelled in the institute's pastry and baking arts program. When I finished, my father gave me the building on the Lower East Side as a gift, and my mother hired her favorite interior designer to remodel the first floor into a bakery.

I handled the baking; Mary took care of the rest. Within a year of opening, The Sweet Spot was being featured in magazines, blogs, newspapers, and was labeled as one of the must-visit food destinations in New York City. Part of it was my name linked to the bakery, but we also ran the best bakery in Manhattan, let alone the entire city.

I was born into privilege, but wealth and recognition were new to Mary. She reveled in it, and each night, she sought out the hottest clubs and parties. I did a bump of cocaine to ease my tension over the crowds and the noise, and braced with that high, I followed her.

Looking back, I could not imagine being that painfully young and unaware of the world ever again. But at the time, it was our own Bacchanalia, and the laughter and highs—drug induced or not—we shared in those years were something I could still smile about, though now it was bittersweet. I had more fun with Mary in those years than I ever had.

Until the night I looked across the club. There was a gap in the writhing bodies glistening in the strobe lights. The pulse of the music was heavy and driving, and with the aid of the coke still singing in my system, it felt exciting and primal. I knew who he was. The highest level of society was a small set. He did not look away when I met his gaze, and I was caught in his stare as he placed his drink on the bar and cut through the crowd toward where Mary and I sat.

Someone bumped into him, but he never wavered from his path. When a girl danced in front of him, he grasped her shoulders and moved her aside. The entire time, I was snared by his eyes. At the time, I thought the heat of his gaze was the sexiest thing I had ever seen. Now, if someone stared at me with that amount of intensity, I would recognize him for what he was: a predator.

As he walked through the club, my breath caught in my throat. I did not have a sense of self-preservation at that point, but I remembered that moment with startling clarity. I stared at him and thought, *This is it. This man changes everything.*

And he did.

I poured the batter onto the griddle and dropped a smattering of berries in each one. I went through the motions of making pancakes. This was easy, soothing. It was why I decided to purchase the inn when I saw it was for sale. A wrong turn led Sam and me to Raven's Gap, but once I reached the end of the road, remote and cut off from the rest of the world, I knew this place was perfect. It was as far from New York City as I could get in terms of culture and noise.

I poured batter, added berries, and flipped the pancakes until we both had a fluffy stack. When I turned from the griddle, I found Evelyn had made coffee and warmed some of the homemade huckleberry syrup I kept in the refrigerator.

We were sitting down at the small table in the corner

of the kitchen when the screams split the quiet. I started violently, sloshing hot coffee over my hand, transported for an instant into the past.

The scream came again, galvanizing me and yanking me back to the present. My plate clattered to the table. Evelyn was already limping down the hallway toward my apartment, and I darted past her. I ran to Sam's room and found him twisting in his bed, the covers tangled around him as he writhed in the grip of a nightmare.

I put a knee on the mattress and a hand on his shoulder. "Sam." My voice was firm and loud. It had been years now since he was plagued by nightmares, but in the first two years, he awakened me regularly with haunting whimpers. He never screamed, though. The sound raised the hair on the nape of my neck. "You're safe. It's just a dream." He went rigid under my hand the instant he finally roused from sleep. "It's me, honey. It's okay."

Evelyn turned the lamp on behind me. Sam sagged, and then he lunged up from the tangle of sheets and wrapped his arms around my neck. Caught off balance, I braced a hand on the bed to keep from toppling over. "It's okay. It wasn't real. You're fine. I'm here."

He buried his damp face against my throat, arms tight around me. He trembled against me as I rubbed his back, and I wondered how I was supposed to comfort a child when I had no idea what frightened him. I twisted to sit on the bed, pulling him with me until he was sprawled across my lap.

I held him tightly, and the shudders wracking him gradually lessened. When he took a deep breath and his hold on me loosened, I asked, "Do you think you can go back to sleep?"

He shook his head, his forehead rolling against my collarbone.

"Your mom and I were about to have pancakes," Evelyn said. "Want to join us?"

He pulled back from me and scrubbed his cheeks with his palms. He smiled at her shyly and nodded.

In the kitchen, I warmed the pancakes as Evelyn heated our coffee and poured Sam a glass of milk. My mind churned. Sam had not been sleeping well for several months now, but a nightmare had never made him cry out in such a way. I did not think the timing was coincidental.

I needed to find out what happened at Grant Larson's ranch.

ELEVEN

GRANT

"WHAT PART OF *make it look like an accident* did you not understand?" My voice held a sharp bite that startled Iago, and the wild horse danced away from me.

"You didn't tell me he was a one-man army," John Smith said as he approached the pen.

"What's the damage?"

"He blew Rogers's head off. Not to mention the injuries from the IEDs. What civilian has access to dynamite?"

"I meant," I said between clenched teeth, "can this be traced back to me?"

John smirked. "Relax, Senator. We cleaned up and were gone before the police and fire department arrived."

"And Hector Lewis is still alive."

"He won't be for long," he assured me.

"I expect you to make this right."

His smile was not a pleasant expression. "Don't I always?"

"And I want no mistakes with the woman and the boy."

He mimicked doffing his hat to me before he turned and strode away.

Rage made my hands tremble, and I took slow, deep

breaths to calm the fury. But there was something else there, beneath the anger at the blitheness and disrespect.

I had felt it so infrequently in my life, it took me a moment to recognize the emotion as fear. I could count on one hand the number of times I had been afraid. The last instances of fear both revolved around Winona.

The first occurred several months after she started working for me.

I heard the commotion before I saw it. One of the voices that was contributing to the yelling and swearing had me breaking into a jog as I rounded the corner of the barn.

I reached the corral in time to see Winona yank the bullwhip out of the new hire's hand and swing it. The tail caught the man across the cheek, leaving a knife-like wound across his face that immediately welled with blood.

The sudden silence was thick with tension.

"You crazy bitch," the man breathed. When he lunged for her, she hit him across the face again with the whip. Before he could reach her, three of the other ranch hands had him face down in the dirt.

"What is going on here?" I snapped.

Winona whirled toward me, and I almost stepped back since the whip was still clenched in her hand. "It's pretty clear what was going on here. And if this is the kind of treatment you allow your horses to receive, I quit." She tossed the whip at my feet and moved slowly across the corral to the quivering, sweating horse at the far end.

She could not quit. The very thought of never seeing her again almost cut my knees out from under me. I fired the newly hired hand on the spot. She never knew

I had my men take him out behind the north barn and flay the flesh from his back with the very whip he used on the horse and she marked his face with.

I convinced her to stay by allowing her to set up her own training program, not for the horses but for my own trainers. It was a genius move on my part. She was brilliant and gentle with horses, and as soon as she began teaching the other trainers her methods, I saw results across the board.

The second time I felt that gut-clench of fear was when I knew she discovered the truth and I realized I would have to kill her to keep her quiet.

TWELVE

HECTOR

THE FOOTSTEPS ON the front porch were quiet and stealthy. The evening light spilled in a bright pool through the windows of the cabin. The location was remote, several miles back from the highway, and only a handful of people knew about the old hunting lodge from bygone decades.

As soon as I heard the cry of the magpies, I locked Frank in the bedroom, inserted a loaded magazine into the CZ, and pulled the slide to chamber a round as I crept across the room. The ragged hooked rug muffled my footsteps, and I pressed back against the wall adjacent to the door.

The porch creaked and groaned underfoot, and then I heard a voice call softly, "Hector? Are you here?"

I set the CZ aside and jerked open the door. "What the hell are you doing here?"

She gave a start of surprise, leaned her shotgun against the porch railing, and then flew into my arms. I grunted at the impact and almost staggered back a step.

"Goddamn, Hec," Maggie whispered, "goddamn." Her voice cracked.

I folded my arms around her and cupped my hand around the back of her head. "It's alright. Everything's fine."

Her fist hit me in the stomach, though there was no force behind the blow. "Everything is *not* fine," she snapped. "I've been waiting all day to hear if you were found inside your trailer. They have your whole place barricaded off and wouldn't let me through. And you have blood on your shirt." She leaned back to peer up at me, and her eyes were bright with tears. "You're okay? Frank's okay?"

"We're a little singed and reek of smoke, but we're in one piece."

She sniffed, and that unflappable steel backbone showed itself as she gave a final squeeze and stepped back. "Let me look at your arm."

She collected her shotgun and followed me inside, placing the old Browning on the rickety table. I opened the bedroom door, and Maggie knelt as Frank rushed out. He was frantic for her attention, still traumatized by the events of the morning.

I cleaned his wound as best I could. Her face turned ashen as she took in the blood on his coat.

"I want you to take him home with you," I said, and a cough strangled my words.

She looked up at me from where she crouched on the floor, her brow furrowed. "Sit down and let me see your arm."

I obeyed, easing carefully into the one chair in the near-derelict cabin. She moved to my side and unwound the scrap of cloth I bound around my bicep. Blood had dried the makeshift bandage to the edges of the wound. As she gently tugged at it, I clenched my teeth against the feel of the wound tearing open again.

Maggie sucked in a breath. "This is a bullet wound. On both you and Frank."

"It is," I agreed, grimacing as another cough scraped my throat.

"This was not just a fire."

I sighed and tilted my head back as she carefully worked the makeshift bandage free. "Someone tried to kill me. They set a fire and then shot at me when I tried to escape." Anger flared again, as hot as the flames had been. "They shot at Frank, too, as he was running for the woods."

She swore under her breath. "Who was it?" She met my gaze when I remained silent. "People have moved on. It takes effort to hold a grudge that long, and only—"

"Only Jack or Ed are still burning that candle."

"Ed would shoot you in the face," she said. "He would never hurt Frank." Her face was pinched as she took in the ugly furrow the bullet left in my arm. "You need to see a doctor."

"I'll be fine. I want you to take Frank and go home, Maggie."

"I'm not leaving you here. Come with—"

"Please," I said quietly.

Her gaze searched my face. "What are you not telling me?"

"I think Winona discovered something about Grant Larson. If I had to guess after this morning, I would say I think it may have gotten her killed." Her eyes widened, and I continued. "I wager he thinks I know what she discovered."

"You're coming home with me," Maggie said. When I opened my mouth to argue, she snapped, "It wasn't a suggestion. If your stubborn ass is staying here, then so am I."

Frank leaned against my knees. He was still panting nervously, and he had not even bothered to investigate the squeaking nest in the corner. "You're not staying here."

"Then we're going home. I'll patch up your arm and Frank's neck as best I can. I'll feed you both. You can tell me everything while we hike back to my car."

Her chin was set, and I knew there was no arguing with her. As we hiked back to where she parked her vehicle, I told her about the thumb drive, the camera traps in the woods along the border of Larson's property, and the safety deposit box key.

Out of the corner of my eye, I thought I saw the white wolf keeping pace with us through the woods, but every time I turned my head to try to spot her, she disappeared into the shadows.

We bathed Frank in Maggie's old clawfoot bathtub, cleaning him of the soot, the smell of smoke, and the blood. Once he had eaten and was settled on Maggie's couch as she bandaged his neck, I claimed her shower.

Later, when I sat in her bright, fragrant kitchen as she swabbed antibiotic ointment on my arm and bandaged it, she quietly asked, "Why didn't you come to me this morning? I was worried sick."

"I went to the cabin to think through what I need to do next. Larson is a powerful man. A dangerous man."

"What are we going to do?"

I slanted her a look at the use of *we*. "I don't want you involved in this."

"Too late. Winona was my dearest friend. Now you are. What can I do to help?"

I stood and moved down the hall to her guest bedroom, where I left the contents of my pockets on the bedside table before I tossed my clothes in the washing machine. I returned to the kitchen and slid the small key across the table to her. "I need you to find out which bank this key belongs to. I need to know what Winona hid there."

She turned the key over and studied it. "I'll start calling banks tomorrow morning."

"And I don't want you telling anyone I'm here." Her brow creased, but I continued before she could argue with me. "This morning, it was a coordinated attack. Larson's men or not, I don't want this to come to your doorstep." She let out a sigh and nodded. "Do you mind if I borrow your cell?"

"Not at all." When I moved toward the guest bedroom, she called after me, "Supper will be ready in fifteen."

William answered on the first ring. "Hey, Ma."

"It's Hector. Your mother's fine. I'm just borrowing her phone."

"I tried to call you earlier today, and your phone went straight to voicemail. Your girl is off the grid, Hec. No passport, no bank account, no line of credit. She's a ghost."

It took me a moment to realize of whom he spoke. "You couldn't find anything at all on Faye Anders?"

He chuckled. "Oh, I found plenty on Faye Anders. Small town librarian in Iowa. A regular volunteer at the local hospital and animal shelter. She was single, no children, and died in a car accident twenty years ago at the age of thirty-three when she was driving home from volunteering at the hospital one night and was hit by a drunk driver."

"And I'm guessing there is no Sam Anders?"

"Your girl's son? He doesn't exist. At least not on paper. It sounds like Raven's Gap has gotten a lot more interesting since I left."

"And it just got even more interesting." I told him of this morning's events.

He was quiet for a moment when I finished. "Do I need to get Ma out of town?"

It was my turn to chuckle. "You really think you could manage that?"

He let out a breath. "No."

"Tell me what you know about Larson."

"As a rancher or a politician?" he asked.

"Politician." I could find out about the ranching angle. The DC connection was beyond me.

"Off the top of my head, I know he was sworn into the Senate in the '90s. He's pretty moderate but leans left on agriculture, environmental issues, education, and healthcare. He's more right wing about guns and Israel. Serves on a number of committees, especially ones related to energy interests, public lands, and national parks. He's well liked, seen as approachable and honest."

"Does the man have any secrets?"

"He's a politician. Of course he does. He's in someone's pocket, and he's a pathological liar."

"I need to know whose pocket he's in, and what he's lying about."

"Give me a couple of days. And, Hector? I'm counting on you."

"I know. Someone will have to get through me to get to Maggie."

"Don't let them get through you," he ordered, and hung up.

I STARTLED INTO wakefulness dreaming I could smell smoke. It was a phantom scent, but it drew me from bed. I moved silently through Maggie's dark house, checking the locks on the windows and the front and back doors. I cracked the door to Maggie's room to check on her. She was curled up on one side of the bed with Louie, the little Bichon, tucked into the bend of her knees. I retreated.

Everything was secure, but I stood in the kitchen staring out the window over the sink. All was dark and quiet, but I watched the shadows until I felt Frank lean against my legs.

I rested a hand on his head. The mattress in Maggie's guest bedroom was comfortable, but I did not return to it. I grabbed a comb from the bathroom and moved to the couch. Frank sprawled beside me, content to let me work the fine-toothed implement through his hair as long as I did not get too close to the tender wound on the back of his neck.

I never had a dog as a boy, but desperately wanted one. Once, when I was ten, a stray that was half wild and all bones and mangy fur wandered up to our shack. I shared the fish I caught with him, and he stayed for three days until he disappeared. I searched for hours until I found his broken body by the railroad tracks. I cried harder over that nameless dog than I had over anything else in my life.

When I first brought Bill, Frank's predecessor, home, I saw him as little more than a tool to aid my search for Winona and Emma. But the brown poodle puppy viewed our relationship differently. When I lost Bill at the age of ten to cancer, I was gutted. I lasted six months after his passing before I went back to Bill's breeder for another puppy.

I did not know why I was incapable of loving my wife and daughter. Until I brought Bill home, I thought it was simply an emotion I was not equipped to feel. The emotion I felt for my dog, though, surpassed anything I had ever felt for another human. I stopped questioning it. I could not be bothered to sit on the proverbial couch and parse out my feelings.

When all the snarls were combed free from Frank's hair, I set the comb aside. Maggie's laptop was sitting on the coffee table in the living room, and I powered it up and retrieved the flash drive from the night stand in the bedroom. I pulled up the spreadsheets Winona had created and studied the one with what appeared to be surnames in one column, date ranges in the next, and coordinates in the third column. If they were surnames, out of the three hundred fifty plus names, only one stood out to me as familiar. *Harrington-Moore.*

I pulled up the internet browser and searched for Harrington-Moore. Entries for Johnson Harrington-Moore showed up on the screen. I always thought it asinine when a man had three last names. Johnson Harrington-Moore owned one of the largest pharmaceutical companies in the world. Harrington-Moore was an American company that developed a number of drugs, vaccines, and biologics. An internet search showed its top drugs and devices were in the areas of cancer, diabetes, and infectious diseases.

The lobbying group for the pharmaceutical industry was legendary. I did a search for the senator and Harrington-Moore and found a number of images of the two men together. At high-end restaurants, at sporting events, at what looked to be an opera or a symphony.

I studied the list. Some of the surnames were too generic to bother searching. Nelson, Carmichael, Jefferson. I skimmed over the long list of names for another that was more unique. *Navarro*. The name sounded familiar, but when I performed a search on it, too many results came back. Instead, I queried Larson and Navarro together, and the search returned a news article from a few years ago. Grant Larson was mentioned in the article along with Edmond Navarro, president and CEO of the largest natural gas producer in the Appalachian Basin.

I searched both Navarro and Harrington-Moore in coordination with the dates listed on the spreadsheet for each, but the results that came back told me nothing.

The blue-white glare of the computer screen against the background of the dark living room gave me a headache, and light spots flickered across my vision when I closed the laptop. I placed the laptop on the coffee table, and Frank shifted to rest his chin on my knee. I placed my hand on his side and tilted my head against the back of the couch.

Two wealthy, powerful men were on Winona's list. I would place bets on the other names on her list being just as wealthy and powerful. These were the kinds of connections a man in Larson's position would have, both as one of the largest land owners in America and as a senator. Had the coordinates not led me to the camera traps in the national park borderlands, I would assume it was a list of campaign donors.

I needed to get eyes on Larson's operation, and knew of only one way of doing that.

By the time I heard Maggie stirring in the next room, I was almost finished cooking breakfast. When she stumbled into the kitchen, bleary eyed, I slid a freshly poured cup of coffee across the counter to her. She clutched it in her hands and staggered to the table. She buried her face in the mug and did not come up for air until I placed a plate laden with an omelet, hash browns, and toast in front of her.

I sat across from her and ate my share, waiting until she stood and poured a second cup of coffee before speaking to her. "Do you still have Jose's photography equipment and camping gear?"

"I do. I should have sold it, but I just left it stored in the garage."

"May I borrow some of it?"

Her brow furrowed. "What are you planning?"

I told her. "I'll be gone for a few days. Do you mind keeping Frank for me?"

"You know I don't, but I don't like this one bit."

"I'll be fine. I'm not going to get too close. I just want to see what I'm up against."

She reached across the table and touched the back of my hand. "It doesn't have to just be *you*, Hector."

I smiled at her and could feel the bitter edge to it. "Who's going to back me up? What friend am I going to call on other than you?"

Her frustrated silence told me she knew the answer as well as I did. "And I'm useless to you in this. I hate that."

"You're not useless. Keep my dog safe and hidden. Keep an eye on his wound. Don't let on to anyone that you know of what happened. As far as you and anyone else knows at this point, I've disappeared."

She smirked. "You're just going to let everyone think you're dead?"

This time when I smiled, there was real humor to it. "And won't they all be disappointed when they find out the news of my demise is greatly exaggerated."

THIRTEEN

FAYE

AFTER I DROPPED Sam off at his friend's house to spend the night, I came home and went straight to his bedroom. As I searched the room, I told myself that at the age of eight, he did not have any privacy to invade. It staved off my guilt as I looked through his collection of books and sifted through his toys.

I found the notebook he liked to draw in tucked under his pillow. I perched on the edge of the bed and flipped through the pages. The drawings consisted of what I imagined most young boys' drawings consisted of. Superheroes and cars, monsters and trains. I thought several of the drawings depicted life here at the inn, guests at breakfast in the dining room, the fire pit in use beside the river. The drawings made me smile, until I turned to the most recent pages.

This was what I had been searching for, but as I studied the heavy lines drawn in pencil and crayon, I could not make sense of the scenes. I was looking for pictures with the heavy red marks of blood or of men touching him inappropriately. I imagined that was what a psychiatrist would look for. But I was a baker and an innkeeper, not a shrink, and the pictures he drew of what looked like fat dogs and eyeballs struck me as odd but not disturbing hints of trauma.

I slipped his notebook back under his pillow and retreated to the kitchen. I originally thought to run the
inn as a bed and breakfast, but it was too difficult to
manage that alone if I had a full guest list. If I had one
or two guests, I cooked breakfast, but when the inn
was full, I usually set out muffins along with coffee
and tea in the mornings, and one day a week, I served
pancakes for breakfast.

I never set out to feed the town, but Ed Decker, the
local mechanic, showed up one morning to tow a guest's
vehicle. It was bitterly cold, and I offered him coffee
and pancakes. The next week, Ed showed up again on
pancake morning, this time with his wife and a dozen
people from town. I had been serving breakfast weekly
ever since.

On Friday evenings, I set out cookies. I perused my
pantry to see what tonight's cookie would be. I settled
on double chocolate mint cookies and within the hour
had a tray laden with fragrant cookies ready for the
sideboard in the great room.

The fire was low in the massive fireplace, more for
ambiance than for heat, though spring here was a fickle
creature. The family of four from Kentucky was playing
a card game at one of the sitting areas near the windows
overlooking the deck. The older couple from Massachu-
setts were reading by the fire. Two middle aged couples, one set from Florida, the other from California,
had drawn a set of chairs together in a loose circle and
chatted animatedly.

I donned the facade of friendly innkeeper and
stopped to talk with each group for several minutes.
I told the older couple about the bookstore in town,
though I left out the fact that one of the managers had

been a serial killer. The middle-aged couples asked about restaurants in the area, and I gave them a list of suggestions. The family of four was curious about which trails in the national park would be suitable for children.

I breathed slowly through the exchanges, keeping my smile in place and my tone friendly. The casual back and forth conversation with strangers had never come easily to me. I was completely at a loss when it came to small talk. But answering questions and keeping the professional guise of hostess in place made things easier and kept a barrier between us that prohibited the anxiety from crawling up my chest and into my throat.

I was fluent in four languages and never mastered the art of conversation in any of them. But as the innkeeper, no one wanted to know what my favorite music was or what movies I enjoyed or which books I reread the most. No one asked what I thought of the current state of politics or my opinion on the latest headline events. That made speaking with my guests easier. They did not see me as an individual. They saw me in a role that extended to aiding them in enjoying and planning their vacation.

It was refreshing that they did not ask anything of me personally, and over the last year, my hands had stopped sweating when I approached people sitting together talking. The hot flush of nerves did not stain my chest and throat as I spoke to my guests. I managed to cobble together a confident approach that did not involve a line of cocaine.

I walked into a bathroom at boarding school the year I was fifteen and stumbled upon a group of girls snorting lines off of the marble edge of the sink. They were all lovely and nubile and confident, and I was miserable and painfully shy and lonely. I had led a sheltered life, but I was not ignorant. I knew drug use when I saw it, even though I was shocked by it.

When one girl turned to me with a smile and said, "Want to try?" it was not out of curiosity that I joined them around the sink. Now, I would not even call it peer pressure. Instead, it was the intense euphoria of being included.

I did not anticipate the rush of confidence. When I held one nostril closed as I leaned over and swiftly inhaled, I did not expect the happiness I felt when the drug hit my system. I felt lovely and invincible. When I went back to the classroom, I did not hesitate when the instructor called my name. For the first time in my life, I strode to the front of the room without pause and recited my assigned portion of *The Love Song of J. Alfred Prufrock*. I had dreaded this assignment since it was given to me. But with the drug singing in my veins, I did not even stammer. *Let us go then, you and I, When the evening is spread out against the sky Like a patient etherized upon a table; Let us go, through certain half-deserted streets, The muttering retreats Of restless nights in one-night cheap hotels And sawdust restaurants with oyster-shells.*

It was an addictive feeling, such a sense of poise and élan when all my life I had been plagued with crippling shyness. It was an addiction I precariously balanced on a razor's edge for a dozen years. And it was ammunition he could have used against me to take Sam.

When we fled the city, I needed more than social aplomb. I needed tenacity, courage, and a plan. So I quit cold turkey. The withdrawals almost killed me. I still was not certain how many days I lost at the rundown motel in New Jersey in the midst of the hallucinations, sweating, and blind craving. *The muttering retreats Of restless nights in one-night cheap hotels.* Eliot's poem, J. Alfred's love song, swirled around and around in my head when I was conscious.

I was still haunted by what Sam must have witnessed and gone through locked in the room with me while I was insensible. I did not know how many days he went without eating. His diaper had been so full when I finally came to that the rash he developed took months to heal. He was pale with shadows under his eyes as dark as bruises when I finally had the strength to lift him into my arms. He did not cry. He simply stared at me silently. It turned my stomach and filled me with self-loathing even now.

I blinked and brought myself back to the present, snagging a handful of cookies from the platter and venturing out onto the back deck. I found Evelyn in an Adirondack chair with her feet propped against the railing. I dragged a chair close and offered her several cookies as I propped my feet up beside hers.

We ate in companionable silence and watched the late evening light gild the river. Nothing about Evelyn reminded me of Mary. The woman next to me was reserved, taciturn, and forthright. Every now and then, sorrow etched itself into her features. It made me wonder what had brought her, alone, to such a remote and unfamiliar town. But her expression no longer held the tense brittleness it had when she first showed up on my doorstep.

I left her to her secrets. I knew there were some things a woman could not share, even with a friend.

My cell phone buzzed in my pocket, and when I pulled it free, I recognized the number. I slid my thumb across the screen to accept the call. "Madeline."

"Hi, Faye. Nothing is wrong, but Sam seems to want to come home."

"Did something happen?" I asked.

She hesitated. The silence stretched for a brief pause, and her voice held a false brightness when she spoke again. "Not that I've been able to gather from the boys. They played for a bit after dinner, but when I just went to put a movie on for them, Sam wrote a note saying he wants to go home. Shall I meet you in Gardiner?"

Sam rarely wrote as a form of communication. Even if her moment of silence had not clued me in that she lied, her claim of Sam writing a note did. "No, you don't need to load everyone up and come out. I'll just come to the house. Tell him I'm on my way."

I hung up as I got to my feet. Evelyn tipped her head back against the chair and smiled at me. "I'll hold down the fort for you."

I usually hired help in the spring, summer, and fall months. I had hired housekeeping help, but held off hiring anyone to help with dealing with guests. Evelyn had readily fallen into that role, but now, as I grabbed my purse and headed to my old Ford Explorer parked out front, I wondered if I was taking advantage of her friendship. I would put an ad out in town next week.

A vehicle was parked in a neighboring driveway, but I did not recognize it. I glanced automatically in the rearview mirror as I passed, and the vehicle pulled out after me. It did not get too close when I braked for the stop sign, but it turned onto the state road behind me.

Tension swept through me. My gaze darted between

the pavement in front of me and my rearview mirror. I did not realize how tightly my hands were clenched around the steering wheel or how knotted my stomach had become until the vehicle turned off on a side street. I relaxed marginally, taking a deep breath to get my nerves under control. But as I drove the winding canyon road to Gardiner, passed through town, and turned onto the dirt road the Carters lived off of, I kept glancing behind me to see if anyone followed.

The road leading to the Carters' house was steep and winding, cut into the mountain so that a craggy embankment girded one side while a steep drop-off flanked the other. It was a road typical to the area, with no guardrail for reassurance, and I drove with care as the evening deepened.

Sam was waiting for me when I pulled up in front of the house ten minutes later. He stood at the front door, and when Madeline opened it for me, he walked into me, pressed his head against my chest, and clung to me.

"I'm sorry," Madeline said.

"Don't worry about it," I said with forced lightness. "He's been having a hard time sleeping lately. I imagine that is part of the issue."

He clung to my hand as we walked back to my SUV. The sun had sunk low over the mountains, and the last of the day's light died as he clambered into the backseat.

"Did anything happen?" I asked as I buckled my seatbelt. "Did someone say anything to you or do something?"

He shook his head, and when I glanced in the rearview mirror, he was staring out the window. I watched him for a moment. I knew his small face so well. Every curve, every quirk of his eyebrows, every rare gap-

toothed smile. But his internal landscape was so unfamiliar to me. I knew nothing of his thoughts, and
didn't know how to protect him when I did not know
what frightened him.

I put the SUV in gear, flicked on the headlights,
and drove slowly down the mountain road. A couple
of miles later, headlights pierced the dark behind us.
I flinched as the reflection of the bright lights in my
mirrors blinded me for an instant. Unease gripped me
as the vehicle approached and descended the mountain
almost on my bumper.

"Do you have your seatbelt on, Sam?" I asked, careful to keep the tension from my voice. I felt an affirma-
tive bump from his foot in the back of my seat.

Night fell quickly here, and the road was dark. There
were no streetlights. Only the glow of my headlights
created a sliver of relief against the black. The road felt
more treacherous in the dark, and the vehicle only a few
feet from my bumper felt like a threat. I sped up as much
as I dared on the winding unpaved road. Around the
next curve, I lost sight of the other vehicle for an instant.

The road stretched straight before me for twenty-five
yards before the next curve, and I hit the gas. My Explorer was old and cantankerous. It gave a lurch and a
groan but then darted forward and raced down the road.

I was always armed, but I could not reach the holster on my ankle without lifting my foot from the gas
pedal. I slowed going into the curve. My headlights did
not penetrate the yawning expanse of the drop beyond
the nonexistent shoulder. Keeping an eye on the road
and one hand on the wheel, I leaned over and grappled
for the handle on the glove compartment. I had a Glock
43 tucked within.

The headlights of the other vehicle illuminated the inside of the Explorer, and then I heard the roar of the engine before I felt the lurch of impact. I straightened and grappled with the steering wheel as the Explorer swerved dangerously toward the side of the road.

Sam's foot beat a frightened tattoo against my back through the seat. I could not risk a glance toward him. "It's okay, honey. We're okay. We're going to be fine, Sam." I chanted the words over and over.

The old SUV coughed, and the engine revved as I floored the accelerator. I took the next curve in the road sharply and, for an instant, lost sight of the other vehicle in the rearview mirror. But then it was back, racing up on my bumper so swiftly and aggressively all I could do was brace myself.

There was no time to cry out. The force of the impact slung me forward before the seatbelt locked and yanked me back. My vision went dark at the edges, and then another jolt shuddered through the vehicle. Metal screamed, and then my own voice joined in when I lost control of the Explorer with a final strike from the other car.

The world spun violently around me and then exploded when my SUV flew off the road.

It was as if I had been thrown into the center of a tornado. My car was tossed end over end. I wrapped my arms around my head to shield my face. Trees snapped, and metal crumpled with shrieking groans.

And then there was an agony that felt as if my body were being wrenched apart.

Everything went black.

PART TWO

FOURTEEN

GRANT

"WELL?" I ASKED when he darkened the doorway of my study. I preferred to deal with John Smith in the daylight. He always looked larger and more menacing in the shadows of the night, and I was careful to keep my unease from my voice.

He still heard it, though, if the sardonic curve of his mouth was any testament. He prowled across the room and took one of the chairs across from my desk. "It's done."

"You're certain?"

"I didn't think you liked to hear the details. You've mentioned culpability before."

"And you screwed up last time. Forgive me for needing a little reassurance," I said, voice dry.

"When someone does find her vehicle at the bottom of the mountain along Snowshoe Lane, it will look like she lost control and drove right off the road. Single car accident. We cleaned up the scene. Shortly after she went over the edge, her SUV caught fire and exploded."

I hid a grimace. "Her son?"

John, I noticed, was not the least bit squeamish about the news. He was matter of fact to the point of being disconcertingly cold. Granted, that was why I hired him.

"He was with her. We waited until she had the boy in the car before we made our move."

"Good." I thought again of how familiar the pair of them seemed to me and pushed aside any hint of guilt. "What are you doing to find Hector Lewis?"

"He's gone off the grid, but I'm working on it."

"Work on it faster," I snapped. "Boudreaux is arriving in two days."

It was one of Boudreaux's previous visits years ago that was the beginning of the end with Winona. They passed one another as he left the barn and she entered. I was too far away to hear what he said to her, but I could see her face. The distaste in her expression was clear.

"What did he say to you?" I asked when she reached me.

She glanced over her shoulder toward the open barn doorway. When she turned back to me, all expression was wiped clean. She shrugged. "Nothing I haven't heard before." She hesitated, mouth opening to say more before she closed it with a click of her teeth.

"Go on," I said. "What were you going to say?"

"The man is a pig. I hope you're not planning on letting him near any of my horses."

I hid a smile and refrained from reminding her that these were my horses. "No, he isn't here for the horses."

She studied me. "Why is he here? He's not the only rich prick I've seen come through here. None of them have been here for the horses."

I kept my expression carefully blank. "They're just here for business."

And they were, but it was not a business dealing Winona would ever approve of.

I hid a smile at the memory of her impression of Boudreaux. She was right. The man was a pig.

I shook myself and focused on the matter at hand. "I want this situation taken care of yesterday," I said. "I pay you and your team enough that you shouldn't need a second chance. Especially not to handle one man."

John's expression remained passive. "It will be taken care of. This time, we'll go in expecting a war."

FIFTEEN

HECTOR

MAGGIE DROPPED ME OFF on the outskirts of Gardiner hours before sunrise. "You'll be careful?" she asked, holding my rifle as I shouldered my pack.

I grimaced as the shoulder strap scored across the bandage wrapped around my upper arm. The graze from the bullet was a warm pulse I had swallowed a handful of pain relievers to dull. "I won't get caught."

She sighed and handed me the Henry. "That wasn't what I meant."

I switched on my headlamp and set off into the hills, pressing west and north. There was no trail to follow. The handheld GPS led me deeper into Grant Larson's land.

The predawn hours were dark, and my headlamp only illuminated a slender swath of forest ahead of me. The wilderness was monochromatic at this hour. The world that fell within the light of my headlamp was shaded in grays. The yawning black beyond my light seemed cavernous and empty. The world dropped away outside of my narrow field of vision.

The early morning air was steeped in the scent of spruce, fir, and pine, and it still held the crisp bite of winter. All was quiet and still until the white wolf crossed between the trees at the ragged edge of my light's beam. I stumbled to a halt. She paused to glance over her shoulder and, this time, I was certain she smiled at me.

She wove in and out of my light, always just ahead of me, frequently glancing back to check my pace. The trek was a rolling one of mountains and valleys and streams, and the miles passed quickly underfoot.

"Are you following me, or are you leading me?" I called to her.

My light caught in the golden gleam of her eyes as she looked back at me. With a flick of her tail, she disappeared into the night. Though I searched for her as I continued my hike, she never showed herself to me again.

I was a mile from the main compound of Larson's ranch when the first pale precursors of sunrise lightened the eastern horizon. I climbed a rugged low mountain and set up camp below the ridge well within the tree line, clearing off a section of the ground and using a small shovel in my pack to level the area for my tent. Once that task was completed, I shouldered my pack once more and climbed to the summit.

I was half a mile from the main compound of Grant Larson's ranch. Any closer and I risked setting off any perimeter alarms he might have in place. I did not need to be closer. From the crest of the low mountain, I could see the first rays of sunlight gleam on the roofs.

I set up the tripod low to the ground and mounted the high-powered binoculars. The field of view was a thousand yards. Close at hand, I set up a second tripod and mounted the Nikon FX with the Sigma 150-600mm Sport lens attached. I had no doubt Larson's security team patrolled the area immediately surrounding his home and barns. The mountaintop was craggy and tree-less. I stayed low and lay flat, settling in on my stomach.

I put my eyes to the sights on the binoculars, ad-justed the focus, and Grant's sprawling compound came into sharp relief. There were signs of life already, even though the sun had not fully risen. The ranch hands were already about, and I settled in to watch.

The daily inner workings of a ranch were not unfa-miliar to me. As a boy, I awakened one morning, and when I peeked around the curtain that served as the wall to my mother's bedroom in the ramshackle two-room house we squatted in, I found her still abed. I snuck away for the day, escaping the monotonous confine-ment of school and the countless fights I had with the boys who jeered about their fathers doing my mother in the alley behind the bar.

I did not fight for my mother. I was certainly not de-fending her honor, as she had none for me to care about. My first memory was of cleaning up her vomit when she returned from a bender. I was four at the time, and in all of my memories, I could never recall a kind word or a gentle touch from the woman.

I fought to release some of the rage that simmered in-side me constantly. Only when I felt the crack of knuck-les against my cheekbone and drove my fist into the tender belly of the other boy did I feel some sense of release from the pressure of being so angry.

But on this day, I simply wanted the peace of sitting alone by the Platte River with my fishing rod. I dis-tinctly remembered not catching any fish that day, but being perfectly content with the hours spent under the endless, harsh Nebraska sky. When the sun began to list in the western sky toward the horizon, I wandered through the rows of wheat toward home. My stomach was gnawing on my backbone in hunger. It was a feeling I was well familiar with.

In my head, I envisioned my mother reprimanding me when I returned home, scolding me severely in a soft, even, caring tone before hugging me and telling me she had been worried sick. I laughed at the fantasy, knowing she would not have even noticed I was gone. She rarely acknowledged my presence even when I was home.

But when I made it back to our derelict shack, she was still abed. Not even a shuffle of stirring or the whisper of breath came around the curtain, and when I pushed it aside, a slant of light from the dying sun spilled through the open door and fell across her face. Her eyes were closed. Her face was gray, and her blue lips were speckled with her own vomit.

I stared at her, willing myself to feel sorrow and empathy for this bitter husk of a woman who never had any love for me. But instead, I felt nothing. Not even the anger that was always bubbling just beneath the surface. It was gone, as certainly as she was.

I rolled my few belongings into a paper sack and then searched the cupboards. One can of beans and a moldy hunk of bread were all that lined the shelves. I scraped the mold off and deposited both in my paper sack. I did not glance behind the curtain as I walked out of the house. And as I strode into the wheat fields, heading toward the highway, I did not look back.

I slept in a ditch that first night, with my spare shirt as my blanket and coyote song as my lullaby. The next day, I began hitchhiking west. Though I was rail thin, I was tall for my age, and no one thought I was anything less than a young man making his way across the country for work.

Until an old, weathered man in an equally old and weathered pickup pulled onto the gravel shoulder near the Montana state line and offered me a ride. When I climbed into the front seat, his eyes narrowed, and he studied my face with a keen gaze.

"Bologna sandwich in the glove box if you want it," he said.

I had not eaten in days, and my head swam with lightness. I ate the sandwich in three bites.

"Where you headed?" he asked.

I gave him my standard answer. "To a job in California."

"Bullshit," he drawled. "You're not older than twelve."

Juvenile indignation had me correcting him. "I'm fourteen!"

"Hm," was all he said in response. Fifty miles of rolling plains passed before he spoke again. "Do you have a place to stay tonight?" When I remained quiet, he continued. "Got a room in my barn no one is using at the moment. Warm and dry, clean. I don't have a big spread, but it's more than I can manage now on my own. You help me out on the ranch, and you'll get three square meals a day."

I stared at his grizzled face, the glint of white in his whiskers, the deep lines around his eyes and mouth. Though his clothes were worn, he was dressed neatly. His truck was old, but the inside was clean. He was old enough, I figured I could outrun him if need be.

"Okay."

"Name's Jed Lewis. What's yours, kid?" he asked.

The work had been grueling, but it was as he promised. I had plenty to eat. I had a bed to sleep in at night that was not eaten by mice. The long hours day in and day out emptied me of any residual anger and resentment. Jed was a hard man, but he was fair. For the first time in my life, I thought I might be happy.

As I watched the comings and goings on Larson's ranch, I spotted no children among his hands. But Larson worked side by side with his men. Nothing looked amiss throughout the first day as I studied each man, each paddock, and each barn.

Except for the north barn. None of the ranch hands entered the barn. Had it not been for the numerous cameras on the eaves of the barn, I would have thought the building in disuse.

I studied each face of Larson's security team but did not recognize anyone. It had been too dark and chaotic during the ambush for me to see any faces in the light of my burning Airstream.

The first day passed without event, and after darkness fell, the ranch hands and security team retreated to separate bunkhouses, each steering well clear of the other. When Larson emerged from one of the barns and entered his home, I folded the tripods, packed the binoculars, camera, and lens away, and retreated to camp.

I did not light a fire. I cooked a can of soup over the gas camp stove and then settled into the sleeping bag in the tent with my rifle close at hand.

The next morning before dawn, I set up my position once more on the mountain's crest and settled in to surveil. Today, I took photos of each man and each building. The sun crept through the sky steadily, and a wind that smelled of spring snow blew through the valley sprawled before me and raced over my vantage point.

At midday, my vigilance was rewarded. A lone man arrived at the ranch, and Larson met him in the front circular drive. I zoomed in with the camera lens and snapped photos of the newcomer as they crossed the compound. Larson led him directly to the north barn, and the two men paused before a side door. Larson punched a code into a keypad and preceded the other man as they entered. It was over an hour before they reappeared, and before the man left, he shook Larson's hand.

In the late afternoon, someone else arrived. This newcomer was not alone. Two younger men were with him, and they bore such similarity that I guessed them to be father and sons. I zoomed the camera further in on the father and felt a bolt of recognition. The president's brother was as notorious for his edgy lifestyle as he was for his ability to sway the opinion of the leader of the free world. Larson led the three men into his home.

I had been lying in the dirt for over an hour with the binoculars trained on the house to see when the men reappeared when the bullet came out of nowhere. It bit into the rocks several feet from where I lay. I flinched back with a curse. Shards of stone stung against my skin, flung like shrapnel from the shot.

The shot had come from my left, angled upward from the north side of the mountain's crest. I grabbed the binoculars and camera and scrambled backward. My rifle and pack were only a few feet away. Another bullet kicked up rocks and dirt inches from my hand as I reached out and snagged the rifle.

I brought the Henry to my shoulder, thumbed the hammer down, and fired in the direction from which the shots had come before ducking out of sight behind a rocky outcropping. I disassembled the tripods as quickly as I could, folding them away and tucking the stands, lens, camera, and binoculars into my pack. I shoved sixteen more rounds of ammo into my pockets and shouldered the pack.

Since firing my shot, it had been quiet. I stayed crouched down as I left the summit, walking at an angle so I could keep one eye at my back. I retreated down the mountain to the tree line. Shielded from view from the crest, I waited and watched, and within minutes, a man appeared on the ridge.

He wore tactical gear and carried an AR-15 with a scope on it. He studied the ground where I had set up watch. The sun must have glinted on the lens of the camera or on the eyes of the binoculars, giving away my position. After a moment, the man spoke into a radio.

I left the tent. It could easily be replaced, and I was not going to take the time to dismantle it and pack it away. I set off at a fast clip down the mountain, keeping well within the cover of the trees.

Larson was notorious for not tolerating trespassers on his land. The men he hired to patrol his property acted like they were still in Afghanistan or Iraq or some other hell hole where they shot first and asked questions later. It could be little more than that.

But when I heard the helicopter, I knew it was not so simple a matter as that. I was not going to stick around to confirm my suspicions, though.

I ran.

SIXTEEN

GRANT

THE REPORT OF a rifle echoed through the valley. Laurence Boudreaux choked on a swallow of Springbank 1919 he had helped himself to as soon as he saw it.

I forced a smile. "Gentlemen, if you'll excuse me for a moment." I had to fight the urge to take the bottle of whiskey with me as I strode from the study. John Smith met me at the front door. "What the hell is going on?" I asked.

"Antonio thought he saw a reflection off of a rifle scope in the hills and went to investigate. He just radioed in. It looks like someone has been camped out watching the area."

"Shit."

"Think it's him?"

I would put money on it being Hector Lewis. The man was swiftly becoming more than just a concern. "Call Jack and get up in the air. When you find him, don't bother bringing him in."

"You got it," he said, and turned on his heel, already calling out orders.

I pulled in a breath that was meant to be calming, but I had to suck in several more before I felt a modicum of calm.

I always suspected this day would come. Since the

moment I saw Winona slip away from the paddocks and head toward the north barn, a clock began to count down.

I followed her, keeping out of sight as I watched the careful way she crept around the buildings angling toward the northern end of my compound. I ducked around a corner when she darted a cautious glance over her shoulder.

Don't do it, Winona, I pleaded with her silently.

But she headed straight for the north barn. She tried the front entrance, but, of course, it was locked. She circled the building, and dread built in my gut as I followed her.

I stayed just out of her line of sight. She tried the back entrance, rattling the doorknob in frustration.

There were no windows on the north barn, no weaknesses in the construction, even though she tested the door's strength by jamming her shoulder against it.

I did not say anything to alert her to my presence. I simply waited until she stepped back from the door, forehead wrinkled. She turned, studying the façade of the barn. She startled violently when she spotted me, the color draining from her face.

"What are you doing here?" I asked, keeping my voice soft.

"I couldn't find the bridle Cyrus prefers," she said, and I had to admire her quick thinking. "I thought one of the hands might have misplaced it."

She cut a wide berth around me and hurried past. That careful distance she kept between us killed me.

"Winona," I said. I waited until she turned back to me. "Be careful."

Now I retreated to the study and went straight to the

sideboard. I poured a finger of the Springbank 1919 and tossed it back, not even bothering to enjoy it.

"Well?" Laurence Boudreaux barked.

I hid a grimace. Had it not been for his money and connections, I would not have bothered to extend the invitation to him again. He always made a mess when he came and left it for me to clean up. "Nothing to be concerned about. Just a coyote that has been giving us trouble."

A moment later the thump of the helicopter's rotors pulsed through the air.

Boudreaux's heavy brows arched. "A coyote, you said?"

I smiled and forced my teeth to unclench. "One that has become a fucking nuisance."

SEVENTEEN

HECTOR

I WAS TOO old for this shit. I slowed from a run as soon as I heard the helicopter veer to the west. I was no runner, and my heart thundered in my chest.

I kept my ears pricked for the sounds of voices. At one point, I thought I heard the roar of ATVs in the distance, but the sound never drew closer. I crept through the forest at a fast clip. I stayed deep within the shelter of the trees and scrambled downhill, rocks rolling dangerously underfoot.

Between the danger of crossing paths with a grizzly and the danger of crossing paths with Larson's well-armed men, I thought the prior would be more manageable. I moved swiftly and silently. Every now and then, I thought I caught a flash of white in the corner of my eye.

I needed to see what was inside the north barn, and I contemplated what the security and secrecy around the building meant. It had to be a storehouse or a factory. There was nothing unusual about the building, no excess of ventilation or odd piping going in or out above ground. Drugs could be easily procured without wealthy, powerful, connected men coming all the way to Montana. Women as well.

The only thing I could think of that the west boasted

that someone could not easily procure elsewhere was its wildlife.

I hiked into Gardiner early in the evening as the sun was sinking toward the horizon. I skirted town and stuck to the shoulder of the narrow, curving road to Raven's Gap. I had been walking along the side of the road for a mere ten minutes when I heard the rumble of an approaching engine. I moved off the road to let the vehicle pass. I carried my rifle over my shoulder, but I lowered it now and held it loosely at my side. The car drove past without incident, and I continued on my trek. My arm ached, and a glance at my sleeve showed a stain from where I had bled through the bandage.

When I reached the turnoff for my land, I detoured from the state road and followed the rough path I had worn into a lane over the last thirty years. I purchased fifty acres of land in the rugged northern reaches of the Black Canyon of the Yellowstone when Winona and I first moved here from Cody, Wyoming. She had dreams of horses and alpacas, and my dreams had been crushed on the dirt floor of the arena beneath a bull's horns and hooves. I let my bitterness over my own loss delay fulfilling the promise to her until it was too late to give her horses, alpacas, or the house on the hill.

There was no hint of what transpired over the course of the two-mile walk to the meadow where I had parked the Airstream, but yellow caution tape was tied between two trees at the end of the drive and the clearing looked as if a bomb had been detonated in it. Trees were snapped and splintered. Dirt and debris were flung like shrapnel in the explosions. And at the center of the meadow sat the burned, warped carcass of my home.

I tugged the caution tape free and moved across the

expanse of the wounded meadow toward the scorched earth and destruction. It had been little more than a tin can, but I bought it in place of a ring for Winona. I was seventeen when Jed died and had no desire to spend my years toiling day in and day out in backbreaking labor. I found homes for his horses on neighboring ranches and sold off his two hundred head of cattle before I took to the road.

I was in Wyoming a year later at the Cheyenne Frontier Days Rodeo when I saw the prize money and decided to take my chances. I paid the entry fee and stole a bull rope from another contestant. I did not have a leather riding glove and had not known I needed one until my hand was scored and shredded after that first ride. I watched the bull I was slated, a cantankerous bastard named Nero, paying attention to the way he spun to the right as soon as he left the chute.

When it was my turn, I held onto the rope like my life depended on it, kept my hips square and my weight down, and squeezed Nero's sides with my thighs and knees. When the crossbred Charbray flew out of the gate, it felt as if I had been thrown from the top of a skyscraper with a fifteen-hundred-pound weight tied to my arm. It was all light and sound and a down-force that felt as if it were going to yank my arm out of socket.

The eight seconds felt as if they crept by at the pace of centuries, and when the buzzer finally screeched, I hit the dirt with a broken thumb, a score of eighty, and, in the end, thirty-five hundred dollars in cash.

I applied for membership with the Professional Rodeo Cowboys Association. I kept riding, and I kept winning. Within a few years, I was able to apply for membership to the Professional Bull Riders. I raked in the buckles and the prizes, but I was still sleeping in my truck seven years later when I met Winona.

She was a barrel racer, and the dark banner of her hair, the wide, white gleam of her smile, and the bounce of her tits caught my eye the first time I saw her in the saddle. I did not know anything about love, but I knew about lust. In the ensuing year, I never tired of sleeping with her, and when she began talking about marriage, the idea of having her in my bed every night appealed to me.

First, though, I had to buy a proper bed. I bought the Airstream trailer brand new, the exterior gleaming, the interior so clean I took my boots off before I entered. Winona had known what my purchase meant the instant she saw it, and she had always jokingly called it her aluminum engagement ring.

It was now reduced to ash and rubble, and a lump was hard in my throat as I took in the ruins. The only thing that remained intact and recognizable was the trailer hitch, charred and warped. That and the cinder block that once served as my front step.

My eyes burned as I crossed the pockmarked, scorched expanse of earth. Stepping within the ring of ash lifted the smell of the fire sharply into the air. I brushed the soot and debris off of the cinder block and lifted it.

The white wolf was there when I turned around. I was not even surprised to see her. I was beginning to expect her presence.

"She never told me she was unhappy," I said to the wolf. "But she didn't need to." I pointed toward the ridge to the north of where we stood. "That's the spot she picked out for a house. She wanted to have a view of the entire valley." The breeze smelled of spruce and melted metal.

I dropped my gaze. The white wolf moved closer, and I held myself still. She passed so close I could have reached out and touched her. She padded to the edge of the scorched earth and sniffed the air before lowering her nose to the ground.

"It would have been the first real house I ever lived in," I admitted to her. She lifted her head and looked at me, ears pricked. "What's the opposite of claustrophobia? I think that's how I'd feel in a real house. Too much space."

She shook her head, and I could almost imagine the gesture was aimed at me instead of the result of something tickling her ear.

"Does she know I'm trying?" I asked, voice dropping. "Does she know I haven't given up, and I'm doing my damnedest to bring her and Emma home?"

The wolf stared at me. There was intelligence and wisdom in those golden eyes. Winona's eyes had been a deep, rich brown, so dark they were almost black.

The wolf did not reassure me. Instead, she turned, skirted the stretch of ash, and moved toward the woods. At the tree line, she stopped and looked back at me before disappearing into the shadows. She was, I realized, headed north toward the ridge I pointed out to her.

My truck was parked nearby, virtually untouched save for a riddling of bullet holes across the driver's side from bumper to bumper. I placed the cinder block in the bed of the pickup and lifted the bed liner in the corner. The spare key to the truck was still tucked beneath it.

I searched under the truck, under the hood, and through the cab, but I found nothing that indicated a bomb might have been rigged to the vehicle. Even so, I held my breath as I turned the key in the ignition and shifted the truck into gear. Everything operated as normal, and I was not blown sky high.

I took one last look at the remnants of my home before turning the truck down the drive and heading into town. It was fully dark by the time I pulled into the lot in front of Maggie's diner. There were only a handful of tables occupied, but whispers and stares met my arrival. Maggie was standing beside a booth talking, but she turned when she heard the commotion. Her face went lax with relief when she spotted me, and she placed the coffee pot on the table and crossed to me.

I leaned down and accepted her tight hug.

"I've been worried," she said quietly. "Are you hungry?"

"Starving," I admitted.

I looked over her shoulder and recognized the woman Maggie had been speaking to when I arrived. Evelyn Hutto sat at the booth. The younger woman's hands were wrapped around a coffee mug, and I could not miss the spaces in her grip. After Jeff Roosevelt kidnapped her from the museum and she managed to kill him and escape, she became lost in a whiteout. By the time Frank found her, frostbite had already done irreparable damage to one of her hands, one of her feet, and an ear.

Maggie moved to retrieve her coffee pot, and I followed her to the booth. "You'll want to hear this. While you talk to Evelyn, I'll make you dinner."

I gestured to the bench across from Evelyn. She nodded and took a sip from her mug before speaking. "I see you're not dead." Her voice was low and even.

If ever a woman fit the old adage of *still waters run*

deep, Evelyn certainly did. I had a feeling a lot went on beneath the surface that she never allowed to show. I still wondered if she played a role in the disappearance of the man who stalked her for a year when she lived in Atlanta. The five-year-old case had grown cold, from what William dug up. Even though it seemed I was wrong about Jeff Roosevelt killing Winona and Emma, he had proven himself to be a dangerous predator. She and I were the only ones who saw it. And she was the one to end his killing spree.

"Not yet," I agreed. I slipped the pack from my shoulders, grimacing as the strap slid across my arm, and placed it on the bench before sliding in across from her.

She did not bother with any other pleasantries before she said, "Faye and Sam are missing."

I stilled.

"Sam was going to spend the night with friends," Evelyn said. "The friends live on the other side of Gardiner, and their mom called Faye Friday night and said Sam had changed his mind about staying the night. Faye went to pick him up, but they never came home."

I remembered the fear on Faye's face when Sam was missing, the secrets boiling beneath that masked exterior. "You're certain she intended to return?"

Evelyn simply nodded. "She was coming back." I noticed for the first time the tension in her face, the exhaustion stamped in the dark circles under her eyes.

"Do you know how she's connected to Grant Larson?" I asked Evelyn bluntly.

"The senator? No, I don't." The wrinkle of her brow said she spoke the truth, but I was not certain she would tell me even if she did know. "The first time I heard her mention him was the day Sam didn't come home from school." She met my gaze. "Something is wrong, Hector. I can feel it."

"Have you reported her missing to the police?"

She looked away, silent for a long moment before she spoke. "She wouldn't want me to go to the police."

Evelyn was an astute woman, and her admission confirmed what I already suspected about Faye. "You do recall I'm the police," I pointed out.

She arched a brow at me. "Are you really?"

I smiled before I could check the reaction. Her point hit home, but it also made me realize that if Grant Larson were trying to kill me, the public nature of my position as a police officer might afford me some amount of protection.

Maggie appeared at my side and slid a plate laden with a club sandwich and fries onto the table before me. She paused by my side when Evelyn quietly asked, "Will you help me?"

I felt Maggie's gaze on me as I studied the woman sitting across from me. I had seen Jeff Roosevelt's fixation on Evelyn. Obsessed with bringing him to justice, I saw that fixation as a means to an end with no thought toward Jeff's intended victim. I had banked on Jeff killing her, but had not counted on Evelyn's tenacity or her refusal to be a victim.

There was no room in my conscience to feel guilt. My reserves were completely used for my wife and daughter and the regrets I carried for them. Truth be told, if I were in the same situation with Jeff Roosevelt, I would do the same thing all over again. I could fight my guilt over seeing the woman before me as a pawn, but I could also acknowledge that I owed Evelyn.

"I think it's time I went back to work."

MAGGIE WAVED AWAY the loss of the camping gear as I told her what transpired. "I don't care about a tent and sleeping bag. Shooting trespassers is a bit extreme, though, even in this area."

"Is it?" I asked. I combed my fingers through Frank's topknot. He lay sprawled beside me on the couch with his chin resting on my knee. The poodle had been glued to my side since I walked into Maggie's house. The wound on his neck was already scabbing over. "If you have something to hide, something you don't want to be discovered?"

"Shit," she whispered, cuddling Louie in her arms. "What is he doing on the Broken Arrow?"

I had my suspicions, but I did not know how I would prove it. "Will you take Frank and go visit William for a few weeks?"

"No."

"Please. Larson is a dangerous enemy to have."

"I won't be driven from my home. And before you say it, you won't be either," she said. "I've been calling the banks in the area. I haven't found the safe deposit box yet, though."

"Maggie—"

"You've been on this crusade for Winona and Emma for a long time," she said, voice quiet and firm. "When I thought it was leading to self-destruction, I hated it. I felt helpless watching it eat at you. I need you to let me help you." She was staring down at Louie but now she looked up and met my gaze. "Please."

"I won't have you hurt."

"Then we need to figure out what Larson is up to and how to stop him."

I still had no ideas for how to do so the next morning as I walked into the police department. Joan Marsden, the wife of the chief and the receptionist during the weekdays at the station, looked up from her computer screen, her eyes widened and her lips formed my name before she composed herself. "Officer Lewis," she said, with only a slight tremor in her voice.

"Mrs. Marsden. Is the chief in his office?"

"He is, with the commander. Go on in, though. We've all been concerned about you, and I know they'll be relieved to see you."

That was a gross overstatement, but the two men listened to my statement of the events at my home. I did not tell them about my suspicions regarding Grant Larson. I knew they had their own suspicions about me. I had been a thorn in the Raven's Gap Police Department's side for thirty years now.

When I left Donald Marsden's office, I had a new service-issued pistol to replace the one lost in the fire and a new badge. I had a spare uniform in the locker room and headed there to change.

I turned when the locker room door opened behind me. Joan slipped into the room and closed the door behind her. She flicked the deadbolt into place before turning to me.

"What's wrong?" I asked, keeping my voice low. Here at the police department, we were never anything more than Mrs. Marsden and Officer Lewis to one another.

She moved to stand in front of me and placed her hand on my chest over my heart. Her eyes slid closed.

I pressed my hand over hers. "Are you okay?"

She swallowed, and when she opened her eyes and

smiled up at me, her lips trembled and her eyes were bright. "I should be asking you that. I was so worried."

"I'm fine," I said. I was not certain where this concern was coming from. I had never considered us lovers. That was too intimate a term. We shared our bodies on occasion and little more.

She nodded and sucked in a tremulous breath before her fingers dropped to my belt. I caught her wrist, stilling her movements.

"Are you certain about this? Here?"

She went up on her toes and pressed her lips against my throat. "Yes."

Joan had come to me for gentleness after her husband beat her. She had shown up on my doorstep ten years ago, and then she kept coming back. I was not a gentle man, but I gave her what she needed as best I could. This was not gentle. It was hard and fast, and both of us were breathless when we finished.

She leaned against me for a moment, arms tight around my neck. When she leaned back, I smoothed my hands over her hair, straightening the mess made by clenching it in my fists. She pressed a kiss to my jaw and retreated into the bathroom stall.

I cleaned up and straightened my clothing. When she exited the stall, she looked as polished as ever. She cupped my cheek in her palm. "I'm glad you're okay," she said, voice soft.

And then she turned away, unlocked the door, and slipped out of the locker room.

When I exited the locker room minutes later, Ted Peters called my name from the end of the hallway.

"I'm sorry about what happened to your home," he

said as I approached. "I processed the scene meticulously so I didn't miss anything."

"I appreciate it," I said.

"You're going to want to see this." He offered me a file folder. "Those prints you had me run came back with some interesting results. Who was it?"

Something in his voice caught my attention before I answered. "A hitchhiker I picked up outside of Bozeman," I lied. "Her behavior raised my suspicions."

He nodded at the folder. "It should have."

"Thanks for pulling this together for me," I said. I waited until I was sitting at my desk to flip the folder open.

Frank left his spot on the dog bed in the corner and crossed to my side. I rested a hand on his back as I flipped through the case report. I remembered the case from the news reports five years ago. It was plastered in the headlines and dominated news coverage.

No wonder Faye and Sam were in hiding.

I was still mulling over the implications of their identity an hour later as I drove to Snowshoe Lane. It was well out of my jurisdiction, but I drove the treacherous stretch of road slowly. Evelyn had given me the name of Sam's friend, and it was easy enough to find the Carters' address outside of Gardiner.

The road was only paved for the first quarter mile outside of town, and then it became a narrow dirt lane, not quite wide enough for two vehicles, that twisted and turned up into the mountains. I drove to the address listed and knocked on the front door of a neatly kept home.

A woman came to the door after a moment. "May I help you?"

"Madeline Carter?" I asked.

"Yes?"

"I'm Hector Lewis, with the Raven's Gap Police Department," I said. "Did Faye Anders come to your house Friday evening?"

She opened the door, and I stepped back as she joined me on the porch. "Yes, she did. Her son changed his mind about spending the night with my boys." She glanced away from me as she spoke. "I called her and offered to meet her in Gardiner, but she said she would just come to the house."

"Why did he change his mind?"

She hesitated, hands twisting together.

"What did he do that made you decide he couldn't spend the night?" I asked.

She let out a breath. "My oldest apparently was teasing Sam. I've reprimanded him for it. But...when I heard a commotion and checked on the boys, Sam had Adam on the floor with his hands wrapped around my son's throat. It scared the boys. They were screaming at him and trying to pull Sam off of Adam. My son's face was turning purple by the time I reached them." She hurried to add, "I've always thought Sam was a sweet boy. He has played with my sons a number of times without any issues. I probably overreacted to the situation Friday night and should have done more to smooth things over, but...it made me nervous."

"Did you tell Faye this?"

"No," she admitted. "I was still figuring out how I wanted to handle it."

"Did it seem as if anything was wrong when she was at your house?" I asked.

"With Faye?" Her brow creased. "No, she was only

at the house for a minute or two, but I didn't notice anything. Are they okay?"

I pulled a card with the number to the police department on one side and the number to my desk extension on the other. "If you think of anything else, give me a call at the number on the back."

She frowned at the card but accepted it. "Yes, of course."

I drove the dirt lane that descended toward Gardiner slowly. If I had not been looking, I would have missed it. I braked and glanced in my rearview mirror, but I was right on a curve. I drove on until I was able to pull off to the side enough that another vehicle could pass safely.

I parked and walked back uphill with Frank at my side, gaze focused on the dirt at my feet. When I reached the spot where I caught a glimpse of it, it took me several minutes to find it again. I moved so the sun was at my back once more, and then I saw the glint of red in the dirt. I knelt and studied the shards of red plastic. They were the remains of a shattered tail light.

I straightened and moved across the narrow stretch of road. There was less than two feet of shoulder between the edge of the road and a steep drop down the mountainside. I walked along the road, peering carefully over the drop.

Frank found what I was looking for before I did. He stood barking at the edge of the road fifty yards along the mountainside.

"I'm coming," I called to him. "Get back from the edge."

Had we not been looking for it, I never would have spotted the destruction out of sight from the road.

It was not a sheer cliff, but the land fell away at a

sharp, steep angle. The mountainside was scored open, scarred with snapped trees and metal and glass debris. It was a five-hundred-foot drop on this stretch of road, and deep below, I could see the crumpled carcass of a burnt wreck.

"Fuck."

Frank whimpered and moved too close to the edge for my comfort. I called him to my side and retreated to my truck.

I backed my truck into position and set the emergency brake before retrieving the climbing equipment from the lockbox in the truck bed. I locked Frank in the cab so he would not try to follow me down the mountain.

Once the rope was anchored to the tow hitch, I strapped into the harness and inserted the rope through the GriGri. I connected the GriGri to the harness with a locking carabiner, tested the blocking mechanism, and then backed over the edge.

I could have rappelled swiftly if I were going over a vertical cliff, but with the loose scree precarious underfoot, I climbed down cautiously. When I reached the bottom, I could still feel the heat coming from the wreckage.

The comparison to my Airstream could not be missed. The smell of the ash, the warped metal, the twisted, skeletal ruin. I unclipped from the rope and approached what remained of the vehicle. Years ago, I responded to a car accident at the request of the sheriff's department when the deputies were shorthanded. A father and son on vacation at Yellowstone swerved to miss an elk standing in the road one night. Trapped within the wreckage, neither had been able to escape when their vehicle caught fire. By the time the first responders were alerted to the wreck and arrived on scene, it was too late. Twelve years later, though, I could still remember the smell of burnt flesh.

I braced myself for the stench now as I crouched to peer into the wreckage. The memory of the two blackened skeletons, burned into the pugilistic posture, from the accident a dozen years ago was at the forefront of my mind. It took me several moments of staring into the present scorched vehicle to realize it was empty.

EIGHTEEN

FAYE

CONSCIOUSNESS CREPT IN and receded in waves. Pain pressed at me from all sides, sharp and insistent, only ebbing when everything went dark again.

Awareness returned like a blow, and the shock of realizing I was still alive made my breath catch in a sob. I was hanging upside down, my head pressed to the side against the roof of the SUV. Everything hurt. I could not distinguish one flair of pain from the other. It was constant and livid. My mouth was filled with the sharp metallic flavor of blood.

"Sam?" It took several attempts for my voice to work and my words to be audible. "Sam?" I tried to turn my head to glance into the backseat, but I could not move. Panic beat a steady drum alongside the pain coursing through me, and I fainted.

When next I came to, I grappled to hang on to consciousness. "Sam! Answer me, buddy!" Silence was the only response I received.

I reached for the clip on my seatbelt, and the pain went from a constant flair to a bolt that made me cry out and made my vision darken. I struggled to breathe as I grappled with the seatbelt clip. It was jammed.

My headlights were still on. The windshield was gone. Dirt and debris, tree limbs and twisted metal filled my vision. I pushed my hands against the roof of my car to try to alleviate the pressure on my head, but I could not lift myself. A sob caught in my throat, and when I sucked in a painful, shuddering breath, I smelled it. Acrid. Sharp. Something was burning.

Terror sliced through me just as a sound reached me, a scrabble of footsteps sliding down the embankment. Relief swept over me. "Help!" My voice was a croak, and I coughed as a curl of smoke caught in the back of my throat. "We're here!"

Someone was there. Rocks rolled, and I heard dirt fall on the upturned undercarriage of my car. Footsteps approached along with a narrow beam of light, and I twisted my head to catch sight of a pair of boots stop beside the car.

The glass in my window was shattered, and I stretched out a hand toward the feet. "Please. Please, help."

Something was wrong. The boots stood still for long minutes, and the smell of smoke grew stronger. No hand caught mine, no voice offered reassurance. There was just stillness and quiet.

And then the boots turned and disappeared from sight.

For an instant, I thought whomever it was had moved to help Sam. But then the sound of rocks rolling and dirt falling came to me again.

"Please," I whispered. And then I screamed it. "Help! *Please!*"

Coughing choked off my desperate cries. The air was hazy with smoke, and horror sliced through me when I heard the crackle of flames.

I scrabbled to feel for my keychain and almost wept

when I found my keys still lodged in the ignition. My fingers did not want to work, and there was no strength in my arm when I tugged at the keys. It took several tries before I was able to yank it free from my ignition.

The tool on my keychain was dual purpose. On one end, there was a point to hammer against glass to break a window. The rest of the tool was designed to slice a seatbelt. I could not turn my head, so I groped blindly for where the seatbelt bit into my hip. The blade on the cutter was sharp, and it slipped through the polyester webbing with ease.

The tension released so quickly across my hips and chest that I did not have time to brace, and my shoulder slammed into the roof of the SUV. Consciousness wavered. I groaned in pain, twisted at an awkward angle, still caught upside down with the steering wheel biting into my thighs.

"Sam?" I wheezed as the smoke turned the air to a gray haze. I could not see the flames, but I could hear them. I felt heat begin to creep up my legs. "I'm coming, baby. Hold on."

I stretched, turning my upper body as much as I could so both shoulders were pressed into the roof. Glass bit into my palms as I reached back and caught hold of the window frame. I pulled and bit back a scream of pain as I dragged my weight, shifting and twisting until my upper body was free from the wreckage. I could not contain a sob as I caught sight of the flames licking the sky at the accordioned front end of the Explorer.

Rocks bit into my back and scored across my skin as I pushed and tugged and finally shoved myself free from the twisted wreck of my vehicle.

I did not even pause to take stock of my injuries or to try to catch my breath. I groaned when I caught sight of Sam. There was blood on his face, and he hung limply against the binding of his seatbelt, thin arms lax against the roof. His seatbelt was jammed as well. I wrapped an arm around his chest and fumbled to get the seat-belt cutter in place. My fingers trembled and were slick with blood. I lost my grip on the cutter, and it clattered against the ceiling as it fell.

I lunged into the vehicle, ignoring the bite of glass and the cut of warped metal. Flames ate at the dash, and I could feel the heat on my face. The tool was just out of reach, my fingers slipping over the end without gaining purchase. I pushed farther inside and felt my flesh tear.

I snagged the tool and scrabbled backward. The blade cut neatly through Sam's seatbelt, and I caught him in my arms as he fell. I knew the risk of spinal injuries, but I could not take the time to be careful and gentle. My eyes streamed, my lungs staggered against the push of the smoke, and the blistering heat beat at my back.

I dragged his limp, light weight out of the SUV and tried to lift him into my arms. My legs refused to work, and I staggered as I gained my feet and fell. The fire was a roar now, cracking and popping, and the smell bit at the back of my throat. I clutched Sam to me with one arm and crawled away from the flames.

I felt the change in the air, the pressure in my ears, the flair of heat. I had only a second to curl my body around Sam's, and then the explosion rent the air and rolled over us like a crushing wave.

Sam was the first thing I saw when I finally managed to claw my way to consciousness. His face was lax, and blood had dried in the delicate curve of his ear and across his face where it had dripped from his nose.

I dragged myself closer to him, and my hand shook as I reached for him. "Sam?" I whispered, and it felt as if my voice had to crawl over broken glass before it escaped my throat.

His face remained still, and I closed my eyes as I pressed my fingers to his throat. A sob caught in my chest when I felt the faint flutter of a pulse under my fingertips. I clasped his limp hand and pressed it to my cheek. "We're going to be okay," I told him.

I groaned as I pushed myself upright. My vision swam, and I hung my head until the world stopped rotating around me. Pain radiated through my body, so fiercely and sharply it took me long minutes of breathing deeply before the urge to vomit passed. The epicenters were my right ankle and knee, my chest, and my head. My hands and arms bore numerous cuts, but only one still bled heavily. I rolled carefully onto my left knee and struggled to my feet.

My SUV was still burning. The fire dancing wildly over the warped and blackened ruins of my vehicle. The smell burned my eyes and the back of my throat, and the heat did nothing to quell my shivering. The flames were the only source of light in the depth of night. I heard no sirens in the distance.

I took a step, putting weight on my right foot, and my leg collapsed beneath me. I hit the ground hard and cried out, darkness dancing along the edges of my vision. Rocks bit into my cheek where the side of my face was pressed into the ground. Sam's feet were in my field of vision. He remained limp and still, and the laces on one of his shoes were untied.

I clenched my teeth and forced myself to standing, remaining upright through sheer willpower as I limped around my burning car. I gave it a wide berth, but it was my torch in the dark. I peered upward into the night at the wake of devastation my vehicle had left as it plummeted down the mountainside.

What little distance up the incline I could see in the flickering firelight looked as if the land had been scraped raw. Snapped trees, metal and glass debris, gouged earth. The incline was not perfectly vertical, but it was steep enough that when I grit my teeth and tried to scramble up the slope, I only made it a few feet before falling and sliding.

I was breathing hard, lightheaded with pain, and a tremor rattled through my limbs. In the dark, I did not know how far we had fallen, how far the climb up to the road was. The memory of the man standing just out of reach, observing but not helping, before turning around and walking away came back to me. I did not know what waited for us above.

I crawled to Sam. Pain flared through my ribcage as I lifted him in my arms. I staggered under his weight, and his head lolled against my shoulder. It felt as if fire burned through muscle and against the bones in my ankle and knee as I took a step. I tightened my grip on Sam, even as my arms shook to hold him, and refused to fall.

I was disoriented in the dark and from the woozy spinning of my head. Nausea churned in my stomach, and I knew I could add a concussion to the list of my injuries. But we were alive, both of us, and I had to get us out of here if I wanted to keep it that way.

I moved away from the fire still quenching its thirst

with ragged cracks and spark-spitting flairs. The orange glow of the fire faded quickly behind me, and I glanced back when our shadow disappeared into darkness. I stood at the edge of the light for a moment, taking in the horror of the crumbled, scorched wreckage of my vehicle. Then I turned and stumbled into the darkness.

Away from the blinding illumination of the fire, I could see the stars when I glanced up at the sky. The stars spun above me as I tilted my head back, searching the sky. I stumbled and clutched Sam tighter to me. I found the ladle on the Big Dipper and followed its guidance to Polaris.

Gardiner was to the southwest. I just needed to make it a few miles. I turned my back to the North Star and kept it over my right shoulder as I struggled over the rough terrain in the dark. I moved at a shuffle's pace, blindly groping through each foot placed in front of the other. I could not afford to fall.

The night was alive around me. A wolf called for her pack in the distance, and a moment later, she received a mournfully welcoming response. When we moved here, the silence after New York City seemed oppressive. It had taken me months to realize there was just as much traffic here, just not of the human variety. Most of the time, it frightened me. The sounds that pierced the night were wild and untamed and not entirely peaceful. But tonight, there was a comfort in the disquiet. It made me feel less alone.

I lost track of time, focused on putting one foot in front of the other. Breathe in, breathe out. Shut out the pain. Left foot, right foot. Breathe. Hold tight to Sam. Don't stop. Everything else faded away.

My right leg was dragging and I was struggling to

breathe when the first fingers of dawn lightened the black of night to morning gray. I almost walked into the side of the cabin before I realized it was there.

I sagged, and it took every ounce of strength I had to round the corner of the cabin and climb the front steps. There was no vehicle in sight in front of the cabin, and no lights burning within, but the front porch was sound underfoot.

"Hello?" I called, and my voice was a hoarse whisper. As soon as I stopped moving, I felt the strength go out of my limbs, and I gently deposited Sam in the single rocking chair on the porch before I dropped him. I braced a hand against the roughhewn doorframe to steady myself and knocked. There was no response, and I sagged forward, my forehead resting against the smoothly polished wood.

I tested the doorknob only out of habit and staggered when it turned easily underhand. The door swung open, and I peered into the dark interior. "Is anyone there?" I fumbled along the wall for a switch, and light spilled over the interior of the cabin.

The cabin was spartan, but clearly lived in. I could see the kitchen and living room from the threshold, both clean but almost barren. A coffee mug and a clay pipe sat on a small table beside a threadbare recliner. The two pieces were the only furniture in the room. I ventured within, limping down the narrow hallway.

"Hello?"

The cabin was still. The hallway led to a bedroom on one side, a bathroom on the other. The bedroom contained only a neatly made bed and an unadorned dresser. The bathroom was clean, a hand towel folded precisely on the vanity. I did not see a phone anywhere.

I had to brace myself with one hand against the wall as I retreated. On the porch, it took me several attempts before I could lift Sam into my arms. Black spots danced at the edges of my vision as I carried him into the cabin and nudged the door closed behind us. As we entered the hallway, Sam's dangling feet clipped the edge of the wall. Knocked off balance, I stumbled and went down, twisting so I took the brunt of the fall.

Pain exploded through me, white and hot and sharp, and everything went dark.

I was not certain how much time had passed when I finally managed to drag my eyes open again. It took me long moments to recall where I was and what had happened. I barely had the strength to push myself upright, and even that simple motion forced a sob from me.

I dragged Sam into the bedroom but could not manage to lift him onto the bed. I curled up beside him and rested my palm over his heart, and then I was pulled under once again.

The slam of a car door outside wrenched me to awareness. Grappling with consciousness, I held onto it tenuously, pushed myself to a seated position, and rolled the cuff of my jeans back to retrieve the Beretta Pico from the holster around my right ankle. It was another thing I learned once I arrived in Montana. The people who thought New Yorkers were unfriendly and rude had never met a territorial Montanan. And we were trespassing.

I used the bed to struggle to my feet, and waited deep in the shadows of the hall as I heard footfalls on the front porch. When I searched the cabin earlier, I saw nothing that identified the owner. No photographs or bills lying about. But I knew to whom the cabin belonged the moment he walked through the door.

I stood in the shadows, watching, leaning against the wall for support. He hung his head and rubbed the back of his neck as he toed off his boots and left them neatly aligned by the front door. Exhaustion was written into every line of his body as he crossed into the kitchen.

The light from the refrigerator edged the harsh angles of his face in an unforgiving glow. His father was white, but he had inherited his Native American mother's high cheekbones, swarthy complexion, and dark hair and eyes.

Those dark eyes flared when he spotted me as he straightened and turned, and the exhaustion disappeared in an instant. I knew him by sight and name, though I had never interacted with him the handful of times I saw him around town. He had certainly never come to the inn for pancakes.

The disappearance of his sister and niece happened years before I arrived in town, but it was something that was still whispered about regularly. Those whispers also spoke of how likely it was Hector Lewis had killed his own wife and daughter and hidden their bodies. I did not know whether that was true or not, but it was no secret in town how much Jack Decker hated his brother-in-law.

My fingers flexed on the grip of the Beretta, but I kept it at my side, pointed at the floor. Jack had always struck me as an angry, bitter man. I did not know how he would react to our invasion of his home.

"I don't want any trouble," I said.

"Then what do you want?" he asked. "This is the second time this week I've come home and found someone in my house uninvited."

I started to tell him his door had been unlocked, but I thought better of it. I was off balance and uncertain and so tired. I just wanted to lie down and close my eyes. It was difficult to remain upright, let alone maintain my grip on the pistol.

"I just need..." I swallowed. "I need help."

He said nothing for a long moment, and he studied me as closely as I studied him before he finally spoke. "Larson thinks you and your boy are dead." I put a hand against the wall to steady myself as I leveled the pistol at him. He held up his own hands. "Before you shoot, I had nothing to do with you going off that mountain road."

Disbelief scored through me, and the irony of whose cabin I sought shelter in almost made me laugh. "You work for the senator."

"Not as part of his security team. I'm just his pilot." He leaned back against the counter and sighed. "You can take a load off, kid. You're safe here."

My wrist shook under the weight of holding up the gun, and I slowly let it drop until my arm hung at my side. I let the doorframe take the brunt of the effort to keep myself upright.

"You haven't seen a doctor, have you?" he asked. "You're bleeding."

I glanced down at my arms. I felt so detached from my body at the moment that I felt genuine surprise at the sight of blood rolling down the inside of my forearm.

"What shape is your boy in?" Jack asked.

"How do I know I can trust you?" My voice sounded far away to my own ears.

"You don't. But I'm guessing since you ended up here, you don't have any other options."

"You were the first cabin I came to," I said, but I could not deny his assumption was correct.

I must have closed my eyes for a split second, because suddenly he was in front of me, and his hand on my elbow halted my downward slide toward the floor. He eased the Beretta from my clenched fingers.

"Sam won't wake up," I whispered.

"We'll get him help," he said, and I thought there was a thread of gentleness in his voice. It surprised me. Everything about him struck me as hard and severe.

"We can't go to a hospital. Too dangerous."

"Even Larson is not foolish enough to try something in a hospital."

I clutched his sleeve. "Not Larson." I could not force myself to say his name. He had connections everywhere, and he bought loyalty as easily as he purchased a new suit. "He can't find us."

"No one is going to find you."

"He'll kill us." I could no longer feel my legs, and the dark hallway tilted as he lifted me in his arms.

"That's not going to happen. No one is going to hurt you or your boy."

The promise in his voice coaxed me into relinquishing my tenuous grip on consciousness.

NINETEEN

HECTOR

I LEFT MY truck parked at the police department. My return had not gone unnoticed, and I had no doubt Larson would hear of it soon, if he had not already. This was not a fight I wanted to bring to Maggie's doorstep. Exhaustion dogged my steps right alongside Frank as I hiked through the woods to her house. Once I downloaded the photographs I took and printed off copies, I would check in to a hotel.

Her car was already parked in the carport, and a light was on in the kitchen. I let myself in, surprised when neither of the dogs greeted me. "Maggie?"

"In the kitchen," she called.

I paused in the doorway, and fury sliced through me, hot and sharp. "What the hell are you doing here?"

Jack Decker sat across from Maggie at her kitchen table, nursing a cup of coffee. "I would never make trouble for Maggie. But you are just by being here. Larson wants you dead."

I arched an eyebrow and crossed my arms over my chest. "I already got that memo when his men tried to burn me alive and then almost shot me."

"You were trespassing," he reminded me. "I told them the infrared on the chopper picked up a heat signal heading west."

If he wanted gratitude for giving Larson's men a false lead, he was not going to receive it from me. He appeared to be unarmed, but I studied Maggie's face. "Are you okay?"

Her hands were folded together on the tabletop, and though concern was etched into her face, it did not look like she had been threatened or like she was being coerced when she said, "I'm fine." She arched a dark brow at Jack. "He's finally decided, for once in his life, not to act like a spoiled asshole." If the younger man's complexion were any lighter, I would have sworn he flushed.

He took a deep breath and turned to me. For the first time in fifteen years, he met my gaze without a trace of animosity. "Grant Larson is a poacher. And I don't mean a small-time, petty hunter who occasionally picks off an animal he's not supposed to. I mean a full scale, multi-million-dollar operation."

I stayed in the doorway, but he had my complete focus. "Go on."

"It's invitation only, starting at fifty thousand dollars for a seven-day hunt. He specializes in endangered and protected animals."

I suddenly remembered the letters in the column of Winona's spreadsheets. "Wolves, grizzles, and cougars?"

He nodded. "Along with wolverines and bald eagles."

Maggie made a sound of distress low in her throat, and Frank moved to her side.

"In the park?" I asked. Killing for sport was a cowardly, honorless act, but killing within national park boundaries was outright stupid.

"Sometimes within the park, but mainly along the boundary with his land. He uses bait to lure them off park territory. He brings in a taxidermist as well. Everything is kept under wraps. Not even the ranch hands know, although most would look the other way."

The cameras outside of the one building and the surreptitious comings and goings made more sense. "The north barn."

"The north barn," he agreed.

"Jesus Christ." I rubbed the back of my neck. "Harrington-Moore. Navarro. Boudreaux."

"Those are some of his clients, but only a few," Jack said. "It's an elite group. An exclusive bunch of psychopaths."

"More than psychopaths," I said. "Some of those men are movers and shakers in DC. Influential men with deep, deep pockets and far-reaching influence."

He shrugged. "Politics isn't my forte."

"But aiding and abetting a poaching ring is." The animosity returned to his dark eyes, eyes that were so like his sister's. "Winona would be ashamed of you. So would your mother, if she knew." I was not Native American, but my wife's love and respect for the earth and its creatures was something I had witnessed over the years.

His face flinched as if I had struck him, and he looked away, a muscle ticking in his jaw. "I deserved that," he said finally.

I studied him, the harsh lines of his face, the heavy slant of his brow. "Why did you come here?"

"A woman and child are at my cabin right now. I'm willing to overlook a lot, but not the murder of an innocent woman and a kid." He left unsaid that he was willing to overlook my death.

Maggie's eyes widened. "Faye and Sam?" She darted a glance at me.

"I found her vehicle at the bottom of the mountain off of Snowshoe Lane today," I said.

Her face turned ashen. "Christ. They're still alive? That's a five-hundred-foot drop."

"Both are in bad shape," Jack said. "I called my mother to look after them. She's suggesting they go to the hospital. Their injuries are more than what she can bandage with a first aid kit."

"Larson is the reason Faye and her boy went off that mountain?" I asked.

"I wasn't there when they burned your trailer, and I wasn't there when they drove that woman and kid off the mountain," he said, gaze and voice direct. "But I know he sent his men to handle them just like he sent them to your place. Told them to make it look like an accident, both times."

"Why Faye and Sam?" Maggie asked.

"The boy got into the north barn one day when a group of school kids toured the ranch and he wandered off."

"I went with Faye that evening to find him," I said.

"And showed up on his land days later. Larson's men were just to keep an eye on you. But when it became clear the boy talked, the orders changed."

"Sam *doesn't* speak," Maggie said, voice tight. "At all."

Jack's brow wrinkled, and he glanced at me. "If the boy didn't talk, then how did you know about his operation?"

"Winona told me."

His face went completely blank.

I turned to Maggie. "Laptop?"

Her lips were pressed into a grim line. "It's on my bedside table, and the thumb drive is in the safe."

I retreated down the hall. Frank followed me, with Louie close at his heels. I grabbed her laptop and retrieved the flash drive from the gun safe under her bed. The dogs trotted after me as I returned to the kitchen.

I took the seat beside Maggie. When the laptop was powered up and the spreadsheets pulled up on the screen, I turned it and slid the computer across the table to Jack.

He studied the spreadsheets for several long, silent minutes, and the clock on the kitchen wall counted out the seconds as the groove between his eyebrows deepened.

"How did she find out about the poaching?" I asked.

"She didn't know about it."

When he leaned back and rubbed his jaw, I said, "Obviously, she did. That has to be what she was documenting. These hunts. The coordinates led me to camera traps at the edge of Larson's land."

"I didn't know she knew," he said finally. "She never said a word to me about it."

"She had to have. She would have come to you for advice."

His face took on the countenance of granite. "And what? You think she came to me and then I ratted out my own sister to my boss, and he killed her?"

My brows arched, and I almost laughed at the irony. His disbelief echoed the consternation I felt fifteen years ago when the rumors first started to circulate. My wife and I did not have the best relationship, but my disinterest did not make me a murderer. I did not kill my wife and my daughter, even though I had grown tired of being a husband and father. Before I became angry, I was stunned at how quickly people leapt to that conclusion.

He thrust his chin toward the computer screen. "If she knew what he was doing, she would not have kept quiet about it. And Larson is not a man you cross. Everyone working for him knows that. You remain loyal to the man, and the rewards are rich. He is not a man who is stingy with his favors. But if you cross him, it's not just a matter of losing your job. Having your reputation ruined. Not being able to find work afterward. The fire at your trailer. The accident the woman and boy were in. There you have a glimpse of how Larson operates."

"I'm telling you this now for the last time. I won't ever repeat myself. I had nothing to do with Winona and Emma's disappearance."

He held my gaze for a long moment and then hung his head. Silence settled over the kitchen. "Fuck," he finally bit out. After several minutes, he looked up and met my gaze, and I knew the look in his eyes. It was desolation and despair. I had seen it enough in my own eyes over the last months to recognize the emotions. It was the result of certainty and obsession being stripped away, leaving a man without answers and without anyone to blame. "*Fuck.*"

He shoved back from the table, startling Louie and Frank, and strode out of the house. The front door slammed behind him, and then I heard it. A guttural, agonized, wordless roar. I knew he had thrown his head back and shouted his rage at the sky, because it was a move I had made several times myself. Frank and Louie began barking wildly.

Maggie stood and moved to a cabinet. She returned with a bottle of whiskey and three shot glasses. I took the whiskey from her and filled all three glasses to the brim. I set the bottle aside, lifted the shot glass, and threw the whiskey back. A cough from Maggie indicated she had done the same. When Jack stalked back into the kitchen, he followed suit when Maggie pushed the shot glass toward him.

Brother, best friend, and husband. We sat in silence for several minutes.

When Jack looked me in the eye, for the first time since I met him when he was a pissant teenager, I saw a shred of decency in the man. "I'll help you bring him down."

I KEPT COMING back to the photos of the first man who had shown up at Larson's. I pulled an image in close and cropped it into a headshot. An image search on the internet took me to the home page of a website for Baxter Taxidermy. The face of Arnold Baxter stared back at me from the website and matched the face of the man I saw at Larson's ranch.

I hooked Maggie's computer up to the printer and printed out the photos I took of the man.

When the task was finished, I turned to where Maggie was curled up at the end of the couch with Frank draped over her feet and Louie occupying her lap. She was so quiet, I thought she had fallen asleep, but her eyes were open and she stared blankly at the opposite wall.

"Mags," I said softly.

When she glanced at me, the lamplight gleamed on the sheen of tears in her eyes. "I wish she had come to me. I hate that she kept this to herself. She must have been so frightened."

My throat closed. "We'll make this right for her," I said finally when the tightness in my throat eased enough to allow words past.

"We have to," she whispered.

I stood and bent to press my lips to the top of her head. "I'm going to be staying in a hotel in town until we see this through."

"Hector—"

I interrupted her. "You saw my Airstream. But you didn't climb down that mountain today and see what was left of Faye's car. I don't know how she and Sam survived that. I won't have that be you. Keep yourself safe for me. Please. I'd like for Frank to stay here with you, too."

She sighed, and I knew she did not have an argument for my request. In the end, though, Frank would not budge from in front of the door as I tried to leave.

I rubbed the poodle's ears. "Stubborn dog," I muttered, but I made no further protests and allowed him to accompany me into the night.

I got a room at one of the cheaper chain motels off the state road in town. Thankfully, my wallet was in the pocket of the pants I pulled on before fleeing my burning Airstream. The bed was unfamiliar but comfortable, and Frank lay beside me with his chin resting over my heart. My mind churned, and sleep eluded me until the early hours of the morning.

At the police department the next day, I ran Arnold Baxter through the system. His driver's license was current. He had one DUI charge on his record from thirty years ago. His registered vehicle was the same one he arrived in at Larson's ranch. The man appeared to be a law-abiding citizen.

When the end of my shift rolled around, I headed north to Livingston. Frank rode in the passenger's seat beside me, his chin propped on the rolled-down window, a pleased canine grin on his face.

Baxter Taxidermy was on the outskirts of Livingston. The shop was located at his home, I realized, when I pulled up at the address. I followed his driveway around the side of the house to a rectangular building with a sign over the door announcing his business.

The sign in the window read OPEN, and a man behind a long counter looked up when the bell over the door rang as I entered the shop. "Hello," he called.

I paused inside the door and glanced around. I could not ever recall being in a taxidermist shop before, and all the glass eyes staring at me were disturbing. Frank moved around me and entered the shop, moving straight toward the front counter.

The man was working on a black bear mount, and he left his work station as I approached the counter. When Frank whined low in his throat, I glanced down and realized the counter was a glass display case. Bugs swarmed over a set of skulls inside the case.

I had never considered myself a squeamish man, but my stomach turned at the sight.

"I use a colony of dermestid beetles to clean my bones," the man said. "Fascinating, isn't it?"

I looked away from the writhing beetles and swallowed. "Not sure that's the term I'd use."

He chuckled. "What may I help you with?"

I studied the heads mounted on the wall behind him. "Any of those from Yellowstone?"

His face, which had been open and friendly, hardened. "Not a one. I run an honest business here. Everything is above board. If you're looking for something else, I'm afraid you'll have to go elsewhere."

"Really?" I said, and pulled the photographs out of my pocket. I placed them on the counter, spreading them out in a neat fan, and slid them toward him. "And what was Grant Larson looking for?" The color drained from his face as he studied the photographs I took of him as he entered the north barn with Larson. "You have run an honest business up to this point, Arnold. I did my research. But I'm pretty certain you won't be keeping a written record of the work you do for Larson for the Fish and Wildlife wardens to inspect."

His throat worked as he swallowed. "Look, I... I can explain."

"Be my guest," I invited, and he flinched.

"He came to me and said he had an offer for me."

"When was this?"

"Last week," he said, and I wondered why Larson had suddenly needed a new taxidermist. "I knew who he was, but I didn't know..." His voice trailed off.

"That he was a poacher."

He nodded. "I didn't know until he invited me to his ranch and told me what the offer entailed."

"Last week was the first time he approached you?"

"Yes, he came by here and took a look at my work and then invited me to his ranch the following day."

"Did you accept his offer?"

He let out an unsteady breath and scrubbed his hands over his face. "My wife has been sick for years. The medical bills... He offered me a lot of money to work for him."

"What does working for him involve?"

He glanced toward the door behind me. "Look," he said, voice low. "The taxidermy community is small. It's not rocket science to put two and two together and realize that Jake Martin must have been working for him."

I made a mental note of the name. "Why do you think that?"

"Because he dropped off the face of the earth last week." Sweat beaded on the line of his brow. "No one has seen him since."

"Was a missing person report filed?"

"Yeah, three days ago. Some hikers found his truck abandoned at a trailhead and called it in. They searched the area but called it off after twelve hours."

I had probably received the call to join the search party with Frank, but my phone was destroyed in the fire. "You think Larson had something to do with his disappearance."

"I have my suspicions," he said. "Jake was no hiker."

"What does working for Larson involve?" I asked again.

"You're not getting what I'm saying," he whispered. "Larson is not a man you double cross."

This was not police business yet, but I drew my badge from my pocket and placed it on top of the photograph on the counter. "You're not getting what I'm saying. You can talk to me, or you can talk to the feds about this. But you're going to talk to one of us."

He leaned his elbows against the countertop and dropped his face into his hands. "Shit," he breathed. I gave him a moment to pull himself together. When he straightened, he drew a handkerchief from his pocket and wiped his brow. He stepped around the counter and moved to the front door, holding up his hands. "I'm not going to make a run for it. I'm not that stupid." He flipped the lock on the door and twisted the sign until the CLOSED notice faced the outside. "Let's go in the back."

I started to follow him but noticed Frank staring into the glass display case. His ears were pricked, tail high. "Frank." The poodle looked at me when I said his name and sat facing the macabre display. "Come away from there," I ordered, and with one last glance at the bugs crawling over the pile of animal skulls, he trotted to my side.

Baxter led me into a small break room and moved toward the coffee pot on the counter. He lifted a mug in my direction, but the memory of those bugs crawling all over the skulls had me shaking my head.

His hands trembled as he drew a flask from a drawer and added a liberal amount of whiskey to his coffee. He drained the mug before taking a seat across from me.

"Those photos you have of me. The barn I'm entering, part of it is set up as a taxidermy workshop. All the equipment is provided. Top-end stuff. He will call me when he has a job. I do all the work there onsite. I don't keep any record of the work done. And he pays me twenty thousand per job."

"For the job and your silence regarding the fact that he is killing protected species inside a protected area."

His eyes slid closed. "It's a life-changing amount of money."

"It is," I agreed. "And prison is a life-changing experience, I hear."

His eyes flew open, and he glared at me. "What do

you want from me? If you're going to arrest me, get on with it."

"I'm not here to arrest you. I'm here to ask for your help. I need to get inside Larson's operation, and I need solid proof."

"I don't know what kind of proof you need," he said. "But any kind of proof I could get you is going to come straight back on me."

"The proper paperwork you should be filling out for the wardens. Photos and recordings. Evidence that unequivocally ties Larson to poaching."

Arnold paled as I spoke. "You're going to get me killed."

I shrugged and moved to stand. "I can take you in right now, then."

He held up his hands. "Okay, okay. I can't get you photos. I'm not allowed to bring a phone, camera, anything like that in on the job. But I can keep a record of each article of wildlife. I don't know names, though. I just deal with the animals."

"Does Larson tell you ahead of time what animals you'll be processing?"

He hesitated. "This upcoming hunt is for grizzlies."

"The U.S. Fish and Wildlife Service is trying to restore federal protections for grizzlies."

A court ruling in 2018 stated the removal of the bears' threatened status violated the Endangered Species Act. There was a massive outcry, both from ranchers claiming the predators were a threat to their livestock and from environmental groups and Native American tribes that knew the grizzly populations would plunge without protection.

I recalled an article I read in which Larson, ironically, publicly sided with the environmental groups and Native American tribes. The wily bastard was probably banking on the protections being restored. It would up the price tag on his trophy hunting trips.

"They haven't made that ruling yet," Arnold said. When my gaze sliced to him, his throat bobbed. "I'm going to need some protection after I do this for you."

He would not be getting protection from me. I fully intended to hang his ass out to dry. But I said, "You get me what I need, and then we'll talk."

"The hunting party went out yesterday. He should be calling me sometime this week or next."

I pulled a card from my pocked and handed it to him. "As soon as you hear from him, I want to know." I stood and moved to the doorway. I glanced back and found him hanging his hand, scrubbing his hands over his face. "And, Arnold?" His head snapped up. "If you even think of not cooperating, I'll bring the feds in and spread it far and wide that you were the leak in Larson's operation. Understand?"

He nodded weakly. I called Frank to my side and strode through his shop, careful to avoid looking at the bugs swarming over the bones as I passed.

TWENTY

GRANT

HUNTING WAS A waiting game, and the wait was even longer when I was accompanied by idiots. The two younger Boudreaux men bickered back and forth as if they were children, not grown men in their thirties.

I refrained from informing them that the noise they were generating was certain to keep our prey away. As long as there was a kill at the end, the longer it took, I reminded myself, the more I got paid. At the moment, though, the thought was little comfort.

The idea came to me forty years ago. I was in a constant battle with Yellowstone over the boundaries of the park and with the Indians over portions of my land they wanted to claim as their own and build a casino on. My horses were not on a winning streak.

I was frustrated, burning the candle at both ends, and losing money like a sieve. When I almost took a whip to a stubborn horse, I knew it was time to take a break and decompress. I headed out into the backcountry for a week of camping and living off the land.

I blamed the stress I had been under when I came across the pair of poachers on my land and shot them in cold blood. I left them to rot in the wilderness along with the carcasses of the adult mountain lion and two kittens they had killed.

The seed was planted, though. The only difference between poaching and trophy hunting was permission and money. I could give permission and arrange the hunts, and I desperately needed the money.

I made it work in the era before predators were reintroduced to Yellowstone. After the wolves, grizzlies, and cougars were reintroduced, business skyrocketed.

I was careful. Everyone who played a role in the trophy hunting side of my ranch was carefully selected, and our clients were top of the line. Presidents and princes, sheiks and businessmen. Vastly wealthy, well connected. Men and women who appreciated quality experience, knew how to keep secrets, and would pay big money for an American safari. Those were the requirements.

I had been on a hunt not unlike this one with the Boudreaux family when a bird cry drew my gaze to the surrounding hillside. I grabbed my binoculars and searched the area where the birds had been startled into flight. I thought I saw a flash of long, blue-black hair between the trees, but I could not be certain.

"There," Laurence Boudreaux whispered suddenly, excitement tight in his voice.

He moved to raise the rifle to his shoulder, but I halted the movement with a hand on the barrel. "Wait until it's closer. You'll have a cleaner, more accurate shot."

The grizzly lumbering toward the slaughtered horse was female. She was thin from hibernation, and, I soon saw, from birthing two cubs. They tumbled after her, clumsy and charming.

Truth be told, I did not have a problem with the predator reintroduction to Yellowstone. An ecosystem needed predators to remain healthy. The trophic cascade was essential for maintaining balance.

I enjoyed watching the predators. They were wily and intelligent, independent and collective thinkers all at once. Ruthless when needed, but not cruel. It was their misfortune that killing them represented a status symbol for so many men and women without conscience.

Laurence Boudreaux and his sons were almost trembling with excitement. "The trio is going to look magnificent mounted on the wall in my study," Laurence whispered. The sow's head came up at the sound, and her nose lifted as she scented the air. "Now?"

"Now," I agreed.

I turned my head away when he pulled the trigger.

TWENTY-ONE

FAYE

WHEN I SURFACED to awareness, light played over my eyelids, creating a kaleidoscopic pattern of brightness and shadow. My eyes were too heavy to open, and my head was stuffed with the cottony feeling of drugs in my system. The quiet sound of beeping pulsed nearby. Panic tried to sink its claws into me, but a soft, low voice sang somewhere nearby.

The language and words were unfamiliar, but the tone soothed me and set me adrift once more.

A HUM OF activity buzzed around me, but I could not quite break the surface.

"Miss? Can you hear me? Can you tell me your name?"

I tried to form words, tried to force sound from my lips, but then I stilled as I remembered. I was not myself any longer.

Fear tried to cut through the haze, but then there was nothing.

THERE WAS PRESSURE on my hand, someone's fingers clasped around mine. *Mary.* I tried to grip her hand, but there was no strength in my fingers.

"You're alright, Faye," a voice said softly. "Everything is going to be okay."

But the voice did not belong to Mary, and my name was not Faye. Confusion tried to permeate the fog that enveloped me, but darkness slipped in like the tide.

I KNEW WHERE I was as soon as I opened my eyes. Hospitals all had the same piercing white light and cold, antiseptic smell. I lay blinking at the ceiling for an indeterminate time before my eyelids became too heavy to hold open. When next I woke, consciousness returned quickly, as did the memories of the accident and aftermath.

Awareness swept in. Machines hummed and beeped quietly around me. An IV line pinched the back of my hand. My head was muddled with drugs. A shard of pain slashed through my side when I tried to draw in a deep breath.

I must have made a noise, because I heard a scrape of a chair nearby and a rustle of movement. I sucked in a breath, bracing myself, but the face that appeared above mine swept away the surge of tension.

"You're in the hospital in Livingston," Evelyn said softly. "Sam is going to be okay. He's in the bed beside yours." I turned my head against the pillow to see past her and had to close my eyes in relief at the sight of the small boy lying so still in the hospital bed. "You're both going to be fine." When I turned my gaze back to her, she said, "His arm is broken, and he was bleeding internally. They had to remove his spleen, and..." She touched my hand. "His brain was swelling." My breath strangled in my throat. "The doctor told me this morning that with the oxygen therapy and medication, the swelling has been relieved enough that he's confident Sam won't need surgery."

"I need to be closer." My voice was a hoarse croak, scraping against my raw throat. I moved to push myself upright, but there was no strength in my arms.

"Don't try to move," Evelyn said. She left my line of sight as she dragged the chair she had been occupying out of the way. The hospital bed shifted as she popped the brake, and then she slowly rolled the bed across the room. She paused at intervals to drag the IV pole and the heart rate and oxygen monitor after us.

She positioned the bed so the bedrails touched. As she set the brake on my bed, I reached through the railing and gingerly touched the back of Sam's hand. His skin was warm.

"He hasn't woken up yet, but the CT scans and MRIs have come back normal." I left my hand over Sam's but turned my gaze back to Evelyn. "You have five fractured ribs, and your ankle and knee are sprained." Evelyn glanced at the door and lowered her voice. "I told them I was your sister."

"How long have we been here?"

"Betty Decker brought you to the hospital two days ago," she said.

"We can't be here."

The panic must have crept into my voice, because she leaned close. "When they asked for your information, she told them your names are Faith and David Jones. She didn't know your birthdays. She said you flagged her down on the road, and once you were in her vehicle, you lost consciousness."

I closed my eyes, the adrenaline ebbing slightly. "We were forced off that mountain."

"I know." Her hand closed around mine. "Just rest now. I'll keep watch."

"If he comes," I whispered, "save Sam."

Her fingers tightened on mine. "Who?"

I tried to answer her, but the darkness drew me under.

I CREPT DOWN the hallway, and the silence breathed around me. The hallway seemed to stretch forever, contracting and expanding around me as if echoing the breath of silence. I placed my hand against the wall to steady myself.

I glanced at the framed photograph hung on the wall immediately to my left. The glass in the frame was shattered, fractures spread in a corona from where a fist had been driven into our smiling faces. Behind the seams of glass, Sam, Mary, and I had been captured one day at Central Park. We were on a blanket in the grass dappled in sunlight. I was lying on my stomach on the blanket, and the timer on the camera I set up caught me mid-laugh as Sam leapt on my back. Sam's head was thrown back with those infectious toddler giggles. Mary sat leaning on a hip, smiling at the pair of us.

As I stared at the photograph, Mary's head turned and she looked straight into my eyes. Her smile was still there for a moment, and then it faded and her lips moved with a single word.

"Run."

I lurched backward, gaze darting to the end of the hallway. It remained empty, but the light at the end of the dark corridor beckoned. The end of the hallway was a precipice, and it seemed as if I looked down on her sprawled body from a great height. She lay twisted, hips canted at an angle, her top knee drawn up, her shoulders flat to the ground and arms outflung. She looked as if she had fallen from a cliff and lay broken and bleeding on a canyon floor.

But the blood was in the wrong place. It was smeared across her face, not pooling below her head. And slowly, painfully, her face turned toward me, though the rest of her body remained deathly still.

She looked across the room and met my gaze. I stood frozen. Her smile was not there, and the blood on her mouth painted her teeth like smudged lipstick when her lips moved. They formed a single word.

"Run."

A hand touched my face, and I lurched out of the darkness. I gasped as I woke, gulping a breath of air as if I had just broken the surface of deep, black water. The hand patted my cheek, and when I blinked, I found Sam's face close to mine.

For a moment, I was still caught in the nightmare that was made of twisted memory, and a bolt of fear shot through me. I reached out to him to cover his eyes, but the IV line in the back of my hand caught my attention and brought me to full awareness.

I cupped his cheek instead of swaddling his eyes with my hand. My smile was shaky around the edges. "Sam," I whispered. "How are you feeling, sweetheart?"

His eyes welled with tears, making my own burn in response, and he patted my cheek frantically. I placed my hand over his to still the movement when my face began to sting.

"I'm okay," I reassured him. "We both are."

"Oh good, you're both awake," a voice said, startling me. I twisted in the bed, wincing as the movement sent a stab of pain through my side.

Evelyn jolted awake where she was slumped in a chair beside my bed asleep as the nurse came into the room.

"I'll go let the doctor know you're awake," the nurse said.

I turned to Evelyn. "The inn?"

"Don't worry about the inn. I'll head back to check on things."

The day was filled with doctors and tests. I saw the concern in the doctor's eyes when Sam did not answer her questions with anything more than a nod or shake of his head and a glance darted my way. After I explained that Sam was nonverbal, the doctor's concern eased, and she assured me that the CT scans and MRIs showed the swelling in his brain had receded.

"Everything looks great," she said. "I'm not concerned about any residual cognitive issues, though he may have headaches and some dizziness over the next couple of weeks."

The orthopedist explained the break in Sam's arm to me, and by the time the surgeon came by to discuss the surgery to remove Sam's spleen, my eyelids were growing heavy. He repeated the news Evelyn told me. Sam was bleeding internally when we arrived at the hospital, the impact from the car wreck having damaged his spleen. He explained the importance of vaccines now that his immune system was compromised and prescribed a round of antibiotics for him to take once the IV was removed and we left the hospital.

As the surgeon left the room, I turned my head against the pillow and studied Sam's face as he slept. Dark shadows marred the skin beneath his eyes, and there was a bruise on his forehead and a scrape on his chin. The cast on his arm was blue.

I closed my eyes when my vision blurred. He was so small lying in the hospital bed, and he was so very fragile. My own aches and cuts and bruises paled in comparison to the injuries that could have stolen him from me. I could have easily awakened and found him gone.

I trembled at the knowledge. Everything I did was in an effort to protect him and keep him safe. But I learned a long time ago that a mother could never shield her child from everything that would harm him. I discovered it was the curse of motherhood. A woman would fight and bleed and willingly trade her life for her child, and still the world snuck in blows she could not absorb or deflect. There was so much fury and heartbreak and agony bound up in the thorny burden of motherhood.

I was not certain if the pain I felt in my chest was from my heart breaking or from my broken ribs as I lost the battle with sleep.

When I woke again, Hector Lewis stood beside Sam's bed. Sam was sitting propped up, and Frank, his standard poodle, was sprawled alongside Sam's legs. I never had a dog of my own, and never thought to get a dog for Sam. The smile that wreathed Sam's face, the gentle way his hand cupped over Frank's head, though, made me rethink that.

"Frank recently had an injury, too," Hector said. Sam's gaze flew to Hector's, his expression pinched with concern as he gently touched the bandage around Frank's neck. "He's starting to heal, though. He seems to be feeling fine now, but I knew he would want to come compare wounds with you." Sam smiled and extended his arm, letting the poodle sniff the cast on his arm. Hector glanced up and caught my eye. "I need to talk with you privately."

I had donned a pair of loose-fitting flannel pants earlier, so I pushed aside the sheet covering me and carefully eased my legs over the side of the bed. Hector rounded the hospital bed as I stood, but I waved aside the wheelchair when he moved to it. I needed to get my feet back under me as swiftly as possible.

I caught hold of the IV pole and tugged it after me as I limped to the doorway. Each step grated like a serrated knife through my ankle and knee, but I ignored the pain. Lying helpless in a hospital bed indefinitely was not an option. When I turned to face Hector once I reached the hallway, I found he had pushed the wheelchair after me.

He parked it beside me and set the brakes. "Sit here if you need to. I don't want to have to pick you up off the ground."

I stiffened my legs and clutched one of the handles of the wheelchair. "I'm fine."

He did not peer at me closely to weigh the veracity of my words. He simply nodded and said, "I think your boy witnessed a murder."

My gaze flew to Sam, and I moved around the wheelchair and carefully took a seat. "What? When?"

"The night at the Broken Arrow," he said. Then he told me everything he discovered about Larson.

"Why do you think Sam saw…?" My gaze darted to him again, but his attention was focused on Frank.

"A man is missing. A taxidermist who was part of Larson's poaching operation. The timing of his disappearance fits. And it explains why he wants the three of us dead."

I blinked. "Three of us?"

The muscles in his jaw tensed. "His men lit my Airstream on fire and tried to keep me from escaping with Frank."

I remembered the explosions I heard in the middle of the night and the ensuing wail of fire engines. I stared at Sam. He was engrossed in playing with the poodle. He hid his hand under the blanket and wriggled his fingers until Frank slapped a paw over the movement. I watched the game unseeingly as I digested what Hector told me.

I thought the nightmare of the last days had been spurred by Senator Larson remembering me or recognizing Sam. That it had nothing to do with the past was something that never occurred to me. I had been caught up in the remembered cycle of fear and fleeing.

But wanting Hector dead as well did not fit the narrative built in my head. Relief pierced me. Perhaps we had hidden so well for so long that we had been forgotten. Perhaps we were safe from the past, safe from being found by him. Perhaps we could continue to call Raven's Gap and the inn home. Perhaps everything I worked to build for Sam over the last four years was not crumbling before my eyes.

I took a cautious breath, realizing I had been holding it. Something loosened tentatively in my chest. But the relief was immediately followed by guilt. If Sam had witnessed what Hector thought he did, I was terrified he would be driven further into silence. How much could one little boy see and maintain his grasp on what was good?

"Are you sure?"

"No," he said. "I'm not. Has Sam ever shown any violent tendencies?"

I recoiled at the suggestion. "No, never. Why do you ask that?"

"I went to see Madeline Carter the other day," he said. "She told me the reason she called you to come get Sam."

"He was homesick," I said quickly, defensiveness already raising its head at the careful way he watched me.

"She said the boys got into it, and she found Sam with his hands wrapped around her oldest son's throat."

I started to deny the accusation, anger and denial making my chest hot and tight. Sam's nature was gentle and kind. He was not capable of violence. But when I glanced across the room and found him watching me, dark eyes wide and narrow face pinched with worry, I had to admit that I did not know what he was capable of.

I had been so afraid of being found that I kept him hidden, cloistered even from other children. Only last year did I put him in public school when guests at the inn started asking why he was not in school. I had never been called into the school to discuss any behavioral issues, but at the parent-teacher conferences, his teachers always expressed concern over the distance he kept from other children, rarely showing any interest in playing with them. The invitation for him to spend the night with the Carters had filled me relief. Though I never attended any in my youth, I thought slumber parties were a normal part of childhood friendships.

But Sam never had a normal childhood. And as he dropped his gaze from mine and focused on the dog lying across his legs, I had to consider the amount of violence he had been witness to and victim of in those first years of his life. Abuse could warp an adult, drive her to desperate measures, imprint the gut-clench of fear as a default emotion.

How much damage would abuse do to a child, to a little boy whose mind and personality were still developing? Bones still held the evidence of spiral fractures for a lifetime after the break healed. The mind must still show the striations of a child seeing his father shove his mother into the wall and wrap his hands around her throat. The psyche must bear the fissures of terror and confusion and pain.

The knowledge broke my heart for Sam all over again, sharper and more bitter than my previous moments of heartache for him. Even now, I could not fully protect him from his father. I had certainly done him damage as well with the secrets he was forced to keep.

Hector cleared his throat, and I dragged my gaze back to him. "I'd like to talk to your boy. He may not have realized what he saw that night. But he could be a witness. One I need to bring Larson down."

"He's been through a lot," I admitted to him. "More than any child should have to go through. And I don't just mean this." I dipped my head to indicate the hospital room.

Impatience hardened his face, but then he looked past me and watched Sam play with Frank. His face was a harsh slab of bone and weathered skin, and his silver goatee did nothing to soften his features. But as I watched him study Sam and Frank, I saw the impatience ebb away.

"I can bring in a psychologist," he said. "The sheriff's department partners with one, and they loan her to us when there's a child involved in a case."

I started to respond, but a nurse walked past us and

glanced into the room. She stopped. "Sir, did you bring a dog into the hospital?"

"No."

She blinked at his clipped denial, and I hid a smile as she squinted at Frank. She arched her eyebrow at Hector. "Ah-huh. Look, I like dogs. But a rule's a rule. We can't have dogs in here."

"By the time you do your next round, we'll be gone."

Her mouth tightened, but Hector dismissed her by turning to face me. I could see the moment she realized it was not worth her time arguing with him. It was apparent to anyone observing that he did what he wanted when he wanted without bothering to ask for permission or forgiveness. She walked away, rubber-soled shoes squeaking on the tiles.

"I'll call the sheriff's office," he said.

"Thank you."

He did not acknowledge my thanks as he moved around me and approached Sam's bed. I did not move from my position in the doorway.

For such a hard man, his hands were gentle as he lifted Frank and placed him on the floor. Both boy and dog deflated at being separated, though.

"Sam," Hector said, and it was the softest I had heard his rough voice. "I hope you feel better. Take care of yourself. I'll be back soon to ask you some questions."

Sam's gaze darted to me, and I forced a reassuring smile to my lips.

"Would you like for me to bring Frank back when I come?" Hector asked.

Sam nodded vigorously and leaned over the bed to rub Frank's head one last time before Hector turned away and the poodle followed him.

"Any word on when you'll be released?" he asked as he stopped at my side.

"Not yet," I said.

"I'll be in touch."

I watched him leave. The night he had gone with me to find Sam at the Broken Arrow, I told him I did not think law and order were high on his list of priorities. He was a man who served himself, and I could understand that.

I told him I thought justice was his priority. But I also knew that justice meant different things to different people. His would be a brutal brand of justice.

And I could appreciate that as well.

TWENTY-TWO

HECTOR

I HAD NEVER cared for hunting. As a boy, hunting, fishing, or theft were the only way to put food in my stomach, but I had never grown immune to ending an animal's life with my own hands. The first time my slingshot made a rabbit scream in pain, I was seven years old. I was desperately hungry, but my vision blurred and my face was damp as I gently lifted the rabbit in my hands and silenced its cries with a quick twist of its neck. There was no thrill in it, and it was not sport.

But even though I now purchased game meat already butchered for me, I still remembered what was required to hunt. It was more than patience, more than stealth, more than aim. A successful hunt hinged on knowing the patterns of your prey, anticipating their move before it was made.

"How do you bring down a poaching organization?" Maggie asked me.

"You don't," I said. "But you can bring down the head of the operation." The psychopaths who enjoyed killing, who stopped a beating heart for sport, would always find an outlet. Even if an operation like Larson's was shut down, his clients would just find someone else to pay to lure prized game into rifle range. It was the way of things.

But Larson was different. He could be held account-
able and exposed. The world would judge him all the
more harshly because of his political status and his lip
service to the protection of public lands and the Endangered Species Act.

And he did exactly as I thought he would. I anticipated being followed. I had counted on it, and watched
for the vehicle to appear behind me as soon as I left Raven's Gap. If you wanted to catch a rabbit, you sprayed
apple cider inside your trap. If you wanted to bring
down a powerful man with vast connections, you used
yourself or the other two people he was desperate to
silence as bait.

The vehicle followed me at a distance all the way to
the hospital in Livingston, and now as I returned to my
truck, I spied the black SUV in the far corner of the lot.
I had parked in the loading zone at the front entrance,
knowing I would not be questioned with the police decal
on the vehicle and banking on the fact that with the security guard desk just inside the door, my truck would
not be tampered with. Bombs did not seem to be Larson's style, but the men he hired were private contractors, and those bastards tended to prefer armor-piercing
rounds and explosions.

I made Frank wait inside the hospital's entrance, and
held my breath as I turned the key in the ignition. The
truck cranked to life and I shifted it into gear without
erupting in a fireball. I called to Frank, and he rushed
through the automatic doors and leapt over me into the
passenger's seat.

The SUV at the corner of the lot remained dark and
still as I drove across the street and parked behind the
neighboring gas station.

I left the truck running and turned the heater on low for Frank before I exited the cab and moved to stand in the shadows at the side of the gas station. I had a clear view of the main entrance to the hospital and of the black SUV that followed me from Raven's Gap.

Ten minutes later, a man exited the hospital and crossed the lot. He spoke into a phone, and I knew from the way he moved he was ex-military. He moved straight to the SUV but did not drive off.

I drew the phone I purchased from the store earlier from my pocket and dialed William's number.

"Silva," he answered on the second ring.

"It's me," I said. "He's a poacher."

William let out a low whistle. "That's awkward given he's the chairman of the Senate Committee on Environment and Public Works."

"Exactly. I hate to ask you…"

"I'm already on my way," he said. "I'll be in Raven's Gap tomorrow morning."

"Come to the hospital in Livingston instead."

Ten hours later, the SUV in the corner of the hospital's lot was still sitting there when William Silva parked beside my truck.

He was not an overly tall man. He stood several inches under six feet, and he shared his mother's wiry frame. He did not look like a formidable man. In fact, he looked like he would be more apt to do your taxes than take down men easily twice his weight. But he was retired Special Forces, and he had a black belt in Brazilian jiu-jitsu. If I had to choose a man to watch my back in dangerous circumstances, William would be my first choice every time.

His head was shaved as close as a cue ball, and he

was dressed neatly in pressed khakis and a polo shirt. The sharp crease was still present even after having driven all night. Even when he was a boy, he always looked completely unruffled. As the only kid in town with a Brazilian father and a black mother, he stood apart from other boys his age. But William was like Maggie, and like his father had been before he died. He would not stand for being judged for anything but his own strength of character, and he had never resorted to using his fists to demand respect.

He thrust his chin toward the SUV in the hospital lot. "I called a buddy of mine. The security company Larson uses is known to be rough and ready. Lots of excessive force. Lots of hires who were dishonorable discharges."

"Doesn't surprise me, given they lit my home on fire and tried to shoot my dog when we were escaping."

"Fill me in on everything you've found out," he said.

I did so as the sun lightened the eastern sky with a gilding of gold. I gave him a description of Faye and Sam. "I need you to keep an eye on them. Now that Larson knows they're still alive, he's bound to make another play."

"What about you?" he asked. "Ma won't be pleased if you get yourself killed."

"Little harder to get away with killing a man with a badge on his chest than it is to kill a woman and child who don't exist in the system."

His eyes narrowed on the SUV still parked in the lot. "You think something will go down soon?"

"I wouldn't put it past him. I think he's desperate." I turned away.

"Where are you going?"

"To work," I said. "I have to actually do my job if I want to keep the badge. They don't like me enough to keep me around otherwise."

William chuckled. "Find that hard to believe, that they don't like you."

I extended a crude gesture his way as I climbed into my truck, but I paused before I closed the door. "Thank you for coming up to help."

"When the stakes are high, desperate men tend to get reckless."

His words resonated in my mind as I drove the winding two-lane highway back to Raven's Gap. I glanced in the rearview mirror, but the road behind me remained empty.

When we arrived at the inn, Frank trotted at my heels down the hallway to our rented room. I had decided to take him to the hospital with me because children always responded more easily to animals. I did not know what had silenced Sam Anders, but I needed him to talk.

Thirty minutes later, showered and shaved, I headed to the police department to begin my shift. I joined the police department thirty years ago for a lack of anything better to do. At thirty years of age, I had a wife I was not entirely certain I wanted anymore who was keen to move back to her hometown as soon as my career on the circuit was over. I had a new knee, hip, and shoulder, and was fresh from rehab with a piss-poor attitude and a bitterness wedged deep inside my gut at the turn life had taken.

At thirty, I was young and angry and stupid. And when I saw the ad in the newspaper, I thought, *Why the hell not?* I had nothing better to do. And I was mad enough at the world that I liked the idea of having a gun strapped to my hip and the authority to use it. I thought myself a real Wyatt Fucking Earp.

At thirty, I was naive enough to expect a brother-hood. I was met with a boys' club. Like me, had the other officers not had a badge pinned to their chests, they would have likely been on the other side of the law. The idea of fraternity was a flimsy thing when you could not be entirely certain the guy next to you would not shoot you in the back.

Raven's Gap Police Department never had more than fifteen officers, including the chief, commander, de-tective, and three sergeants. I had seen a number of faces come and go in the last three decades. Men and women joined the force and then moved up and on. I never sought promotions or special assignments. I did not care enough about the job to spend more time at it than necessary. I did not want the extra assignments, extra responsibility, or extra paperwork.

I had spent half my life as a police officer. Now at the ripe age of sixty, I just wanted to get through the damn day without needing an antacid or having to put in overtime. The idea of heroism attached to the job made me snort. An overblown sense of power was more ac-curate. Most cops were young, dumb kids with twitchy trigger fingers and a point to prove.

But here in this outpost of civilization, the major-ity of calls to dispatch were comprised of cows loose on the road, tourists stuck in a ditch, drunk drivers, or domestic disputes.

Most claimed they were police officers as a matter of pride and honor, but for me it was simply a means of paying the bills. Later, it kept people's anger in check when Winona and Emma disappeared. Rumor could not ruin a man who was above the law, and the police had always held that privilege. The badge had served as the thin line between harassment and routine patrol when Jeff Roosevelt complained to the chief that I was stalking him.

As I sat at my desk going through the routine of paperwork, I thought about retiring. My knee ached from running through the woods and from standing all night long. My eyes were gritty from lack of sleep.

I squinted at the witness statement for the case I had been assigned to follow up on. I did not give a damn that Agatha Thompson left her car unlocked in her driveway last night and she suspected her neighbor's teenage son had taken it out for a joy ride and then returned it with a full tank of gas and cleaner than it had been when she left it. I was of half a mind to tell the old witch she should be thanking the kid next door rather than filing a police report about him.

But I could not. I had promises to keep. When Winona and I were married, I repeated the words of the officiant without giving them any thought. The vows meant nothing to me. They were empty words. All I had been thinking about as I said them was getting Winona out of the dress she wore. It was the first time I had seen her in a dress. It was yellow, molded to her breasts and the deep curve of her waist. The hem flirted around her knees and was edged in lace. All I could think about as I repeated the words was how easy it would be to flip the skirt of her dress up and have her. When she met my gaze and grinned, I knew she could tell exactly what I was thinking.

To have and to hold, from this day forward, for better, for worse, for richer, for poorer, in sickness and in

health, to love and to cherish, till death do us part. I had
been poor and worse. I was young, so I thought myself
invincible to sickness, imagined I would always be in
good health, and had no inkling that a few years later
my luck would run out in the dirt beneath hooves and
horns. I did not know anything about love, nor did I
know how to cherish someone. I had little in the world
I could claim as my own, and I intended to hold on to
what I did have.

Now, the idea of *till death do us part* made me bitter.
I had no clue when I said those words that death part-
ing us would have been easy. I had no notion that there
were more gut-wrenching things than death that could
separate a man and woman.

In the end, I was not certain I wanted Winona and
Emma as my own any longer. I was not built to be a husband and had been apathetic about fatherhood. Now, it
seemed ludicrous that my girls once felt like a ball and
chain around my neck. I would have given anything to
have a second chance, but all I could do was hope they
had not suffered.

In the first days and weeks, I was terrified I would
find them dead. But in the months and years that followed, I was desperate. Dread at finding my girls turned
to despair at not finding them. And so they lingered
still, not alive but not dead, not gone but not in my arms
where I should have cherished and protected them and
failed to do so. They were ghosts who dogged my step,
caught in this unknown purgatory with no answers.

So I made another vow. This one was an oath I intended to keep all the way to my own grave. I would
not rest, and I would not give up. I would do whatever

it took to find out what happened to my girls and bring them home.

I scrubbed my hands over my face and leaned back in my chair. Promises to keep and miles to go before I sleep, as Robert Frost said.

Frank's head came up and he looked toward the door a moment before Donald Marsden appeared in the threshold.

"Chief," I said. "What can I do for you?"

"You have a moment?"

"Sure."

I kept expecting him to sit down before my desk and tell me he knew I was sleeping with his wife, but once again he disappointed me when he took the chair opposite me.

"Do you need anything while you're getting your housing situation straightened out after the fire?" he asked. "Joan suggested we might have a fundraiser for you."

I watched his face carefully as he said her name, but his expression gave nothing away. The man either had an unbeatable poker face, or he did not know.

"That's not necessary," I said.

The chief was a man who was very proud of having been a Marine and found endless opportunities to tell people so. He liked to label himself a Vietnam War combat veteran when I knew for a fact he had never been farther east than Germany during his stint in the military. He also used his fists when he was angry. I wondered how long that poker face would last if I knocked his head right off his shoulders.

"Senator Larson called," he said, and it was my turn to adopt a poker face as he watched me carefully. "He seems to think a member of the police department has been trespassing on his land."

"Why would he think that?"

"He said his men found a campsite on a ridge near his home and what looked like a sniper's nest." I snorted at that melodrama. "He wanted me to know he would press charges."

"Lots of trails in Yellowstone lead right up to the edge of Larson's property. Can't press charges if there are no indicators that someone is venturing onto private property," I said noncommittally.

Marsden sighed. "I thought we wouldn't have these issues with you any longer now that Roosevelt is out of the picture. You don't make it easy on us, Hector."

My temper flared. "Didn't know that was my job."

He gave me a look that was meant to be quelling. "You've done this job long enough that you should know there are some things we have to finesse."

"My job description was to serve and protect," I quoted. "I leave the bullshit to you."

He rubbed a hand over his face. "Good thing, since you have about as much subtlety as an elk in rut."

I remained silent.

"I'll tell you like I told you when you were causing trouble with Roosevelt," he said finally. "Don't give me a reason to fire you."

"Larson's a poacher," I said.

His face went blank. His mouth opened and closed. After a long beat of silence, he sat back in the chair. "You have proof?"

"I'm working on it."

"Solid proof. A full, thorough case report. Otherwise the DA will throw it out."

"This is bigger than the DA. He's operating a hunting organization that specializes in endangered species. A number of them lured out of the park."

He let out a low whistle. "Then make sure it's air tight before we bring in the feds. Larson is a powerful man with powerful connections. If we don't have every T crossed and every I dotted, he'll get off before we even finish reading him his Mirandas."

"I'm on it," I said.

"Air tight, *and* by the book."

I met his gaze and arched an eyebrow. "Would I do things any other way?" I asked, keeping my voice mild.

"Of course not," he muttered as he stood and exited my office.

I glanced at the witness statement again and grabbed the phone to follow up with Agatha about her conscientious car borrower. Miles to go, I reminded myself.

TWENTY-THREE

GRANT

"THE WOMAN AND her boy showed up at the hospital in Livingston."

I looked up. "You told me it was taken care of."

"What can I say? These people have a hard time staying dead."

I started to respond to the retort when something snagged in my memory. "Do you have the security footage from when she and Hector Lewis showed up to get the boy?"

"Yes."

"Bring me stills of her face. And the boy's."

I dropped my face into my hands as soon as he left and rubbed my temples. Pushing back from my desk, I strode out of my house, stopping first by the kitchen, and moved toward the paddock where Iago was grazing on fresh hay.

His head came up as I approached and bobbed in greeting. I waited, leaning against the railing, and he cautiously crossed the paddock to my side. I smiled when he stretched out his neck and nuzzled my arm.

Keeping my movements slow, I offered him the apple I purloined from the kitchen for him. His ears went up as he smelled the fruit, and for the first time, he accepted it directly from my hand.

He crunched through the apple noisily and enthusiastically. He did not shy away when I reached out and placed my hand against his neck. He blew a breath out of his nose, and I echoed the sound.

It was Winona who taught me to not just better understand the language of a horse but to speak it myself.

And I knew there was no turning back when she came into my study after I returned from the hunt where I thought I saw a flash of blue-black hair between the trees. I stood to greet her as she rounded my desk. Her face was set, but I could not discern her mood. Until her palm cracked across my face.

"You are despicable," she whispered as my face was still stinging. "Don't think you'll be able to get away with this."

She was a fierce, intelligent woman. Perhaps I should have expected she would dig and dig until she knew the truth. Perhaps I should never have offered her the job that day on the state road watching her gentle the most violent horse I had ever owned.

Iago danced away from me as John approached with the images I requested. There were several in the stack, shots from the footage showing the woman's face from different angles. I recalled that nagging sense of familiarity, and shuffled through the stack to study the images of the boy.

"What did you say their names are?"

"They go by Faye and Sam Anders."

Her name had not been Faye when I met her at the charity event in New York City years ago. Nor had her hair been black. It had been a deep, vivid red that was almost the hue of blood. She was lucky her face was not memorable and that striking hair color was easily disguised. Otherwise, I would have remembered her much sooner.

I studied the images of the boy again and reached for my cell phone. I dialed the number and had to wait to be put through the channels to speak to him. When he finally answered, I said, "I hope you are in a generous mood."

His chuckle was not a pleasant sound. "You know you need to tread carefully, Grant. You never had much of a poker face."

"No, but tonight I have a royal flush. I know where your son is."

TWENTY-FOUR

FAYE

"Can you believe he's here?"

The hushed words drew me from slumber, and I rubbed the sleep from my eyes before pushing the button to raise the head of my bed. I glanced across the few feet separating our beds and found Sam sleeping peacefully. His chest rose and fell in a smooth rhythm, and the machines he was attached to beeped softly and steadily.

The women outside our room spoke quietly. I closed my eyes, letting my mind drift, until I heard his name. I should have been used to it by now. I saw his face on television advertisements often enough these days. But it still lanced that pocket of fear inside me, letting it spill out and seep into my blood. And then what she said penetrated.

"Excuse me?" I called, trying to keep my voice calm.

One of the nurses stuck her head inside my door. "I'm sorry, honey. Were we too loud?"

"Did you say Kevin Hastings is here?"

"He is. A surprise visit. I didn't even know he was coming through this area. I was planning on driving to one of his events with friends."

"He's *here*. In the hospital?" I darted a glance at Sam.

"Yes, he's down on the second floor right now. He stopped into the nursery. It's a good thing I'm not down there. If I saw him holding a baby, I think my ovaries would explode." She laughed, but I did not follow suit. "He should be up here soon, though. I can see if he'll stop by your room if you'd like to meet him."

I could not manage a smile for her. My mind was racing, and my heart was picking up pace right along with it. Her gaze darted to the heart rate monitor. "Could we get some lunch? I think I slept through the first delivery."

She smiled. "Of course, honey. I'll go put in the request."

As soon as she left the room, I scrambled out of bed. Lightheadedness swamped me, and I grabbed onto the rail of my bed to steady myself. My heart rate monitor was beginning to beep erratically. I stumbled to the wall and unplugged the entire machine before I unclipped the monitor from my finger. I sucked in a breath at the sharp pinch as I pulled the IV line from the back of my hand. Blood welled to the surface, but I did not stop to stem the bleeding.

I ached everywhere. My fractured ribs pinched sharply with each breath I took. My ankle and knee throbbed. I limped to the chair where Evelyn left the duffel bag and slipped on a pair of yoga pants. My hospital gown was spotted with blood from my hand, and I stripped it off carefully and pulled a sweatshirt over my head. A blood trail on tile would be easy to follow, so I slipped a sock over my bleeding hand and shoved my feet into my boots.

I moved to Sam's bedside. "Wake up, bud," I whispered, placing a hand on his chest. His lashes flickered as I unplugged the machine monitoring his vitals and unclipped the heart rate monitor from his finger. I grabbed a piece of tissue from the rollaway table and pressed it against his arm as I removed the IV line as gently as I could. His eyes were open when I looked at his face. "We have to leave," I said. I knew the urgency bled into my voice when his gaze darted past me to the doorway.

I leaned over his bed. He wrapped his arms around my neck as I lifted him. Fire swept through me, and I clenched my jaw to keep from crying out in pain. I sucked in a shuddering breath as Sam tightened his arms around me. I could feel his gaze on my face, but I was not ready to look at him yet. I was not certain I could force a smile past my lips.

I peered around the door into the hallway. The nurse's station was empty, and the nurse who told me of his arrival at the hospital was walking down the hall. She turned a corner and disappeared into another room.

I adjusted my grip on Sam and hurried down the hall in the opposite direction. I moved as quickly as I could, breathing through the knifelike sensation in my ribs and the raw, grating sensation in my knee and ankle. I hesitated at the end of the hall before the bank of elevators. It would be quicker, more comfortable, and far more easily cornered and trapped in. I turned the corner and pushed through the heavy door into the stairwell just as a nurse turned onto the hall.

I leaned a shoulder against the wall as I struggled down the staircase. Sam pressed his forehead against my throat. When dampness hit my collarbone, my throat closed. I made it down the next three flights of stairs and peered around the corner into the hallway.

Kevin always had a veritable army around him. Their uniform consisted of well-tailored suits, concealed weapons, and ear pieces. The two men standing at either end of the hall undeniably fit that bill.

I ducked back into the stairwell, panic fluttering like a trapped bird in my chest. This was how he operated. I had seen it enough times to know the way he flushed out his prey. He was nothing if not a master hunter. He would cut off all escape routes. I knew from experience pulling the fire alarm would not work, because he would have every exit watched. There was no way for a woman and child to disguise they were a woman and child.

Unless we did not look like a woman and child together.

I limped down the stairs to the basement level as quickly as I could. A door slammed open on one of the floors above us, and I froze, arms tight around Sam. I backed into the corner, pressed against the wall, out of sight from the central axis around which the stairs revolved.

"I hear he's even more handsome in person than he looks on TV," a man said.

A woman laughed in response. "Is that all it takes to win your vote?"

"Well, it certainly doesn't hurt," he responded. "I wouldn't mind—"

The sound of another door opening muffled the rest of the exchange, and when the door closed with a thump, it was silent again. The stairwell was empty.

Sam trembled in my arms. I pressed my lips to the top of his head. "I will never let anyone hurt you," I whispered. "I'll do anything it takes to protect you." His thin arms tightened around my neck. "We need to get out of here. Can you be brave for me?"

After a moment, his forehead rubbed against my throat as he nodded.

The door at the bottom of the stairwell was labeled STAFF ONLY, but it swung open easily to allow me access. The basement level was quiet, though behind one door, I could hear voices and the clang of cutlery indicating a kitchen. I hurried past a bank of elevators and slipped through an open doorway when I heard the door into the kitchen swing behind us.

The room I ducked into was a break room, and I leaned against the wall and strained my ears to hear the approach in the hallway. Footsteps squeaked toward us on the polished tile floor. I held my breath when the footsteps paused, but then a ping echoed down the hall, and I heard the slide of the elevator door opening and closing.

A doctor's white coat hung from a peg on the wall. I deposited Sam into a chair and snatched the coat off the hook, shrugging into it and buttoning it over my sweatshirt.

Sam watched me with wide eyes.

"Ready to go?" I whispered.

He nodded, and I picked him up carefully. A glance around the threshold showed the hallway to be empty, and I limped down the corridor toward the double doors labeled LAUNDRY. Sweat beaded on my forehead and gathered at the small of my back.

I pushed through the double doors and found a row of large carts parked along one wall. I hurried to one and lowered Sam within. I braced myself with one hand on the edge of the cart and the other pressed against my side as I fought to catch my breath and swallow past the rising queasiness.

It took me several minutes before I could straighten from my bent position. I moved to the rows of shelves and pulled packages of linens down. I ripped open the sterile wrappings and tossed crisp white sheets and blankets over Sam until the pile filled the cart.

"Think of this as a game," I said, forcing a smile to my lips.

He ducked down, and I made certain he was completely covered by the linens.

"I'll be right back for you," I promised him, and then slipped from the laundry room and followed the hallway around the corner.

The exit signs led to a delivery bay. I retraced my steps, went straight to the bank of elevators, and pulled the fire alarm.

The siren was instantaneous, and I hurried back to the laundry facilities, hand clutched to my side. Hospital employees were already hurrying past me as I reached the linen cart, but few spared me a second glance and none stopped me.

I reached into the linen cart beneath the piles of blankets and sheets, and Sam immediately grasped my hand. "We're going now," I said softly. "Just stay hidden."

I wheeled the cart into the hallway and joined the press toward the exit. No one was panicking or running. It was simply a milling tide of employees on this level exiting the building through the big bay doors and migrating down the loading dock ramp. I pushed my way into the midst of the group and kept my head ducked.

I kept my face down and watched for anyone who came too close from the corner of my eye as we exited the building and crossed the parking lot.

"See her or the boy?" I heard someone call.

My head jerked up, and I glanced through the crowd before I could check the reaction. The man in the suit stood about fifteen feet away, braced against the press of people moving away from the building. As if he were a boulder in a stream, people parted around him. His gaze was directed past me, and I quickly lowered my head before he felt my eyes on him.

"Nothing," another man said to my left.

I had to force myself not to break into a run. I moved slowly with the others across the pavement, striving to remain as invisible as possible to the men obviously searching for us. I pushed through to the fringes of the crowd gathering in the parking lot. Many were clustered in groups talking, a few lit up cigarettes and took advantage of the impromptu break. From this angle, I could see around the corner to the main entrance. There were men in suits gathered there as well.

I had to make a break for it now. I glanced around as I pushed the linen cart between vehicles, weaving through the parking lot to the side street. My heart sank. I had anticipated a maze of buildings surrounding the hospital, a city labyrinth we could escape into. But the hospital sat isolated on a stretch of rough plain. There were no shops or businesses in the immediate vicinity, nothing that might offer a hiding place. There was no shelter. We were exposed.

I should have hidden Sam and stayed inside the sanctuary of the hospital, but it was too late now. There was a gas station across the street, the only other building in the vicinity. I pushed the laundry cart in that direction. There were several trucks parked at the pumps across the street. If we could stowaway in the bed of a one of the pickups and escape this area, we had a chance.

Several people gathered along the sidewalk stared
at me curiously. I avoided eye contact and walked as
quickly as I could.

"Hey!"

I flinched at the shout behind me and kept moving, tension knotting itself tightly between my shoulder blades.

"Hey! Stop!"

I risked a glance back. The man pushed his way
through the crowd, staring right at me, talking into a
microphone in the cuff of his suit. He was closing the
distance between us in long strides, pushing people out
of his way. I looked around desperately, and a woman
caught my gaze. She wore a nurse's scrubs, and she
stared directly at me.

Her head turned to take in the man bulldozing his
way toward me, and with a glance in my direction, she
stepped directly in his path. He tried to pull up, but
they went down in a tangle of limbs. Her pained cry
was muffled by his shout.

I shoved the laundry cart against the curb and pushed
the linens aside. Sam peered up at me, face drained of
color.

I stripped off the doctor's coat and tossed it into the
cart. "Everything is going to be fine," I assured him
as I lifted him into my arms. "Hold onto me, and don't
let go." His legs wrapped around my waist, his arms
around my neck.

It felt as if a knife were shoved through my ribcage. My knee and ankle threatened to give out. I was
winded, my arms shaking. Nausea churned in my stomach, and my vision swam. But I hurried across the parking lot and out into the street.

My own breath and heartbeat were so loud in my ears that the only warning I had was Sam's arms tightening convulsively around my neck. The force with which my arm was grabbed from behind yanked me around. I reacted automatically, kicking the man as hard as I could in the knee and jerking my arm out of his grip.

The man went down with a bellowed curse, hands clutching at his broken kneecap. I turned, took a lurching step as I tried to run, and my leg collapsed beneath me.

I twisted as I fell to take the brunt of the impact, and the ground rushed up to meet me. I clutched Sam to me, trying to shield him. I hit the pavement hard, my right shoulder and hip taking the worst of the blow. Sam jolted against me, and I felt something pop in my ribcage. Darkness sliced across my vision, but instinct brought my arms tight around Sam.

I screamed as the man tried to wrench Sam from me. He clung to me as tightly as I clung to him. I did not dare loosen my grip on him. I kicked out blindly, scuttling backward, struggling to push myself upright and fight the black spots that infringed on my vision.

Tires screeched nearby, so close to me that I felt the heat of the vehicle at my back. The man made another grab for Sam and caught hold of my ankle as I kicked at him. He yanked me toward him. Gravel bit into my back, and my head bounced against the pavement.

A figure flew past me, and then the man's tight grip on my ankle was gone as he was thrown to the ground. The newcomer followed him down. I shoved myself backward and scrambled to get my feet under me.

The two men on the ground were a blur of movement. The man in the suit grunted and fought wildly, but the newcomer was silent, his face set in a frozen snarl, as he straddled the other man. He delivered a series of punishing blows to the other man's face, and when the man in the suit twisted to protect himself, the newcomer flipped to his back.

I staggered to my feet and stumbled against the car abandoned diagonally in the street behind me. For a moment, I thought the newcomer had lost his vantage over the man in the suit now that he was on his back in the street. He was smaller and far less burly than the man now over him, but his legs were wrapped around the other man's middle and his arms were wrapped akimbo around the other man's neck, one arm locked around his throat, the other crossed behind his head. The man in the suit flailed against the choke hold, his face red.

I glanced past the men on the ground and saw half a dozen more men racing toward us.

The man in the suit went limp suddenly, and the newcomer shoved the unconscious man off of him and leapt to his feet. He spared me a single glance before turning to face the other men.

"Get in the car, Faye, and lock the doors."

I did not know how he knew my name, but I fumbled with the handle on the back door. Sam's arms were cinched tightly around my neck as I placed him in the backseat. The engine was still running. I darted a glance toward the front seat. "Let go and get down, sweetheart," I whispered, untangling his arms from about my neck.

I did not follow him into the backseat. I closed him in and scrambled into the front seat. I slammed the door, locking it behind me. Then I shifted the car into drive and stomped on the accelerator. The tires squealed, and the backend fishtailed before the tread gripped the pavement and we shot down the street. I glanced into the rearview mirror just as the six men who were part of Kevin's detail rushed the man who helped us.

PART THREE

TWENTY-FIVE

HECTOR

"She's gone."

William's voice was winded on the other end of the line, and that snapped me to attention even more than his words. "What do you mean gone?"

"The hospital had a visitor today. Showed up with more security than a man like that warrants right now. Your girl has more to worry about than Larson. We need to find out who she is to Kevin Hastings."

"Hastings?" I stood and moved to the door of my office, closing it. "Jesus Christ."

"Who is this woman? She's smart. Bet you anything she was the one who pulled the fire alarm in the hospital. She almost escaped, but the terrain here is wide open. I clocked her as soon as she was in the parking lot, and Hastings's men weren't far behind me in making her."

"They got her?"

"Close. I stepped in, and she stole my car while I was taking care of the situation."

"The boy was with her?"

"Yep," William confirmed. "Hastings's men weren't even subtle about it, Hector. They were going to take her down hard in front of witnesses. We need to find them."

"I can be there in an hour."

"No," he said. "I've got this. I have a modified Lo-Jack on my car, and my phone is busted but still working. I can track her."

My desk phone began to ring. "Keep me posted."

"Will do," he said before hanging up.

I picked up the receiver of the phone on my desk.

"Can you meet me somewhere?" Arnold Baxter asked in a low voice on the other end of the line.

"Where are you?"

"I just left Larson's." Nerves lent a quaver to his voice. "He's going to kill me if he finds out I did this."

"Calm down," I ordered. I rattled off an address. "Meet me there in twenty." I cued up the radio on my shoulder. "Romeo 3, dispatch."

There was a crackle of static, and then a woman said, "Romeo 3, go ahead."

"Take me off of calls for the next hour. Forward any non-emergent calls for me to my desk at the PD."

"Romeo 3, I copy that."

Frank followed me out to my truck, and when we turned off the state road onto the dirt drive, his tail began to thump in recognition.

Arnold was waiting for me, pacing beside his van. "What the hell is this place?" he asked as I climbed out of the truck.

I glanced at the burnt, twisted ruins of my Airstream. Beyond the wreckage of my home, just within the shadow of the trees, the white wolf stood watch.

Deciding that telling Arnold it was my home before Larson's men set it ablaze would only make him more nervous, I said, "Somewhere we can talk in private."

He blew out a breath. He studied me for a moment,

and then he turned and reached into his vehicle. "Here," he said, tossing me the object.

I caught it midair and turned it over in my hands. "A tracking collar?"

"On one of the grizzlies Larson called me in to process," Harold said.

"They shot more than one?"

The taxidermist's face pinched in distaste. "A sow and two cubs." I swore, and he nodded. "They got rid of the transmitter on the collar. I'm guessing as soon as they realized she was tagged."

"You've finished the paperwork?"

"Not yet. I'm still working on the kills."

I ran my thumb along the edge of the collar, noting the fraying where the GPS unit had been ripped away. "They are in the north barn?"

"Yes," he said. "Everything is contained there. I don't even need to bring any of my tools."

"Make yourself scarce at the Broken Arrow tomorrow."

He swallowed. "Shit. What are you going to do?"

I strode back to my truck. "Unless you want to be arrested, stay away."

I did not head back to Raven's Gap. Instead, I headed toward Gardiner. I crossed the river and passed under the Roosevelt Arch. I flashed my badge when I reached the small cabin that served as the gateway to the north entrance of the park.

The five miles to Mammoth were an ascent, winding up through the hills. I came around a curve and crested the ridge. The Lower Terraces gleamed like white marble in the spring sun.

The hotel was still closed for renovations this season,

though it was slated to reopen later in the year. Spring had come to the park, and with it, the crowds. This time of year was busy in the park. We crawled through Mammoth Village. Frank pressed his nose to the window, whining in excitement at the people streaming along the sidewalks. I left my truck near the visitor center and crossed the old fort grounds.

In the years following Yellowstone's establishment as the first national park, the Army sent men from Fort Custer to protect the land. The old structures built at the turn of the century with stone quarried from the Gardner River still stood.

I had dealt with Amon Edwards, a ranger with the Yellowstone Law Enforcement Services Branch, on a number of cases before. When I asked to see him, it was only a few minutes before he came striding down the hall.

"Hector." He held out his hand and shook mine with a firm grip. The man was short and stocky with a boyish face. "What brings you to the park today?"

I handed him the tracking collar, and his brow creased. "Can we talk in your office?"

I told him everything I had discovered about Grant Larson's operation. His expression grew more somber and angry as I spoke.

"I'll put in a call to Montana Fish, Wildlife and Parks on this," he said finally. "I'll talk with the Interagency Grizzly Bear Study Team, too. With the GPS in those collars, they will be able to pinpoint where the signal went dead."

"The sow and cubs are on his ranch right now being processed."

"I can't promise I will be able to get the ball rolling on this tomorrow," he warned me. "But I'll do my best."

"That's all I ask," I said. "As soon as I get the paperwork from the taxidermist, I will pass it on to you."

He scrubbed a hand over his face. "A female with two cubs? Shit. It's been a shitshow since the grizzlies lost their protected status."

When I left the building that now served as park headquarters, I found Jack Decker leaning against the side of my truck. He straightened as I approached and rubbed his thumb in the gouge that marred the paint from fender to bumper where he keyed my truck in January.

"I have a buddy who can fix this for you," he said, and I knew it was the only apology I would ever get from him.

I shrugged. "At least it wasn't blood poured across the seats or graffiti across the side."

He looked away. "Saw you when you were passing through Gardiner, and I wanted to have a word." He met my gaze. "Something is going down."

"Kevin Hastings is in town."

His eyebrows arched. "You're well informed. Larson called him, and he showed up today."

"Do you know how Hastings is connected to Faye and Sam?"

"That's why he's here?" Jack said. "I know Larson and Hastings know one another. Old family friends. But I assumed he was here because of what you've uncovered about the poaching ring."

"I think it's more than that. His men attempted to grab Faye and her boy from the hospital this morning."

"Christ." He glanced toward the park headquarters. "Getting the feds involved now?"

"That adult grizzly Boudreaux killed had a radio tag."

"Larson isn't usually so careless," he said.

I smirked. "I guess he's had a lot on his mind lately."

He studied me. "You got to Baxter, too, didn't you?"

I ignored his question as I climbed into the cab. "You'll keep your ears open about the connection between Faye and Hastings?"

"Larson doesn't exactly share his daily gossip with me over coffee," he said. "But I'll let you know if I hear anything." He put a hand on my door when I moved to close it. "Faye and her boy. They okay?"

"They got away from Hastings's men," I said. "But I don't know if they're okay."

The traffic moved even slower out of the park on account of a bighorn sheep sighting. When I returned to the police station, Joan met me at my office door.

"There's someone here to see you."

"Regarding a case?"

"I don't think so, but he didn't say," she said carefully. "He asked to speak with you privately, so I left him in the victim advocate room."

The tone of her voice told me something was amiss, but she disappeared down the hallway before I could question her. I motioned for Frank to stay on his bed. I cut through the bullpen and down the hall, slowing when I turned the corner and caught sight of the man standing in front of the door into victim services. I recognized him immediately for what he was—a bodyguard.

He turned as I approached. He was an oversized

bruiser of a man, the fluorescent light overhead gleaming off his bald head, his suit expensive and pressed until the creases looked sharp enough to be used as weapons in their own right. "I'm going to need your weapon, sir, before you enter."

I ignored him and went to move around him, but he stepped into my path, blocking my way. "I don't think you realize this is not only my jurisdiction," I said, "but my department. You don't have authority here."

He took a deep breath and seemed to swell in size, filling the doorway. I eyed him for a long moment before I shrugged and turned away. "Your boss must not be that interested in speaking with me."

I did not get very far down the hallway before I heard, "Wait, wait."

I pivoted and only William's call earlier kept my surprise in check. Kevin Hastings was the attorney general of New York for six years before winning the Senate election in 2016. Now, his face was plastered across billboards and commercials all across the United States as the prospective candidate for the nomination for president in the upcoming election. He had come out of the gate early, the first to announce his run for the primary.

He was in his mid-forties, composed and dignified enough to appeal to the older crowd, charming and boyish enough to appeal to the younger one. He came from wealth, and he wore it like a second skin. His smile was practiced, everything about him smooth and polished and open. It immediately put me on my guard.

"Officer Lewis?" He strode toward me with his hand extended.

"Yes," I said. "And you are?"

I hid a smile when his practiced one slipped the

slightest bit before he straightened it. I accepted his handshake, noting the firmness and strength in his grip.

He chuckled. "Kevin Hastings. I see I have not done enough to reach the constituency of Montana."

I kept my face bland. "I'm afraid I don't follow politics."

He grinned, and it set my teeth on edge. "No, I'm sure you have much more important matters to attend to." He swept a hand toward the victim advocate office as if he were royalty inviting me into his chamber. "May we talk in private?"

I glanced at the pit bull and arched an eyebrow.

"Paul is a little overzealous at times. I apologize on his behalf. Of course you don't need to surrender your weapon."

The victim advocate room was large with several couches and chairs. It was brightly lit, and the volunteers who worked in the office had made an effort to make the room less stark with landscapes on the wall and pillows with flowers on them on the couches.

I took the chair across from Kevin and after the man nodded at his pit bull, the bodyguard closed the door and remained in the hallway. The man who was possibly the next president of the United States clasped his hands, propped his elbows on his knees, and leaned toward me.

"What I would like to discuss with you is sensitive in nature. The woman at the front desk told me there are no microphones or cameras in this room."

"That's correct," I said.

"I know an honorable man such as yourself will want to do what's right and will understand why I don't want this spread around."

I arched an eyebrow. He was good. He spoke to the

ingrained code of corruption that a number of old timers in the force lived by. He just did not realize I did not give two shits about codes or a guise of honor.

"Why don't you just spit it out?" I asked, and had the pleasure of seeing his annoyance at being derailed from his script flicker across his face.

He chuckled, but there was an edge to it. "A blunt man. I can respect that. I'm here because it has come to my attention that there is a woman in town who is calling herself Faye Anders. She has a boy with her." He studied me as if searching for confirmation, but I kept my face carefully blank. "She and I have some unresolved history, and I would like to settle it before I get further along in the race. I'm sure you can understand."

"What kind of unresolved history?" I asked.

"The kind tabloids love. Nothing that would cost me the candidacy, let me assure you." He adopted a devastated mien, and watching the bloviating buffoon switch out masks was fascinating. "The tragedy she was involved in is still incredibly painful for me to talk about, and it is an intensely private matter."

"And how do you propose to settle this unresolved history?"

"I was told she was at Mercy Community Hospital, but when I went to visit, she and the boy both were gone."

"The hospital must have discharged them," I said, knowing full well the hospital had not done so yet.

He made a noncommittal noise. "The police will need to be involved eventually, of course, given how dangerous she is. But first, I would like your help in finding her."

"Why come to me?" I asked, curious what his answer would be. "Why not go to the chief with this information? If she's as dangerous as you claim..." I let the sentence hang, and he filled in the silence, as I knew he would. Men like this loved nothing more than the sound of their own voices.

"I can assure you, it's more than just a claim. But I would like to keep this quiet for as long as possible." His smile was full of aggrieved commiseration. I started to ask him if keeping it quiet entailed kidnapping a woman and child in full view of evacuated employees and patients at the hospital, but I refrained. His pit bull standing outside the door had already showed me how overzealous the men he hired tended to be. "As for why you, I think your record speaks for itself."

I leaned back in the chair and crossed my arms over my chest. "What record is that?"

He looked caught off guard for a second. "Your exemplary record with the department, of course."

"Hm." It was the biggest line of bullshit I had ever heard, and now I knew for certain who sent him my way. I stood. "I'll think about it."

He pushed his chair back and followed me to the door. "You'll...think about it?"

"I will," I said, enjoying his discomfort. "I'll get back to you about whether or not I'll help you find the woman and her boy. Do you have a card with a number I can reach you at?"

I opened the door and the pit bull moved aside to let me exit.

"Ah, yes." His expression was perplexed as he pulled a business card made of heavy stock from an inner pocket of his suit jacket and handed it to me. I wagered no one had ever told him anything but *yes, of course, whatever you would like.* "You'll be well compensated for your assistance in this matter."

I wondered if he always spoke like a pompous prick. "I'll take that into consideration." I stepped across the hall and opened the door that led into the lobby, stepping aside to let them pass. "I'll be in touch."

Kevin Hastings's bemused expression was priceless as I shut the door in his face. I dug my phone out of my pocket as I strode back to my office. I called William, but it went straight to voicemail.

I unlocked the top drawer of my desk and retrieved the folder containing the case Ted Peters found after running Faye's fingerprints. I read through the case again. The details had captured the nation's attention when it first happened. A lover's quarrel, a murder, a missing child. But nowhere in the case report was Kevin Hastings mentioned.

I brought up the internet browser on my computer. Frank left his bed, stretched, and came to rest his head on my knee as I searched for Kevin Hastings.

Numerous articles and news reports popped up in response to my query. An intensely private matter, he said. I searched his name linked to Faye's real name, but aside from finding that Faye came from the same echelons of wealth Hastings did, I got nothing back in the search.

Affairs your wife did not know about were usually an intensely private matter. Faye being his mistress and Sam his son was the narrative that made the most sense. But everything I read about Hastings over the next hour painted him as a loving, devoted husband.

His private life was just that, though. Private. I found no references to any scandals, personal or professional.

By all accounts, his work ethic, intellect, and charm were unparalleled.

The fact that I found nothing but positive press about him raised my suspicions. A man with a persona that carefully composed undoubtedly had a number of unsavory secrets he worked hard to hide.

And now I knew Faye and Sam were one of those secrets.

TWENTY-SIX

GRANT

"YOU DIDN'T TELL me Hector Lewis would be difficult," he said as he accepted the snifter from me and leaned back in my leather high back by the cold fireplace as if he owned it.

I snorted. "You look up *difficult* in the dictionary, and it has Hector's picture beside it."

He made a noncommittal noise, and we fell into silence. We had worked together for years now, authoring bills, being courted by the same lobbyists. Kevin Hastings was a shark, ruthless, powerful, and filled with the unflinching confidence of knowing he was at the top of the food chain.

He was also intensely private. The only reason I had known about his mistress and the boy was because his financier father had been a close friend. Kevin had been a young man who still needed an older man's counsel, and with his father's death, he turned to me.

It was a family matter. Nothing inspired loyalty like family. I understood that and honored that code.

I had considered Winona family. It was why I did not resort to drastic measures immediately after she threatened me.

Threats could work both ways. She needed to understand that even though I loved her, I could not let her ruin everything I worked so hard for.

I thought long and hard about how to deliver my threats. I decided the most effective way to frighten her into rethinking what I knew she planned to do was to be subtle about it. The threats were as innocuous as possible, aimed at the very things I knew she cared most about.

I never left the neatly typed messages with her when she was at the Broken Arrow. I waited and left one in her daughter's car seat when the pair were in the grocery store. I slipped one under the pillow that smelled most strongly of her in that ugly trailer she and her family called home. There were other places I left the threats, and all were places I knew would hold the most impact.

At the grocery store, I had waited. I borrowed a ranch hand's truck so she would not recognize me and parked across the lot to ensure she found my message. She had as soon as she leaned into the car to place her daughter in the car seat.

She froze, every line in her body going stiff as she slowly straightened. I watched her, noting the careful way she held the note, the way her beautiful face drained of color, the way her arms tightened around her daughter, the way she glanced around, searching for me.

Kevin swirled the whiskey in the snifter for a moment before meeting my gaze. "What do you want?"

As soon as he announced his running, I saw the opportunity. When I first approached him about it, though, he treated me as if I were a stallion past my prime, ready to be gelded and put out to pasture. I had my pride, but now I had leverage. "The same thing I asked you for several months ago."

His smile was filled with hard edges. "You have me exactly where you want me now."

"I'm not an unreasonable man," I said magnanimously. I left out the fact that he would be doing me a favor, removing the woman and child from the equation. Now all I had left to deal with was Hector before I joined Kevin on the ballot as his nominee for vice president.

TWENTY-SEVEN

FAYE

WE COULD DISAPPEAR AGAIN. We did it once before, and I knew how Kevin operated. This time, there would be no press, there would be no manhunt organized by law enforcement. We would vanish, as if we had never existed in the first place.

I knew his aim. He would bury us in an unmarked grave, somewhere we would never be found. No one would know to look for us. No one would remember us.

My eyes burned. This was what had haunted me for years. We could vanish, and no one would remember a woman with harsh black hair and a silent boy with a haunted face. I braked at a stop sign and pressed the heels of my hands against my eyes.

That would not happen now, I assured myself. Evelyn would remember us. I had made a home for us in Raven's Gap. People knew us. They loved my pancakes.

But the lump in my throat felt sharp and tasted of bitterness. I slipped my arm between the driver's seat and passenger's and held my hand out. Sam's fingers immediately clasped my own, and I blinked rapidly to clear my vision.

We could escape, go on the run again and drop out of existence, surfacing again as a new woman and son. I could find a new town, build a new life for us. We would have to start over completely, sever all ties, even with Evelyn.

First, I had to get back to the inn. All of my money, my weapons, and the extra birth certificates, IDs, and passports I purchased for us were in my safe. He would be watching the inn, though. If he found me in the hospital, he already knew everything about the life I built for us in Raven's Gap.

I glanced in the rearview mirror again. We had not been followed as we fled from the hospital, but we needed to get out of this car before the vehicle was reported as stolen.

I had driven a circuitous route around Livingston, turning at random down narrow, quiet streets in the neatly gridded town. It was such a small town I knew we risked garnering police notice, stolen vehicle or not, if I kept switching back through town.

I drove into the lot of the supercenter and pulled around behind the building until we were out of sight from the road. I parked and tried to twist in the seat to look back at Sam, but the slight movement sent a knife of pain through me. I sucked in a breath and dropped my head back. I clenched my teeth against the urge to cry out. The fingers twisted between mine squeezed my hand.

It took me several moments before I could reassure him. "I'm fine." I could hear the lie in the tremor of my voice, but I hoped Sam could not.

A trickle of warmth slid down the side of my face. I wiped it away and found my fingers stained with blood. I pulled down the visor to peer into the small mirror on the flip side. A gash sliced open the hairline above my temple. Blood was crusted in the edge of my hair and down the side of my face into my ear. I swiped away another teardrop of blood that made its way down my cheek.

I should take the time to wipe the car down, make sure we had not left any fingerprints behind. Fingerprints or blood. I should search through the glovebox and trunk to see if there was anything worth taking.

I made do with sliding the cuff of my sweatshirt over my hand and using the sleeve to give the steering wheel and door handles a cursory polish. I left both the glovebox and trunk untouched.

I swayed as I climbed from the car. I kept the cuff of my sweatshirt pulled down over my hand when I opened the back door and leaned within, wrapping my arms around Sam to lift him from his huddled position on the floorboard behind the driver's seat. I could not bite back the cry that left my lips as I attempted to lift him and staggered, bracing a hand on the backseat before I collapsed on top of him.

I was shaking, a fine tremor rattling through me so hard my teeth chattered with the force of it. I closed my eyes and swallowed against the bile rising in the back of my throat. A sheen of sweat dampened my forehead.

A hand touched my cheek, and I opened my eyes. Sam peered into my face, his own set in tense, pale lines of fear.

"Can you walk?" I asked.

He started to nod, but he winced in pain, hand going to his head. He squeezed his eyes shut, and I stroked his hair gently.

"I'm so sorry you're hurting, sweetheart," I whispered. The cast on his arm was still secure, and when I lifted his shirt to check the incision on his abdomen, I found a row of staples. It turned my stomach, seeing his skin raw and puckered around the staples. None were busted, though, and the incision was neat and clean.

I forced myself to stand upright, and he crawled out of the car. I braced my forearm against my side to try to ease the pain, and Sam caught my hand. He pulled my arm around his shoulders and tucked himself against me. As we left the car behind and rounded the building, I had to force myself not to lean heavily against him.

I tugged him to a stop at the corner. We were out of sight from the main entrance but had a clear vantage point across the parking lot. I waited, watching. Approaching someone in a parking lot was a risk, but going inside was a greater one. In this state, we would draw attention, and the security footage would be more likely to identify us than the grainy, indistinct images from the farther range of the cameras looking out over the parking lot.

I debated between an old man and an old woman. A man would feel more protective but would likely be more curious and would want to involve the police. A woman would be more leery about me approaching her, but Sam's presence would reassure her. She would be less likely to ask questions and more likely to keep our encounter a secret.

After about fifteen minutes, I spotted what I was looking for, and the choice came down to availability.

I tried to hurry across the parking lot, but our progress was more of a pained shuffle toward the old woman crossing to her Oldsmobile.

I called out to her as I approached, and her eyes widened when she turned and saw us. "Please," I said, and did not have to force my voice to tremble. "Will you help us?"

She leaned heavily on her cane, almost overbalanced by the two shopping bags in her other hand. Her hair was a distinct elderly shade of violet, but her gaze was sharp and shrewd. A squeal of tires at the edge of the parking lot made me glance over my shoulder.

"Do you need money or a ride?" the old woman asked.

"Just a ride," I said. "Do you live in Livingston?"

"No," she said carefully.

"I need to get out of town without being seen."

She studied me for a long moment. Her gaze lifted to the cut on my head and then dropped to the child at my side, the cast encasing his arm, the way he squinted painfully in the sun and kept his face ducked against my chest. "I only have half a tank of gas."

My knees weakened in gratitude. "Just whichever direction you're going. If you'll just drop us off somewhere where there is a phone."

She nodded slowly. "Climb in."

"It would be better if we got in the trunk," I told her.

Her eyebrows were drawn on with a neat hand, and they arched upward with the wrinkling of her forehead. "You don't need me to take you somewhere specific?"

The wail of a police siren somewhere nearby startled me. "Just away from here."

Sam hesitated when she opened the trunk, clinging to my hand bandaged with a sock. I stroked my free hand over his hair. "It's okay," I whispered. "Everything is going to be fine."

I wondered at what point those words would be rendered meaningless, if they offered him any comfort even now. The respite and safety of the last four years were wiped away as if they never existed. My words sounded empty to my own ears.

But he nodded and crawled into the trunk. I eased myself inside after him, wincing as I curled on my side.

"Ma'am?"

I stiffened at the male voice, but before I could react, the trunk closed over us.

The darkness was sudden and absolute, and Sam whimpered.

"Shh," I whispered against his ear.

Sound was muffled within the interior of the trunk, but I could still hear the conversation taking place just a few feet away.

"Is everything okay here?" the man asked.

There was a long pause before the old woman responded. When she did, her voice was low and tremulous. "This is my granddaughter and great-grandson," she said softly. "We just saw her abusive ex inside, and I need to get her away from here. He's been threatening to take her son away, and I'm afraid he'll resort to violence."

My eyes slid closed at her too-perceptive lie, but they flew open at the man's next words.

"Do you need me to call the police?" he asked. I was blind in the darkness of the trunk, but I twisted my head, stretching my hand out until I could trace the seam of the hatch. "I can get the manager to kick him out of the store, too."

I held my breath waiting for her answer.

"No, but thank you, young man. The world needs more men like you in the world. I just need to get her home before he notices us."

"Of course."

Sam trembled against me, his head propped on my arm, fingers clutching mine. After a moment, I heard the thump of the car door. The engine rumbled to life, and I rocked with the motion of the Oldsmobile reversing and then being put in drive. The seconds ticked by slowly in my head.

The trunk felt like a quiet, warm cocoon. I closed my eyes in the darkness. I breathed shallowly through my nose, trying to calm my heartbeat that still galloped wildly.

It felt too much like those hours we spent cowering under my bed. Even after Kevin's footsteps faded down the hallway and silence rang through the penthouse, I had been too frightened to leave our hiding place. I was certain the quiet was a ruse, and he would lunge from the shadows as soon as we crawled from beneath the bed. It was not until the room began to darken that I finally left Sam hidden and crept through the apartment.

I forced my mind away from the memory of finding Mary.

When Sam was smaller and he did not fully understand the terror that gripped me, I attempted to make our situation into an adventure, encouraging him to think of our hiding in various hotels across the country as a game. I could not do that now. All I could do was hold him close and press my lips to the back of his head. The scent of smoke still clung to his hair, reminding me of how close I had come to losing him.

It was long minutes before the vehicle finally slowed to a stop. The engine cut off, and the door opened and closed.

When the trunk opened, I blinked rapidly, eyes watering as I struggled to adjust to the sudden painful flare of light after the long minutes in the dark. The pulse in my head and churning in my stomach reminded me of my own concussion and the additional blow my skull received today. The old woman held out a hand to me, and I was careful not to put too much pressure on it as I climbed from the trunk. We were in a garage.

"Come inside for a spell," she said. "I'm not a nurse or a doctor, but you need that checked out." She nodded to my head, and I felt another bead of blood roll down my cheek. "My son makes sure I have a good first aid kit. I can take you somewhere later. Perhaps a women's shelter?"

I left her offer unanswered and simply said, "Thank you for helping us."

Her gaze bounced between us, her tissue-paper face soft. "Come inside," she repeated, voice gentle.

Sam and I followed her into a small, tidy home filled with indoor plants and the smell of cookies. A massive cat greeted her as soon as she walked in the door, and she spoke to the beast lovingly.

"This is Rachmaninoff," she said. "He's very friendly. Have a seat here in the living room. I'll just go get my supplies and see about that wound."

I stood in the doorway, taking in the room, the photographs hung on the wall, the piano situated under the window. This was a happy home. One that was filled with light and frequently with family, it seemed.

It reminded me of Mary's parents' home.

Sam took one of the chairs, and the cat immediately jumped up and made himself at home in Sam's lap. For the first time since he awakened today, some of the tension in Sam's face eased and he smiled.

I crossed the room slowly and lay on the couch, unable to remain upright any longer. I tried to take a deep breath, but a shard of pain pierced my side. I remembered the popping sensation when I hit the ground and knew I had damaged my fractured ribs even further.

The measured thump of the woman's cane announced her return. She dragged an ottoman to my side and splayed the first aid kit across her lap as she sat.

Her hands were steady and cool as she cleaned the area and then secured the cut on my head with butterfly strips. She took the sock off my hand, cleaned the ragged wound I made by yanking out the IV line, and then bandaged it as well.

I did not think anyone had ever tended to me with such care before. I knew my emotions were frayed from the events of the last days when her ministrations made my eyes burn.

Exhaustion threatened to pull me under as the adrenalin wore off. I had been on my own for so long that it took me fading in and out of consciousness as the light playing against the wall waned before I remembered I had an ally.

I struggled upright and realized more time had passed than I realized. Darkness was encroaching outside. Sam slept in the chair with the huge cat draped over him like a blanket, and the old woman sat in the opposite chair knitting.

"Do you have a phone I can use?" I asked.

"Of course. There's a landline in the kitchen."

I pushed myself up off the couch and had to hold on to the arm for a moment as the room tilted. I braced my hand against my side as I crossed to the kitchen.

The phone attached to the wall seemed like such

an antique in this day and age. I collected the receiver from the cradle and moved to the kitchen table. The chair caught me when I sagged into it as the strength went out of my legs.

I always made a point to memorize the phone numbers that were important to me, but my head swam and I had a hard time focusing my eyes on the numbers on the phone. It took several attempts before I managed to punch the number in correctly.

Evelyn answered her phone on the second ring.

"It's me," I said, voice low. "I need your help."

TWENTY-EIGHT

HECTOR

THE PHONE ON my desk rang as I powered down my computer. I glanced at the clock and considered ignoring the call to get out of the station on time. The ringing was insistent, though, and I snatched the receiver from its cradle.

"I need to speak with you, but not over the phone," Evelyn said softly on the other end of the line when I answered. "And not at the inn or at the station. The inn is being watched."

Between Larson and Hastings, they had a veritable army between them. "Meet me at the diner in five," I said.

I whistled for Frank, and we strode down the hall. Joan had already left for the day, but I made a mental note to tell her that if Kevin Hastings showed up again, she should make him wait in the lobby.

The man given the task to follow me made no secret of his presence. He leaned against a nondescript sedan and stubbed out the cigarette he was smoking as I approached my truck. He pulled out of the parking lot behind me and followed me through town to the diner. The man parked in the corner of the lot, but he did not follow me inside.

The dinner rush had not yet arrived, and most of the booths were empty. I slid into the booth behind Evelyn.

"Don't turn around," I said to the empty table in front of me, voice pitched low for her ears. "Not sure if it's one of Hastings's men or Larson's, but I had a tail coming from the station. He's parked outside and can see in the windows."

"Faye told me someone would be watching," she said, voice just as quiet.

"Is she safe?" I asked.

Maggie caught my gaze across the diner, brow wrinkled, and I shook my head to deter her from approaching.

"For right now. But she has nowhere to hide."

I thought over it for a moment. "I have a place in mind. But you and I can't go."

"Can Maggie go get her and Sam?"

"No. I don't want Maggie involved any more than she already is." I gazed across the diner and lifted a hand when Maggie glanced my way. "But I know who we can send." She crossed to my side, concern etched into her face. "May I get two club sandwiches? One of those sandwiches is to go." I had never ordered. She always brought me what she wanted to cook for me.

"I'll have the same," Evelyn said at my back.

"And she'll need the check right away," I said.

Maggie glanced back and forth between us. "Sure thing. That will be coming right up."

"You have the address for where she is right now?" I asked quietly once Maggie walked away.

"Yes."

"Write it on the check for Maggie."

When Maggie returned with two plates, she left a

blank receipt and a pen beside our plates. She caught on quickly.

"Enjoy your meal," she said, holding my gaze for a moment. "I'll have a treat for Frank and the extra sandwich ready in a few minutes."

The club sandwich tasted as phenomenal as always, but I did not take time to savor it. I ate in quick bites, one eye on the vehicle at the edge of the parking lot. I stood before Maggie came back to clear away my plate, and as I turned to leave, Evelyn pushed the pen Maggie left for her off the edge of the table.

I paused and knelt to pick it up.

"She's my friend, Hector," Evelyn said, voice low and fierce. "I don't know what she's been through, but I will help her in any way I can."

I placed the pen back on the table. "We'll get it sorted."

Instead of leaving the diner, I cut down the hall. Out of sight from the front windows, I glanced back. Maggie pocketed the receipt beside Evelyn's plate without even looking at it. She turned and caught my eye. I tipped my head toward the end of the hallway where her office was located.

She met me in her office several minutes later with two to-go boxes. "What's going on?" She pulled the receipt from her pocket and handed it to me.

"Kevin Hastings is the reason Faye and her boy are in Raven's Gap." I moved to her desk and grabbed the desk phone. Louie, the little Bichon, was curled up in her desk chair, and he gave me a disgruntled look at waking him.

"*The* Kevin Hastings?" she asked, eyes wide.

I nodded and dialed William's number. "Did you find her?" I asked when he picked up on the third ring.

"No, but I found my car where she abandoned it. If she skipped town, she either caught a ride or stole a car. I haven't heard any reports of a stolen vehicle across the scanner, though."

"She didn't skip town," I said, and read off the address Evelyn had written. "Wait until tomorrow to go get her. The area will be crawling with men searching for her and her boy right now."

He repeated the address back to me. "Will do."

"She'll be wary," I warned. "And I've never seen her unarmed. Don't get yourself shot."

"I'll do my best, but it wouldn't be the first time," he said.

"I had a visit from Hastings today. He wants to hire me to help him look for the pair. Whatever went on between the two of them, he's not here to kiss and make up."

"Yeah, I got that when they almost snatched her and the boy off the street," William said. "I can take her back to Denver."

"No." I needed her son to bring Larson down. "Take her to Jack's."

The silence on the other end of the line crackled. "You trust Decker?"

"Not any farther than I can throw him," I assured him. "But she and the boy will be safe there." I felt Maggie's presence at my side. I glanced at her, and she held her hand out for the phone. "Call me if things go sideways. I'm passing you to your mother."

I stepped away and tuned out their conversation until Maggie put a hand on my arm as she hung up the phone.

"What can I do?" she asked.

"Don't vary from routine," I said. "Hastings and Larson are both powerful men with a wealth of resources. Whatever secrets they think that woman and boy will reveal, they think they are worth killing over."

She hesitated and then moved behind her desk and opened a drawer. "There are Winona's secrets as well." She slid the safe deposit box key I found hidden in the Airstream across the desk to me.

I put my finger on the key, but I did not pick it up. *Hector, if something happens to me...* I swallowed. "Where?"

"Pinnacle Bank in Bozeman. Safety deposit box 219. Both your name and Winona's are on the box. Hector..." I dragged my gaze from the key. Maggie stared at me, expression tight. "Whatever you find in that box, I want you to remember how much she loved you."

I picked up the key and slid it in my pocket before grabbing the carry-out boxes. I turned back to her in the threshold. "I remember that every day, Mags."

What haunted me was that I had never been able to return her love. Whatever she had endured, she had not known with absolute certainty that I would never stop fighting to find her and our daughter.

And when I allowed myself the honesty, I was not certain that what I felt for her now was love. What I felt for her now was a sharp twist of shame at never knowing how to give her the love she needed and a razor's edge at the remembered resentment and anger I felt for her in the end for having needed that from me.

It ate me up inside. I had never known how to love, and remembering Winona's love was not what spurred me out of bed every morning. It was the bitter reminder that she had never known mine, not even now. So I gave her what I had to give. Obsession. Love paled in comparison.

I crossed the parking lot in ground-eating strides, and the man leaning against the car parked in the corner of the lot straightened warily. He pushed the jacket of his suit aside as I approached but did not reach for his weapon.

I tossed the box containing the extra club sandwich to him, and he juggled the container in surprise.

"You'll want to eat," I said. "Keep up your strength for whatever fight Larson and Hastings thinks they are bringing to my doorstep."

Frank could smell whatever Maggie had cooked for him, but I made him wait until we were back in our hotel room before I let him eat.

If the man followed me to the motel, he did so with more stealth and care than he had used thus far. The next morning as I headed to Bozeman, I did so without a tail. I glanced into my rearview mirror often, but the road behind me remained empty of all traffic but local, battered pickup trucks.

A dusting of snow gleamed blue under the morning light, and mule deer intermingled with a herd of elk grazing on the sparkling plain. I slowed for a coyote to lope across the road, his gaze keen on the young elk and deer in the herd.

The streets of Bozeman were busy with morning traffic. Bridger Range and the Spanish Peaks were still capped with snow.

I had left Frank with Cheryl, the woman who worked the front desk at the motel. They had developed a mutual admiration of one another since we began staying at the inn. I was not certain how long this would take me, and while I could sneak a dog into a hospital, a bank was another matter.

The bank was located on the west side of town, and two women manned the front counter. No one was in line ahead of me, and the teller's smile was polite when I approached the counter. "How may I help you today, sir?"

"I'd like to get the contents of a safety deposit box."

"Certainly. Box number?"

"219."

"I'll just need to see some ID." I fished my wallet out of my pocket and slid my driver's license across the counter. She glanced at it and then clicked away at her keyboard. "I'm seeing here there are some delinquency charges on the safety deposit box."

"You still have the contents, though?"

"We do. But the yearly rental fee has not been paid in…" She squinted at the screen, and then her eyes widened. "In fifteen years."

"How much?"

The clack of her nails on her keyboard as she typed grated on my nerves. "It totals to four hundred dollars."

I drew the bills from my wallet and handed the cash to her. It took her several minutes to complete the transaction, and then she glanced at me and smiled. "I'll take your key and will bring the box out to you if you would like to wait in room four."

I relinquished the key and strode through the lobby to the small cubicle labeled 4. It consisted of a pair of chairs and a narrow table. I stood to wait, and five minutes later the click of heels brought me to the doorway.

"Here you are, sir," the woman said as she approached. "Once you are finished going through the box, you can come back up to the counter."

I closed the door as I retreated into the room and placed the box on the table. It was not heavy, and I pulled up a chair and sat staring at the box for a long moment.

Hector, if something happens to me...

I lifted the lid. There was only one item within the safety deposit box: a bulky manila envelope. I unwound the string from around the buttons and opened the envelope, upending the contents onto the table. A disposable camera slid onto the tabletop, so cracked that it looked as if it had been thrown against a wall or run over by a vehicle.

I thought that was the extent of what the envelope held, but when I shook it, slips of paper fluttered free. Several spiraled to the floor. I leaned over and picked them up.

The neatly typed words froze me in place. I straightened slowly and placed the pieces of paper on the table. The paper was unlined, the words typed in an unassuming font. I read each one and then read them again.

Don't do anything foolish.

Remember, we know where you live.

Emma should grow up knowing her mother.

A police officer's job is always dangerous. Don't make your husband's more so.

What do you think would happen to your brother if you aren't careful? Helicopters crash all the time.

Blacks can still be lynched. How would your friend look with a rope around her neck?

My hands shook as I gathered the threats and tucked them back into the envelope. I slid the battered camera inside as well and took the safety deposit box back to the teller.

"Would you like to renew the box for another year?" she asked when she saw it was empty.

"No," I said shortly. "Where can I get film developed?"

Her polite smile stayed in place despite my abrupt tone. "I believe the pharmacy across the street develops film."

The scrawny kid behind the photo desk at the pharmacy eyed the camera I handed him. "Man, that's gnarly. You toss this off a cliff?"

I ignored his question. "I need to know if you can recover and develop the photos off the film."

"I can send it in and find out. Man, I haven't seen one of these cameras in forever."

"Send it in?" I asked. "You can't develop it right now?"

"No, man, we don't deal with film onsite any longer. We can do digital prints here. But we have to send film off to a lab."

"How long does that take?"

He shrugged. "About two weeks usually."

"I don't have two weeks. This is…" *Hector, if something happens to me…* I let out a breath and rubbed the back of my neck. "This is important. Is there anyone in town who can develop these for me today?"

"No, man, everyone I know of sends them off. No in-house development any longer. That's old school."

I accepted the camera back from him and turned away.

"Hey, man, wait," the kid called when I reached the exit. "How important is what's on the camera?"

I hesitated for a moment. "I think whatever is on this camera may have gotten my wife and daughter killed fifteen years ago."

His eyes went wide. "Damn, man." He glanced at his phone. "I get off of work in an hour. I have a dark room in my apartment. Photography's my hobby. I can develop those for you."

"You can do it today?"

"Yeah, if the film isn't ruined. Developing the negatives just takes about thirty minutes. It's longer for printing. I'll have to expose, develop, fix, wash, and then dry each print." At my blank look, he said, "It might take me a few hours, but I can get it done for you today."

"What's your rate?"

His face screwed up in thought. "Two large supremes from Earth and Stone Pizza here in town?"

I almost chuckled. "Deal."

"My name's Russell, by the way."

I almost told the kid I did not give a damn what his name was, but I tightened my jaw around that response and introduced myself.

His darkroom was set up in the narrow hall bathroom in his small apartment. I sat in the living room four hours later shuffling the neatly typed threats as I waited for him to finish. His place was cluttered, but the couch I sat on was clean and the beer he offered me was ice cold.

"This is some sick shit, man," Russell said as he appeared in the hallway. He glanced at the pizza boxes sitting on the coffee table atop piles of books. "I can't eat anything right now." He handed me the stack of prints. "This is what I could salvage. I need a drink."

I placed the notes back in the envelope and flipped through the photographs. It took me several photos before I understood why he could not stomach food at the moment.

The first scenes were innocuous, but upon closer inspection, I recognized what Winona had captured on film. Over a decade had passed since the photos were taken. The landscape had changed and grown, but when I looked closely at the trees in the shot, I spotted the camera traps.

The dead horse in the next photo was a grim sight. She was an old nag, and the bullet hole in her forehead made my fists clenched. With the next photo, I realized the horse had been used as bait to lure the four dead wolves. One of the wolves was white, and my stomach turned at the striking pale fur stained with blood.

There were other animals, the photos taken at different times as evidence by the change of seasons in the pictures. Poaching was a grisly, brutal business, and the photos highlighted that. I had no idea how Winona got the photos. Most were taken from a distance, the features of the people in the frame indistinguishable. Save for one.

"Jesus," I breathed, taking in the photo of Grant Larson holding a dead bald eagle up by the wings. Even taken from a distance, his face slightly out of focus, he was recognizable.

The next prints were photographs of handwritten entries in ledgers. It looked like an inventory of hunts, including names, dates, price, and kills. The last photo in the stack raised the hair on the back of my neck. It appeared to be taken immediately after the photos of the entries in the ledgers. A desk and papers were a blur in the bottom half of the print. And in the edge of the frame stood the shadowed figure of a man in a darkened doorway.

Fury gripped me. *Hector, if something happens to me...*

I glanced up as the kid slumped into the chair across from me.

"Is this in Yellowstone?" he asked.

"Just outside the park."

"They're luring those animals outside of a protected area." Anguish and anger were threaded through his voice. "What can we do?"

I studied the kid. I guessed him to be no older than early twenties, not much older than Emma would be now. "Can you enhance these photos? I want all the information off of the ledgers."

"I'll work on it tonight. Can we take this to the police?" he asked.

"I am the police, kid, but we need the feds for this." I glanced back through the prints. "I want you to keep the negatives safe for me."

He nodded. "I can do that." He drained his beer and held his hand out for the photographs. He pulled one out of the stack and held it up for me to see. It was the print of Larson holding the dead bald eagle. "My sister is a reporter at the Bozeman Daily Chronicle."

I smiled. Nothing was quite so vicious as the court of public opinion. "Send it to her." I pulled out my phone and scrolled through my contacts list. "And give her this phone number. It's an inside source."

"You want to wait while I enhance these?" he asked when I stood. He handed over the other prints, and I tucked them into the envelope.

"No, I'll be back for them tomorrow." I held my hand out to him. "Thank you."

He shook my hand, and his grip was firm and strong. "Sure, man."

My thoughts churned as I drove the eighty-five miles back to Raven's Gap. Anger left an acid burn in the back of my throat, and my jaw was clenched tight against the knowledge that my wife had been afraid, threatened, and felt like she had no one to turn to.

When the lane branched off of the highway, I did not think. I cranked the wheel to the right and made the turn with a squeal of tires.

There was a single guard at the gate, and, for an instant, I considered not even stopping. He stepped into the center of the lane, though, and I hesitated before letting my foot off the accelerator.

He came around the side of the truck as I pulled to a stop and rolled my window down. His eyes widened when he saw my face, and I knew he recognized me.

"Tell Larson I'm here to see him."

TWENTY-NINE

GRANT

"HE'S HERE."

I looked up from the computer. "What?"

"Everett just called it in on the radio. He's at the front gate. Is this guy an idiot, or is he just insane?"

I was hedging my bets on the latter. "Tell Everett to let him through."

"I can get Antonio on the roof with his rifle. We'll scrap his vehicle."

I stood. "Not yet," I said. "I want to hear what he has to say. Tell your boys to stand down."

I moved through the house and waited on the front porch. He came down the lane quickly, and for a brief instant, as I met his gaze through the windshield as he approached the circular drive in front of my house, I thought he might not even hit the brakes. He did, at the last minute, and came to a grinding halt at the edge of the drive with his front tires braced against the rock edging.

This was not a man who could ever be a politician. He did not know when to smile and charm, he did not know how to finesse. The man went at things like a battering ram.

I strode down the front steps. "Hector. What brings you to the Broken Arrow?"

He exited his truck and approached me. Nothing hinted at his mood aside from the ticking in his jaw. I did not see his fist coming.

Pain exploded in my jaw, and I was sprawled over the stone steps leading down from my porch before I even realized I had fallen. It took several minutes for the ringing in my head to quiet to a dull throb.

I pushed myself into a seated position and had to hang my head a moment as white spots spun around the edges of my vision. I lifted a hand to my face and moved my jaw carefully. I swore as pain scored through me, and I could feel that several of my teeth were loosened.

Noise finally penetrated the fog that enveloped me. Groans reached me, and I slowly managed to lift my head. Three of John Smith's men were on the ground. One was unconscious, another clutched his ribs, and the third cradled his arm against his chest. Three more of John's men held Hector face down in the dirt. John knelt over him, his knee driven into Hector's back between his shoulders.

Even John was winded. "You should have let me have Antonio take him out."

"Is that what you did to Winona, motherfucker?" Hector was breathing heavily, but even pinned down, there was nothing subdued about the malice in his voice. "Did you take her out?"

I stared at him, head swimming. I knew Winona would be my downfall. And the moment I walked in on her taking pictures of the ledgers, I had known the threats were not enough.

I never had to use anything more than words and power to intimidate someone before, but Winona was not just anyone. I slammed her face down on my desk, pressing her cheek against the numbers, dates, and names she had snapped photographs of.

"You're in a precarious position here, my dear," I whispered against her ear, pressing my weight into her back. I heard the camera crack under her chest. I swept her hair back from her face and gave in to the urge to press my nose to that tender spot behind her ear where her skin met her hair. I inhaled deeply, and she smelled as sweet as I imagined she would. Like horse and woman. I felt a tremor move through her. "I want you to think very carefully and reconsider whatever you are thinking of doing with whatever you think you know. And while you're doing that, I want you to think about your parents. About your friends. About your brother. About your husband and daughter." She flinched with each person I named.

When I lifted my weight off of her and stepped back, she staggered upright and scrambled around the desk. She was trembling, but there was fire in her eyes when she turned back to me.

"My husband will kill you."

"Your husband doesn't give a shit about you," I reminded her.

Her entire face moved with that blow. It was far more powerful than anything physical I could have dealt her.

"What did you do to her?" Hector shouted now. His face was red, a vein throbbing in his temple. "What did you do to them?"

I pushed myself to my feet and stumbled. When one of John's men moved to help me, I shook his hand off. I thought he might have broken my jaw, but I managed to force the words out. "I didn't know you cared so much. Little late, don't you think?"

He lunged toward me, and I staggered back a step before I could check the reaction. The four men on top of him scrambled to hold him down.

"I'll tear you to pieces," he whispered, gaze angled straight into mine even with his face shoved into the dirt.

Winona had been right. There was murder in his eyes.

"Boss?" John asked. Sweat beaded his forehead.

"You know what to do," I said, forcing the words out around the beat of pain in my jaw. "And make it hurt before you end it."

THIRTY

FAYE

THE KNOCK ON the front door jerked me awake, and I automatically moved to sit up. My body shrieked in protest. I fell back against the couch cushions with a groan.

The old woman hurried down the hall from her bedroom. She was still belting her robe as she moved to the chair where Sam slept. She woke him with a hand on his shoulder, and then she turned to me.

"Hide in the back bedroom while I get the door," she said, voice hushed. "What is this man's name?"

"Hector," I said. "Hector Lewis."

I pushed myself off the couch and caught Sam's hand as we retreated down the hall to the bedroom at the far end. I closed the door until there was only a sliver of space remaining and leaned against the wall, listening.

The quiet murmur of the old woman's voice reached me, but the low timbre of the response was unfamiliar. A sluice of icy fear went through me, and I twisted the handle of the door to close it silently. I turned the lock, wincing at the snick of sound as it tumbled into place.

It was a flimsy lock. The door would be easy to kick in.

I did not know who was in the house, but it was not Hector. I was not certain how Kevin's men found me so quickly, but I was not going to wait around to ask.

Early morning light spilled into the bedroom. I moved to the window and flipped the latches. The sill groaned as I pushed the lower half of the window up, and I darted a quick glance over my shoulder. A sudden slant of light gleam under the seam of the bedroom door as the light in the hallway was flicked on.

I turned to Sam and realized he held the massive cat draped over his arm not bound in a cast.

"Leave him here," I whispered. "We can't take him with us."

The stress of the last days was taking a toll on him, and his face took on a mulish expression.

"He is not our cat." The measured thump of the old woman's cane announced her approach down the hall. "*Now*, Sam."

The urgency in my voice brooked no argument, and he placed the cat on the bed and swiftly moved to my side. I helped him climb out of the window. The drop to the ground was only a couple of feet, and he managed it easily. I followed him out. When my feet landed in the carefully tended flowerbed beneath the window, I caught his hand.

"Quickly now," I whispered.

We stuck close to the side of the house as we crept around the corner. I hesitated when the front yard came into view. The vehicle I stole yesterday from the man who helped us escape was parked in the old woman's driveway.

"Hector sent me."

I whirled around and stumbled back from the man who approached. I pushed Sam behind me.

He held up his hands and took several measured steps away from us. "I'm not here to hurt you, Faye. Or to take you or Sam back to him. I helped you get away yesterday, remember?" He kept his voice soft and low, as if he were speaking to a wild animal.

I did recognize him. He wore another pairing of crisp khakis and polo, and he did not look any worse for wear after his encounter with Kevin's men. But I did not know him, and I did not know if I could trust him, even though he knew Hector's name.

"Hector called me," he said. "Hastings paid him a visit yesterday, and he's being followed. He didn't want to risk leading anyone to you, so he called me." He watched me carefully and slowly lowered his hands. "I'm Maggie's son. I think you know her from the diner. She told me you make the best huckleberry pancakes, and she cannot figure out what makes them so light and fluffy."

I sagged and placed a hand against the side of the house to steady myself. I sucked in a shuddering breath. "I'm glad you found your car. We needed to get away from there." I would not apologize for stealing it in the first place, or for leaving him to fend for himself against half a dozen men.

"Is this man not who he says he is?"

I turned and found the old woman approaching us, her weight leaning on her cane, a wicked-looking kitchen knife clutched in hand.

"He is," I assured her. "The man I thought would come sent—" I glanced at him.

"William," he supplied.

"Sent William instead."

"Let me help you back inside," he said, stepping around me and offering his elbow to the woman.

She handed him the knife as politely as if she were

handing him a cookie and then accepted his arm. Sam wrapped his arm around my waist as we followed them up the front steps into the house. The behemoth of a cat twined around his ankles as soon as we stepped inside.

As William moved into the kitchen, the old woman turned to me. "Will the two of you be alright?"

I was not certain how to answer that question. Kevin's arrival meant our safe, quiet existence in Raven's Gap was over. There would be no going back to the inn I loved in the little town I had begun to call home. I knew this was a possibility and tried to prepare for it. But the sense of loss and despair was keen and sharp.

She must have seen all of that on my face, because she reached up and cupped my cheek, her skin as soft and worn as crumpled tissue paper.

We had not exchanged names. She had not asked for my story. She simply bandaged our wounds and gave us a safe place to hide.

"Thank you," I said.

She patted my cheek gently and then rested her hand on Sam's shoulder. "We women have to stick together."

Sam knelt and rubbed his fingers under the cat's chin. Dark circles bruised the skin under Sam's eyes, and he leaned against me as we followed William to his car. I sat in the backseat with Sam lying across the seat with his head in my lap. I glanced back as William pulled out of the driveway and lifted a hand in farewell to the woman. She returned the gesture before she retreated inside.

I leaned my head back against the seat rest and closed my eyes. I did not realize I had fallen asleep until William said quietly, "Duck down now."

I glanced out the window and saw we were approaching the turnoff for the Broken Arrow. Sam was asleep, his face lax and peaceful, and I shifted him carefully in order to lie down on the seat beside him. I stayed that way even after we passed the turnoff for Grant Larson's ranch.

I felt when the car left the state road, for the ride became rougher, rocking me back and forth. When William parked, I gingerly pressed myself upright and was startled to realize where we were.

"I don't think we should be here," I said.

"Hector arranged this," he said. "But I can take you somewhere else."

I stared at the cabin. "No," I said finally. "There's nowhere else to go." I needed to rest and think of how to get what I needed from the inn without being seen.

"Wait here," William said.

He glanced around as he climbed the front steps of the cabin and then knocked on the door. He waited for a long moment before knocking again. After stepping to the side to peer around the corner of the cabin, he tried the door. It swung open, and he disappeared inside.

Jack Decker needed to learn to lock his door.

William reappeared a few minutes later. He opened the car door and extended a hand toward me. "Let's get you inside."

It would not be the first time the man returned home to find us within. I let William assist me out of the car and then moved aside as he leaned into the backseat to lift Sam into his arms.

I followed William inside, steps slow and measured. I had to grip the porch railing to make it up the steps, and I paused in the doorway, leaning against the threshold for support. I hated this feeling of weakness and helplessness.

"Do you need help?" William asked when he reappeared in the hallway.

"Yes," I said, even as I hated it.

He carried me into the living room and deposited me in the recliner. I watched him warily as he moved back to the porch. He grabbed the single rocker and brought it inside. He took a seat across from me, and I held his gaze as he studied me and waited him out.

He spoke first. "Hastings is Sam's father?"

I had expected a question of this ilk and debated how to answer it. I had no reason to lie about this. "Yes."

"I take it you don't have full custody."

I smiled. It tasted bitter on my lips. "If only it were that simple."

"Did Hastings's wife know about you?" he asked. When my gaze lifted to his, I saw no condemnation in his face, simply curiosity.

"No," I said finally. "No one knew. At least, not outside of Kevin and some of the men he contracts from private military companies." I let out a humorless chuckle and winced at the lance of pain. "He always was good at hiding things." I swallowed at the memory of the bruises so deliberately dealt where no one would see them.

"Hector thinks your boy saw something the night he was at Larson's ranch that put a target on your back."

I darted a glance down the hallway when I thought I heard the creak of a floorboard, but the corridor was empty. "He told me. But I don't know what Sam saw, and I won't put him in further danger." I turned my gaze back to him. "And Larson knows who I am now. That's why Hastings is here."

"And who are you?"

"For right now, I'm Faye Anders," I said, and he smiled.

He stood and held out his hand, helping me from the depths of the recliner to my feet. "Get some rest, Faye."

I shuffled down the hall to Jack's bedroom and climbed into bed beside Sam. I let out a breath as I lay flat and the sharp pinch of discomfort eased in my ribs. I felt bruised all over.

I reached across the bed and placed my hand on Sam. His back rose and fell with his breath, and he did not stir at my touch. I slipped into sleep quickly and deeply.

It seemed as if I had only just closed my eyes when the low, urgent murmur of voices roused me. I struggled to fully surface from slumber, but I kept slipping back into the dark until a touch on my shoulder startled me awake.

"Something has happened to Hector," William said quietly. "You'll be safe here, but I have to go." He tucked his car key under my hand. "If you need it, my car is out front."

He was gone before I could respond, and before I could grasp consciousness, I faded again.

I crept down the hallway, and the silence breathed around me. The hallway seemed to stretch forever, contracting and expanding around me as if echoing the breath of silence. I placed my hand against the wall to steady myself.

I glanced at the framed photograph hung on the wall immediately to my left. The glass in the frame was shattered, fractures spread in a corona from where a fist had been driven into our smiling faces. Behind the seams of glass, Sam, Mary, and I had been captured one day at Central Park. We were on a blanket in the grass dappled in sunlight. I was lying on my stomach on the blanket, and the timer on the camera I set up caught me mid-laugh as Sam leapt on my back. Sam's head was thrown back with those infectious toddler giggles. Mary sat leaning on a hip, smiling at the pair of us.

As I stared at the photograph, Mary's head turned and she looked straight into my eyes. Her smile was still there for a moment, and then it faded and her lips moved with a single word.

"Run."

I lurched backward, gaze darting to the end of the hallway. It remained empty, but the light at the end of the dark corridor beckoned. The end of the hallway was a precipice, and it seemed as if I looked down on her sprawled body from a great height. She lay twisted, hips canted at an angle, her top knee drawn up, her shoulders flat to the ground and arms outflung. She looked as if she had fallen from a cliff and lay broken and bleeding on a canyon floor.

But the blood was in the wrong place. It was smeared across her face, not pooling below her head. And slowly, painfully, her face turned toward me, though the rest of her body remained deathly still.

She looked across the room and met my gaze. I stood frozen. Her smile was not there, and the blood on her mouth painted her teeth like smudged lipstick when her lips moved. They formed a single word.

"Run."

I jerked awake, heart lodged in my throat.

It was dark. The cabin was silent. I breathed slowly until my heart returned to its normal pace.

I stretched my hand out across the mattress and encountered cool sheets. Fear pierced me, and I shoved myself upright too quickly. I ignored the stab of pain in my side as I leaned over to turn on the lamp on the bedside table.

The bed beside me was empty. Sam was gone.

THIRTY-ONE

HECTOR

THE HOT PULSE of pain drummed through me. The blows came from all directions. I curled in on myself on the arena floor, unable to avoid the pulverizing blows from Kamikaze's hooves.

The roar of the Sunday crowd was strangely quiet, and I could not hear Winona screaming my name. I could always pick her voice out of the crowd. Everything slid away in that tunnel of silence when we burst from the shoot, except for her voice. But I could not hear it, no matter how I strained to catch it.

The blows stopped suddenly. The bullfighters—the only clownish thing about them was the face paint—must have driven Kamikaze away. I was supposed to get up and run, but I could not even open my eyes and lift my head.

Where was Winona?

"Get rid of him," a voice said through the pounding in my skull.

The paramedics. They needed to call medical. Parts of me were broken inside. I could feel the shards grating against one another as I struggled to breathe.

"I'll do it," another voice said, and this one I recognized. He adored his older sister, and when Winona introduced me to the family, he had been just a teenager.

He hated me on sight. But since Winona and Emma disappeared, his hatred had festered into something entirely more dangerous.

I recognized obsession. I understood it. I knew he would try to kill me one day. He had simply been biding his time until he thought he could do it and get away with it.

And today was that day.

I realized with a start I was not ground into the dirt on the arena floor by a rank bull.

"I don't care how messy you are, just don't forget to clean up after yourself," the first man said.

"When I'm finished with him," Jack said, "there won't be enough left for the crows. I need access to the north barn."

"Probably going to scalp him," another voice murmured. "Dirty Injun."

The words were followed by the sound of a blow and a yelp.

"Keep your insults behind my back unless you want me to rearrange your face," Jack snapped. "Toss him in the back of the Gator. I'm not dragging him all the way there."

Rough hands grabbed me, and I could not keep a cry of agony contained. Then all went dark.

"MAGGIE," A VOICE SAID, low and urgent. I started. Maggie could not be here. "I need you to record this conversation. Right now." I faded, drifting on waves of pain, before I heard, "—calling the police—north barn—ambulance."

I lost track of the one-sided conversation until I heard

Jack's voice close by. "You crazy bastard. What were you thinking?"

"Winona," I whispered.

SIRENS WAILED IN the distance, a battering ram against the pounding in my head.

"The cavalry," a voice said nearby. I struggled to place it. "About damn time."

I lost time between those words and the shouting that hit me like a sudden blow. I could not make sense of the cacophony until one voice said, "Jesus, what is this place?"

"—think we need to call in Fish and Wildlife—"

"—assaulted the senator—"

"—under arrest—"

"—sir, can you—"

The words swirled around me. It was like being caught in a whirlpool, and I could not keep my head from going under.

I GROANED AT the white flair of light that bit at my eyelids and tried to lift a hand to shield my eyes. The movement was snared as metal bit into my wrist.

"Just relax," a voice said softly. "You're in the hospital, Hector."

I tried to blink my eyes, but they only opened in slits. It felt as if there were a jackhammer on a rampage in my head. A knife of pain was lodged in my side and in my back. The rest of my body hurt so fiercely I could not distinguish one ache from another.

"Are you in pain?" Maggie. It was Maggie's low voice spoken near my ear. "Don't try to speak. Squeeze my fingers."

My hand clenched around hers before I could control the motion.

In a few moments, I heard another voice, one I did not know, and then there was cool relief from the pain that swept through my veins.

"You stupid idiot," Maggie whispered, and then the darkness sucked me under.

WAKING WAS A painful experience accompanied by the alarming surge of nausea.

"Sick," I managed to gasp, and hands were immediately there to roll me to my side and thrust a bucket beneath my face.

Vomiting was even more painful than waking. When my stomach was empty, I let my head hang off the side of the bed. A cool, damp cloth bathed my face, and then I was eased back into the bed.

"Let me get him something for the nausea," a nurse said softly.

I could not find the strength to open my eyes. My throat was raw, but I was afraid that if I asked for water even that would come up with the heaving in my stomach. I shifted restlessly, sucking in a breath at the discomfort. Metal clanged as the handcuff tethering my wrist to the bedrail wrenched my arm when I tried to move.

"Can you please take this ridiculous thing off of him?" Maggie's voice snapped like the crack of a whip.

"I can't do that," an unfamiliar voice said. "He's still under arrest."

"You haven't charged him," another voice said, and I realized William was in the room.

"Only because Senator Larson is in surgery having his jaw wired shut. We need to speak with him first."

"This is bullshit," Maggie said. "Can't you see he—?"

"Maggie," I whispered.

Her hand clasped mine immediately, and I felt the ghost of her other palm against my swollen face. "I'm here, Hector."

"Frank?"

"He's at my house. He's fine," she assured me.

The squeak of rubber-soled shoes alerted me to the nurse's return to the room. "I have some Zofran," she said. "That should have you feeling better in no time."

I tried to cling to Maggie's hand, but the darkness swept over me once again.

"GRADE THREE CONCUSSION, broken nose, punctured lung, broken ribs, lacerated kidney." I listened as the doctor listed off the litany of my injuries. "You're lucky to be alive, Mr. Lewis."

At the moment, I did not feel lucky. I felt like I had been through a meat grinder.

"We've told the sheriff's department that we will be keeping you for several days for observation." The doctor must have seen the look of protest on my face, because he nodded toward the cuff chaining me to the bed. "You don't have much of a choice right now."

I did not have the energy to argue.

"Just focus on resting right now," the doctor said. "And I think you should consider pressing charges yourself."

As the doctor left the room, William strode in with

Edwards, the ranger from the Yellowstone Law Enforcement Services Branch.

"Jesus, Hector," Edwards said. "I told you to give me a little time, not blaze in on your own."

"Can you nail the bastard?" I asked, voice scraping along my throat.

Edwards's smile was edged. "Oh yeah. Someone called 9-1-1 anonymously to report that you attacked the senator. Whoever it was led us right to his processing barn, where you were being held. Police called Fish and Wildlife when they saw the grizzlies." He pulled out his phone, clicked on the screen, and extended it toward me. The handcuff clinked against the railing and hampered my reach for it. He stepped forward and placed it in my hand. "This doesn't help his case either."

His phone was open to a news story released this morning in the *Bozeman Daily Chronicle* about a photograph that surfaced of the senator proudly displaying a dead bald eagle. There were millions of hits already on the article and thousands of comments.

If it would not have hurt so much, I would have chuckled. The kid had come through for me.

"There are more photos like this," I said to Edwards. "I have names and dates. My wife began documenting this operation years ago."

I gave him the name and address of the kid in Bozeman who was working on the photographs. When he left, I glanced at the deputy from the sheriff's department.

William followed my gaze. "Can you give us a moment?" he asked.

The deputy looked reluctant, but he moved out into the hallway.

I lowered my voice. "Where's Jack?"

"Detained with the rest of Larson's men for questioning." He glanced toward the door. "I don't think anyone realizes he was the anonymous caller."

"Faye and her son?" I whispered.

"Safe," he said, voice just as low. "They're at Jack's."

I closed my eyes.

"How are you feeling?"

"About like I did when I was trampled by a bull," I said.

"What were you thinking?" he asked. "His men would have killed you, and you would've been staked out as bait on his next hunt."

I leaned my head back against the pillow. "My head hurts too badly to have this discussion."

He snorted and fell silent for a moment. "Don't think that excuse is going to work for very long with my mother."

Blacks can still be lynched. How would your friend look with a rope around her neck? I forced my eyes open and met his gaze. "If I go to jail, I need you to stay in town and make sure none of this blows back on her."

"I think with the story that just broke, you're not going to go to jail."

"Please," I said.

His gaze sharpened on my face. "Something you want to tell me, Hec?"

The last photo from the camera in the safety deposit box flashed across my mind, the desk and papers a blur in the bottom half of the print. In the edge of the frame, the shadowed figure of a man in a darkened doorway.

Hector, if something happens to me...

Something had happened to her, and the knowledge ate at me.

How often had she lain awake at night consumed with fear for the people she loved? How many risks had she taken to try to preserve the ecosystem she loved so much? How badly had he hurt her after she took that last photograph?

"Hector?" William asked, voice quiet.

"Nothing to tell," I said. This was mine to bear.

THIRTY-TWO

FAYE

"SAM?" I STRUGGLED to keep the panic from my voice as I searched the cabin. He was nowhere to be found inside. I staggered outside. "Sam!"

The moonlight was a heavy blue, and the night shadows were deep. The woods were clustered close around Jack Decker's cabin. Nothing but silence answered my frantic call.

He was gone, and I knew there was only one place he would go. Home, to the inn. I remembered the creak of a floorboard underfoot earlier and knew he had heard William's words.

I hurried back inside and into the bedroom. I pulled out drawers in the bureau, searching through them, and felt along the tall shelf overhead in the closet. If Jack kept my Beretta Pico I had on me after the accident, he had hidden it too well for me to find.

In the bathroom, it appeared Jack was in the process of mounting a towel rod on the wall. A screwdriver was left on the counter. I picked it up and slipped it into the waistband of my leggings in case I needed to pop a lock at the inn. I found the key to William's car under the pillow on the bed.

In the car, my hands shook so badly it took me three tries to insert the key into the ignition. Kevin would have the inn watched. If he had already spotted Sam, he would be long gone, and I would never see him again.

I kept a tight lid on my panic as I drove toward Raven's Gap. The clock on the dashboard said it was just past midnight. When I reached town, I pulled off and parked around the side of Ed's Garage, the mechanic shop owned by Jack's father. I avoided the sidewalks and lit pathways and instead cut through alleys and backyards.

A dog barked nearby, his alert at my presence echoing through the night. I froze in the shadows between houses and waited for lights to flick, but all remained dark and quiet. I crept on, moving into the narrow stretch of woods. The shadows felt sinister and grasping, and I fought the urge to run toward the dim glow of streetlights I could see through the reaching fingers of the trees.

When I did reach the edge of the trees, I stopped and ducked into deeper shadows. I had a clear vantage point of the inn and the street. The street was empty. There were no strange cars parked along the edge. The semicircular drive in front of the inn was lined with cars, but I recognized them as the guests' vehicles. I could see no one and nothing that indicated the inn was being watched.

Even so, I cut back through the trees until I was out of sight from the road and circled behind the houses across the street all the way to the dead end of the cul de sac. There were no houses on this side of the street, and I crept carefully down the embankment to the river's edge.

The route led me straight to the back of the inn, and again I hesitated, hidden in the shadow of the trees, watching. The lawn was exposed. For anyone observing, my movements toward the inn would not go unnoticed. It was a risk I had to take.

I was not certain where Sam gained entry to the inn, but I left the sanctuary of the woods and shadows and hurried toward the back deck. The deck wrapped around the inn, which was built into the hillside with the front at ground level and the back of the building on seven-foot stilts. The side and front doors to the inn were likely all being watched, but I was counting on the back not being guarded, since there was no access into the inn unless one was prepared to climb.

I pulled an Adirondack chair from where it was stored between two kayaks and a canoe and dragged it into position against one of the deck's support beams. I stepped into the seat and then climbed to the arms of the chair before carefully balancing on the back of the chair. The Adirondack tilted with my weight, but the beam it leaned against kept the chair from tipping as I reached up and caught hold of the deck's railing.

My knee and ankle protested viciously as I hooked a foot over the edge of the deck, and my ribs shrieked as I pulled myself up. I clung to the deck railing, quivering with the strain and struggling to calm my breathing. The feeling of being so exposed urged me to rush, but I moved carefully as I adjusted my grip and hoisted myself over the railing onto the deck.

I dropped into a crouch. There were no shouts to alert my presence, no movement within the shadowed interior of the inn. The deck remained empty.

I crept to the sliding glass door that opened off of the great room. The glass door had always made me nervous. They were notoriously easy to pop open. When I first bought the inn and was working on renovations, I used a security bar to give me peace of mind about it. Once the inn opened to guests, I knew I could not keep the place locked up like a fortress. I removed the security bar and purchased a security system for the wing of the building we lived in.

Tonight, the door was a boon. I knelt beside it and slipped the screwdriver from the waistband of my leggings. I made short work of jumping the door off its track. I caught the glass door before it fell, moving it aside and propping it against the exterior wall.

I tucked the screwdriver back into my waistband before I stepped into the inn. I moved away from the moonlit threshold and stood with my back to the wall, letting my eyes adjust to the dark interior. My eyes roved the room, looking for movement, for shadows not consistent with the shape of furniture, but I saw nothing.

Instead of putting me at ease, the stillness and quiet only set me further on edge. My footsteps were silent as I moved through the inn, and I found myself holding my breath.

Breathe, I reminded myself as I moved through the sunroom and into the kitchen.

I crept down the hallway, and it felt so much like the nightmare that had haunted me for the last five years that I had to stop and brace a hand against the wall to ground myself.

I looked to the wall immediately to my left, expecting to see the framed photograph. The glass in the frame would be shattered, fractures spread in a corona from where a fist had been driven into our smiling faces.

But this was not the same hallway. The fractured photograph was not there.

The door to our apartment was ajar. I eased it open, braced for Kevin or one of his men to lunge at me. The living room was empty. I let out a shuddering breath.

Light flickered in Sam's bedroom. When I crossed to the doorway, I found Sam kneeling in front of his dresser. As I watched, he pulled the shelf free from its rollers, set it aside, and reached into the cavern left behind.

He pulled something free from this secret hiding place.

"Sam," I said quietly, trying not to scare him.

A sound like a frightened, cornered animal came out of him. He started violently and spun toward me, blinding me with the beam of his flashlight. He lowered the light as I moved into the room and knelt beside him.

I held out my hand, and he hesitated for a moment before reluctantly placing what he held in my palm. At first, I thought it was a set of marbles, but when I realized what they were, I had to check my reaction to lurch away and drop them.

Four eyeballs peered back at me from the palm of my hand. They were fake, I assured myself. The kind of glass eyes a taxidermist would use.

"Did you take these from the senator's ranch?" He dropped his gaze from mine. "You're not in trouble, sweetheart. I know you heard what William said to me tonight, but I can promise you that none of this is your fault. Did you find these when you were at Senator Larson's?" He nodded, still avoiding my eyes. "Did you take anything else?" He shook his head immediately. "Do you have a pocket?" I asked. He glanced up at me and shifted to pull his pant pocket inside out to show me. I offered him the eyeballs. "I'll let you carry these. We need to get out of here."

"So soon?"

His voice sliced through me like a razor. I shoved to my feet and spun, pushing Sam behind me.

Kevin Hastings stood in the doorway of the bedroom, leaning casually against the frame. He met my gaze and smiled.

Once, I thought his smile was seductive and confident. That was before I realized how dangerous he was.

I backed away from him, nudging Sam behind me. Kevin did not move, but he watched us as idly as a hawk studying its prey. That gaze was calculating, and the mind behind it was ruthless and cruel.

Our bedrooms were set up with a bathroom between them, and I angled toward the bathroom. Sam clutched the back of my sweatshirt in his fist.

"What do you want?" I was relieved my voice sounded sharp and biting rather than quavering.

"You had to know I would find you one day. Faye is what you're calling yourself now, isn't it?" He straightened, and I suppressed a flinch. He shook his head, disapproval written into the perfectly handsome mask of his face. "I never gave up. I want you to know that. But I lost hope."

"Hope," I scoffed. I did not take my gaze off him as I reached back and pried Sam's hand from my shirt. "You know what I want you to do, sweetheart." I could feel his resistance, but this was something I made him practice over and over. The safe room in the closet in my bedroom was the best money could buy. Indestructible, impenetrable. "Now," I said, the whip of urgency making my voice crack. And then his small, frail little body behind mine was gone, racing to safety. I braced myself, expecting Kevin to lunge after him, but he only watched me, smile sharp and predatory. "Where are your guard dogs?"

"It's just us tonight. They messed up at the hospital and drew too much attention. This is a private matter." He sighed. "Faye, Faye. You can't keep him from me."

"You lost any claims to him a long time ago."

He chuckled, low and smooth. It made the hair on the back of my neck stand on end. "You should know you don't get to keep what is mine. Didn't you learn that last time?"

The words were exactly the blow he intended. Then again, he always knew exactly how to inflict the most pain while leaving the smallest mark.

I turned and bolted. My knee and ankle almost gave out, but I ignored the grating agony and ran. The dark bathroom made it feel as if I were running through a cave, and the predator was right on my heels.

I burst into my bedroom. I kept a pistol in the bedside table. I scrambled over the bed and yanked the drawer open. My tug was so forceful it almost yanked the drawer free from the table. I snatched the pistol from its resting place and whirled.

He hit me in a flying tackle as he leapt over the bed. The force threw me off my feet, and the gun went flying. My head bounced against the floor with such force my vision went bright white for an instant before black crept in.

He swung in a wide arc so when his hand cracked across my cheek it felt like it had the force of an anvil behind it. The slap stunned me. The swift succession of blows that followed drove consciousness to the edges of my brain.

He reared back and plowed a fist into my stomach. I retched, trying to curl onto my side to protect myself, but he straddled my chest, his weight crushing me into the floor.

"You thought you could get away with stealing what was mine, you stupid cunt? I know all of your tricks, and this time, you won't get away. I came prepared for them." His voice was winded. He leaned over me. "I'm going to rip you apart," he breathed into my ear before his teeth latched onto the lobe with such strength that I felt the skin break.

The pain was sharp, bringing awareness rushing back in when a dull, steady throb had set up a reverberating tempo through my head and face. I could not keep a whimper from escaping. He wrapped his hands over my mouth and nose, jolting me out of the pained daze, and I scrabbled for a hold on his wrists.

"When I'm done with you," he whispered, "you'll be begging me to kill you."

His fingers tightened around my cheeks. Panic flooded through me as I felt my throat work uselessly, my access to air cut off. I scoured my nails down his face and arms, flinging blows frantically, kicking and bucking against his weight on my torso, but he was unmoving, staring into my eyes.

I scrabbled for the handle tucked into my waistband, but I could not reach it with his grip on me. I could feel my arms and legs growing weighted and wooden, and darkness crept closer around the edges of my vision.

It was the same way Mary died, suffocated at his

hands. My chest burned with the knowledge of the pain she felt in her last moments. I struggled harder.

"*No!*" It was a voice I did not recognize, hoarse and small and tremulous.

Kevin flinched suddenly, falling to my side. I sucked in a frantic, raw breath that scraped along my windpipe and filled my starving lungs with such pain tears leaked from the corners of my eyes.

Even though the voice was unfamiliar, I knew it, and it galvanized me. *No, no, no.*

"Sam," I tried to whisper, but my voice was soundless.

I blinked my vision into focus, rolling my head against the floor to find Sam standing beside me, baseball bat gripped tightly in his hands, face ashen in the moonlight pouring through the window.

Kevin sat rubbing the side of his head. His smile was full of menace even as his voice was soft. "Look how much you've grown. Do you know who I am?"

Sam stared at him for a long, taut moment. His grip did not relax on the bat when he nodded. "You're the monster in my nightmares," he whispered, voice raw.

My eyes slid closed, and a pained moan escaped me. Oh, this boy. My sweet, fragile ghost of a boy. He could not see this unfold before him. Not again.

My fumbling efforts found the handle tucked in my waistband, and I clenched my fingers around it. I would not get another chance.

Kevin laughed and extended a hand toward him. Sam took a quick step back, lifting the bat like a weapon. "No, son, I'm your dad."

Sam's gaze darted to mine, and in that instant, Kevin lunged toward him.

It was the opportunity I needed. I yanked the screwdriver free, shoved myself up with every last ounce of strength I possessed, and plunged the narrow blade of the tool into the side of Kevin's neck.

Blood hit me in the face, hot and metallic, and a choked gurgle escaped from Kevin as he staggered, going down on a knee and then onto his side. His wide gaze met mine, dark in the moonlight, his blood black in the low light as it spurted over his hands when they flew to his throat. He tried to say something, but the only thing that came from his mouth was a spill of more blood.

"I was ready for your tricks, too," I whispered.

THIRTY-THREE

GRANT

IT WOULD HAVE given me some satisfaction seeing him handcuffed to the bed had drool not trickled down my chin as I entered his hospital room. Swearing silently, I turned away and fished a handkerchief from my pocket. I wiped my face and considered changing my mind.

He stared at me as I approached his bedside. Even beaten, his gaze was hard and direct. The man had too much pride by far. I was disappointed to see it had not been kicked out of him.

"I came to let you know you haven't ruined me."

"What's that, Larson?" he rasped. "I can't understand your mumbling." He smiled, sharp-edged and mocking.

In that moment, with my jaw wired shut, my tongue seeming to fill my mouth, my face numb, I wished I had killed him myself and been done with him.

I needed to do something before I lunged at him. I pulled a chair close to his bedside and took a seat. "What you don't understand, what your wife didn't understand, is that with men like me, things like this get swept under the rug."

"You'll be impeached, and you can kiss your political dreams goodbye."

I clasped my hands together so I would not clasp them around his neck. "You're right. And I'll have to pay fines. But there will be no prison time, no loss of finances I can't recover from. I'll keep doing what I'm doing, largely without consequences."

"There are always consequences."

"You're not that naive, Hector," I reminded him, and was gratified when he looked away. "That's why I warned Winona to rethink what she was going to do with the information she collected."

His gaze came back to mine. I was glad he was chained to the bed. "What did you do to her?"

I remembered the day with startling clarity. Winona had not shown up at the ranch for three days, and I thought it meant she had finally heeded my warnings and was too frightened to return. When the police had shown up on my doorstep asking about Winona, I feigned shock when the officer told me she and her daughter were missing.

At first, I thought she had run. But the more I thought about the woman I loved, the more I realized those actions did not suit her character. She was not a woman who would have run. She had too much honor, too exacerbated a sense of right and wrong. It was why I knew I would have to kill her as soon as I realized she knew.

"I threatened her," I admitted. "She disappeared before I needed to do more."

"And you expect me to believe you," he said, that blunt voice dry and scathing.

"I'm not lying."

"You're a politician. Every word out of your mouth is a lie."

I told him the truth. "I admired Winona. Immensely. Had she not been so loyal to you—misplaced as it was—I would have wanted her in my bed." His hand tethered to the railing by the cuff clenched. "I would have hated to hurt her, but I'm telling you I never needed to." I stood and moved to the foot of his bed. "I could have not only had you stripped of your badge but also thrown in jail. I've spoken with the chief, though, and the cuffs will be off within an hour. I'd say you owe me one, wouldn't you?"

"I know what type of politics you play, and I'm not interested."

I shook my head and moved to the doorway. "A little gratitude would not be amiss." I should have known better than to expect it of him.

But truth be told, I did not do it for him. I did it for the memory of Winona. I missed her every damn day.

"What about Jake Martin?" he asked suddenly.

I turned back. "Who?"

"The taxidermist."

"I've never heard of Jake Martin." I held his gaze. "I was feeling generous toward you this time. I won't feel that way again. If you set foot on my land, I'll shoot you myself."

I strode down the bright corridor. My grief over losing Winona was tangled up in relief. I mourned the loss of her swift smile, of the glint of the sun on her hair, of her laughter, of the gentle magic she worked on a horse. I frequently wished I had ignored her refusal. But even in that regard, Winona was different. She was the first woman whose *no* I had respected.

Her loss was something I felt the twinge of every day. But over the last fifteen years, I had been so damn thankful that I had not had to kill her.

I had avoided Hector Lewis for years. I hated the man on principle. He had what I desperately wanted.

But I should have known. He had ruined my chances with Winona. Of course, he would ruin this for me, too.

Winona would have loved the irony of her husband being my downfall. I could picture the satisfaction in her dark, flashing eyes.

I had expected to feel a level of triumph to see Hector broken and bruised. I thought I would relish seeing defeat in his eyes. There had been nothing in his gaze but animosity, though.

As I wiped a trickle of drool from my chin, the feeling of victory was far out of reach.

THIRTY-FOUR

FAYE

"Wake up," a voice whispered urgently. "Faye, you have to wake up."

My face throbbed with heat, and fire was tracing through my midsection. I whimpered as the darkness receded.

Awareness returned like a blow. I sucked in a gasp of air, blinking rapidly. Evelyn's face hovered above mine, tension etched between her brows.

"Sam," I whispered, voice hoarse.

"He's right here." Evelyn moved aside and caught Sam's hand, drawing him forward into my line of sight. "Easy," she said, holding him back when he would have flung himself at me.

I groaned as I struggled to push myself upright. Sam's face was damp with tears and tight with terror. I propped myself up with one hand and held the other out to him, nodding to Evelyn. She released him, and he crept toward me on his knees. He leaned against me, hugging me carefully, but his narrow shoulder glanced across my cheek. I hid a flinch and ran my hand over his trembling back.

"I'm okay," I assured him.

"He came to my room and woke me," Evelyn said quietly. "I didn't hear his knock until…" She hesitated, and I glanced at her. "Until I heard him calling my name."

I cupped the back of Sam's head as he buried his face deeper into my neck. *You're the monster in my nightmares.* I shuddered, then felt the same shiver course through Sam.

I looked around. I was still sprawled in my bedroom floor. The lamp on the bedside table was turned on. If it were not for the pool of blood on the floor, it would seem as if nothing out of the ordinary had happened. "Where is he?"

Evelyn nodded toward the living room. "We need to hurry. The inn is probably being watched." Sam moved back as Evelyn crouched at my side and draped my arm around her shoulders. "Ready?"

I told her I was, but the room swam as she drew me to my feet and my stomach crawled into my throat. I swallowed convulsively. Sam tucked himself against my other side as I swayed. It took long moments before I was steady on my feet and my stomach ceased its escape attempts.

When I could speak, I said, "He told me it was just him tonight. There shouldn't be anyone watching."

"Good. That will help." She kept her arm around my waist as she led me into the living room. "But we need to move quickly. The sun will be up in a few hours. We need to be finished by then."

I knew immediately what the rolled rug in the center of the floor contained. My legs were so shaky that my gate was off kilter and drunken. I stopped and stared, dazed.

Terror and relief coursed through me in such a torrent that my knees threatened to turn to water. Evelyn's arm tightened around me, and Sam leaned against me. A sob crept into my throat. I contained it with a hand pressed hard enough against my lips that I tasted blood. All these years of fear. Now it was done.

"I can't carry him by myself," Evelyn said.

I glanced to the windows. Dawn had not yet lightened the darkness of the sky to gray. "I can do it," I said in response to her unspoken question.

She took one end of the rug, and I grasped the other. It was heavy, far heavier than I anticipated. I staggered at the awkwardness of carrying it.

"Close and lock the door," I told Sam.

He darted back into the bedrooms as Evelyn and I maneuvered into the hallway. When the door closed behind us and the lock tumbled into place, he reappeared at my side carrying his baseball bat. My heart ached for him.

It took us long, tense minutes to get the rolled rug through the inn to the side door leading off of the dining room.

"Wait here," Evelyn whispered, easing her half of the burden to the ground.

She darted outside, and a moment later, her new hatchback pulled around the side of the inn and backed up to park at the bottom of the steps leading down from the deck.

Anyone passing on the road could have seen us struggling to load a heavy, thickly rolled length of rug into the back of her vehicle. But the road remained dark and empty.

We had to lay the backseat flat to fit him into the back, and even then the end of the rug jutted up between the driver's seat and the passenger's seat.

Sam sat in the floorboard at my feet with his head resting against my knee. Evelyn drove, not flicking on her headlights until she turned onto the state road leading through town. Her gaze darted between the road ahead and the rearview mirror, but her hands were steady on the steering wheel.

I watched the side mirror as she drove out of town, but the road behind us remained deserted.

When we were almost to Gardiner, she turned off the state road. The Yellowstone River curved north in an oxbow. An old track angled off of the state road and crossed the curve of the river over a narrow single-lane bridge. The spring thaw had the river flowing high and white under the bridge.

The bridge did not appear to be well used any longer. It was more suitable to traffic on foot than on wheels. But Evelyn drove slowly across the rickety planks. I did not realize I was holding my breath until we reached the far side of the river.

The old road was more of a trail, though it had seen more traffic recently with the FBI coming and going from the area. The turnoff five miles down the road was almost hidden by the spring overgrowth. Evelyn pulled carefully down the rutted lane. When we rounded a curve, the derelict ruins of the old Labelle Hot Springs Resort were a dark shadow against the night-cloistered woods.

"The FBI has been over this area with a fine-tooth comb for months," Evelyn said. "All the women Jeff buried here have been found. No one will think to look here when they start to search."

I studied Evelyn's face in the pale moonlight. Her words were matter of fact, but her face was set in tense lines. She pushed her glasses up her nose before turning off the car and opening her door.

The greenhouse I heard about had been torn down. The thorny tangle of rose bushes that had been hacked down lay at the back of the ruins of the resort like discarded carcasses. The breeze that drifted through the trees made the yellow police tape seem to crawl across the ground to investigate our movements. I scuffed it aside with the toe of my shoe when it wandered too close.

Much of the work of digging a grave had already been done for us by law enforcement. They had dug up the bed of roses that served as a tomb for Jeff Roosevelt's fifty-six known victims. I shuddered looking at the turned dirt. When I glanced at Evelyn, she stood frozen, staring at the remnants of her own nightmarish encounter with the serial killer.

She dropped her end of the rug to the ground and walked back to her car, returning a moment later with a shovel. She climbed carefully down into the pit the forensics team left behind and crossed slowly to the deepest depression in the earth. She stood beside it, staring into the dirt.

I let my end of the rug fall and placed a hand on Sam's shoulder when he moved to follow me. I pointed. "Sit under that tree over there," I said quietly.

When I reached Evelyn's side, she said, "It could have been me in this hole."

It was about four feet deep, two feet wide, and six feet long. "But it wasn't." I took the shovel from her and climbed carefully into the grave. "We'll take turns."

The eastern horizon was gray by the time the hole was deep enough. My hands were raw and blistered, and I was drenched in sweat and coated in dirt. I leaned down and extended my hand to Evelyn to help her climb free of the grave we dug. She was in the same state I was with blisters and dirt.

She flexed the hand missing her pinky, ring, and half of her middle finger and shook it briskly. As she moved to the rug, though, her steps were quicker and steadier than I had seen them since she came home from the hospital.

We hauled the rug entombing Kevin Hastings to the edge of the hole and dropped him within. The sun's dawn bled across the sky from the east.

I was breathing heavily, woozy from pain and exertion, and when I glanced at Evelyn, she leaned forward and braced her hands on her knees. I let the shovel hold me upright until Evelyn held out her hand for it.

"Almost done," she said breathlessly.

I had to sit down as she began to toss dirt over the rug in the bottom of the hole. I tilted my head back as I caught my breath, studying the dense canopy of forest overhead. I glanced over my shoulder and my gaze found Sam, curled on his side under a tree. His eyes were closed, but I was not certain he slept. The baseball bat was clutched close.

I turned back and watched Evelyn shovel dirt into the grave. Her hair was falling into her face. Her hands and arms were smudged, and there was a streak of dirt across her cheek from where she adjusted her glasses. But she worked steadily, and her face was calm and set.

I often wondered what brought her west to this remote outpost. Her friendly but pragmatic nature made her seem forthright and engaging, but there was a reserve to her, a careful distance she kept even though I knew she considered me a friend. She handled the horror of Jeff Roosevelt with a strength that impressed me.

Watching her calmly and unquestioningly shovel dirt over a man I killed assured me she had dealt with her own nightmares. And I did not think this was the first time she had helped hide a body.

We made quick work of filling in the grave and sweeping away the evidence of our traffic through the dirt. My entire body was protesting and trembling by the time Evelyn retreated to her car and returned with bottles of water to wash away the worst of the dirt from our skin.

What water I did not pour over my hands, arms, and shoes, I drank thirstily. I turned and looked back at the loamy tomb.

"I feel like I know them," Evelyn said quietly. When I glanced at her, I found her staring at the discarded, dead rose bushes. "I don't know their faces or their names. I might never know. But I think of them often and want them to know they will be remembered." She met my gaze. "I think they would understand us using their grave for someone who deserved what they did not."

I swallowed. "You haven't asked me what he did."

Her gaze moved past me. I did not have to turn to know she was looking at Sam. "I don't need to know the details."

"Thank you," I whispered.

Her gaze returned to mine. She studied me for a long moment before stepping forward and wrapping her arms around me. My ribs ached, but I hugged her back tightly. For an instant, she was the only thing keeping me upright.

Then there was a rustle of movement behind me. I

stepped back and turned to Sam. He moved straight into my arms. He tipped his head back, and I gently brushed the hair away from his forehead. His eyes studied me with a gravity far older than his years.

His gaze darted over the site of the greenhouse, and then he asked, "Are we safe now?" His voice was raw and hoarse from disuse.

We were not. I had just sentenced us to an entire lifetime of hiding, of leaving the home we had grown to love, of always looking over our shoulders. But it would not be the monster who showed up in Sam's nightmares that we were fleeing. Not any longer.

I cupped his small face in my hands. "Yes," I promised him.

THIRTY-FIVE

HECTOR

THIS TIME, I WAITED on his front porch instead of breaking into his home and availing myself of his beer and his recliner.

I sat on the steps and closed my eyes. The wind sighed in the limbs overhead, and the trees creaked and groaned as they swayed. Birds called out to one another above. I thought I could make out a warbler, a junco, and a robin. A woodpecker hammered away somewhere nearby. The sun was bright against my eyelids, mottled with shadow as the wind moved in the trees, casting the boughs into the path of the sunlight.

Spring was settling firmly over the Greater Yellowstone area. The chill was diminishing in the air, and the wind was fragrant with new growth. Frank sprawled beside me with his head resting on my knee.

I could not recall the last time I had simply taken a moment to exist with nothing on my mind but the feel of the sun and wind against my skin and the taste of the shifting seasons lingering in my mouth when I inhaled.

I felt like a fucking poet sitting there enjoying the peace and quiet of the moment. Maybe it was the head injury.

The day was fading into evening when I heard the rumble of an approaching vehicle. Frank sat up beside me as Jack's truck appeared around the bend in the dirt drive. The other man did not say anything after he parked beside his cabin and approached me.

I did not say anything either for a long moment. "You could have killed me," I said finally.

He nodded. "Thought about it, to tell you the truth. But Maggie would have been pissed."

"She already is pissed."

"Yes," he said. "But at you, not me."

I grunted in acknowledgment. "Thanks for having me arrested."

He stared at me for a long moment, and then he threw his head back and laughed. "It was my pleasure. It really was." He sat on the other side of Frank and passed his hand over the poodle's head before mimicking my pose of elbows on his knees. "We're never going to be friends."

"Nope," I agreed. "Though I think she would have liked for us to be."

He sighed. "What the hell happened to her and to Em?"

"I ask myself that every day. And one day, I'll find the answers. Larson claims he didn't kill her. He would have done so to silence her, but she disappeared before he had a chance."

"He could be lying," Jack said.

"Possibly. But I don't think so." A man had his tells, and Larson had not shown any when he spoke to me of Winona. Or when I asked him about Jake Martin. Which led me here. "In Yellowstone, you said I had gotten to Baxter."

"Shifty little weasel," he said.

"What about Jake Martin?"

"Who?"

"The taxidermist Larson had working for him before he brought Baxter in."

"Baxter has been the only taxidermist working for Larson as long as I've been around," Jack said, confirming my suspicions.

The sun gleamed gold as it sank below the trees. I stood and moved carefully down the steps. I checked myself out of the hospital today. A hot shower and a decent meal had gone a long way toward making me feel human again.

"Hector."

I turned back and met Jack's gaze.

"I'm sorry you lost your job. Calling the police was the only way I could think of getting you out of there."

I nodded. "You saved my life."

"Well," he said, "don't get sentimental on me."

I chuckled. "I'll try not to." From the corner of my eye, I thought I saw a flash of white in the trees. When I turned my head, though, I did not see her. "Winona told me once about skin-walkers."

Jack made a noncommittal sound. "A Diné legend, not Lakota."

"That's what she said. Are there similar legends in Lakota culture about people appearing as wolves?" I asked.

He was silent for a long moment. I stared into the trees, searching the shadows for the white wolf, and did not meet his curious gaze.

"In Lakota culture," he said finally, "we believe in a *wakan*. A man or a woman capable of mediating between the supernatural and the common people."

"Do they appear as wolves?"

"No, but there are a group of the *wakan* who all experience similar visions. *Šung'manitu ihanblapi.*"

"What does that mean?" I asked.

"*They dream of wolves.*"

I turned and met his gaze. His eyes searched mine.

"All Native peoples revere the wolf," he said. "We admire them for their strength and endurance, for their courage and loyalty, and for their extreme devotion to family."

Bitterness wrapped tightly around my throat. I called Frank to my side as I headed down the drive. I possessed no devotion to my girls when I had them. What I felt for them now was not exactly fidelity.

But still the white wolf dogged my steps at the very fringe of my vision.

THE LOCK ON the back door of the shop offered little resistance. I eased the door open and slipped within, Frank close at my heels.

I twisted the flashlight on and grimaced as I panned the narrow beam of light around the room. We were in a storehouse section of the shop. My light glinted dimly in the dull glass eyes of the dead animals around the room. The place was the perfect fodder for nightmares.

I crossed through the storage facility and tried the door at the opposite end of the room. It opened into a dark hallway. I paused in the doorway, ears pricked, but all was still and quiet.

My tread was silent down the hall, and I darted the light from my flashlight into the two open doorways on either side of the corridor. One was a neatly arranged office, the other was the break room I remembered from my previous visit.

The storefront was filled with moonlight, and all of the animal heads seemed to peer over my shoulder as I moved to the glass counter. The bugs within the case kept up their work even at night. I fought a shudder as I clenched the end of the flashlight between my teeth and slid the glass top aside.

I had to steel myself to reach within, and I was thankful I had donned gloves before breaking and entering as I swept the beetles aside. I could feel their creeping movement even through the gloves I wore. It was a sensation I would not soon be able to forget.

I moved the mule deer and elk skulls to the side and brushed away the mulch. Hidden beneath, beetles crawling over it, was a human skull.

"What gave me away?"

I turned, and my flashlight's beam caught Arnold Baxter in the doorway. The gun in his hand looked like a Ruger. It was pointed at me unwaveringly. I glanced at my hands to be certain no beetles had latched onto my gloves before I reached up and took the flashlight from my mouth.

"Put the flashlight on the counter," he said. "Nice and slow. Your pistol, too." I hesitated, and his gun jerked. "You can do it in one piece or with holes in you. Makes no difference to me."

"Alright," I said. "Take it easy."

Frank was no longer by my side. No surprise there with the human skull in the glass case. Though we had attempted human remains detection training, the poodle had a strong aversion to the smell of decomposing human tissue. I did not glance around to see where he was. I placed the flashlight on the counter and then eased my CZ out of the holster on my hip and laid it beside the flashlight.

He motioned with his gun. "Step aside and put your hands on your head." I obeyed with a grimace, the motion feeling as if my broken ribs were grating together. "So? How did you know?"

"You were the one who told me about Martin. But you've been Larson's taxidermist this entire time, haven't you?"

"I'm the best in the area," he said matter-of-factly. "He came to me when he first started selling hunting trips."

"And Jake Martin?" I asked. Sam had never seen the man murdered as I thought.

"He followed me one day and saw that I went to the Broken Arrow. He was able to guess the rest. He wanted a cut. When I refused, he had the nerve to try to blackmail me."

"So you killed him," I said flatly.

"I had to. He was going to ruin everything. Jake had a hot head and a big mouth." His face tightened. "Now you've gone and ruined everything as well."

I tensed as his hand tightened on the pistol. "I think you and Larson managed that easily enough on your own."

His finger moved to the trigger. "You don't—"

Frank hit him from behind, a silent, ghostly shadow launched from the depths of the hallway. I dove to the side as Arnold screamed, and his finger tightened on the trigger.

The bullet hit the case beside me, and glass exploded. I landed hard on the floor. Pain ricocheted through me. My breath stuttered in my chest, and white stars spun in

my vision. I lay on the floor for a long moment struggling to catch my breath and not lose the contents of
my stomach.

When I finally managed to push myself upright, Arnold was writhing on the ground. He had lost his grip on
the gun. I kicked it aside. The elbow of his gun arm was
clenched between Frank's jaws. Arnold swung wildly
at him, fist glancing off of the poodle's head, but Frank
maintained his grip, snarling low in his throat.

Arnold drew his fist back, but I caught it in my own
before he could strike my dog again. I grabbed his forearm and shoved his clenched fist toward his body in a
swift movement that snapped his wrist. I heard the pop
of bones even as he howled.

I patted him down roughly as he curled into a fetal
position, sniveling and moaning. He carried no other
weapons on him.

"Ease up, Frank," I said. I knelt as the poodle came
to my side. I ran my hands over him gently and found
no wound or places that made him cry out. I rubbed his
ears and peered into his dark eyes. "Good boy."

"Fuck," Arnold groaned. "You snapped my damn
arm in two."

I stood and holstered my CZ before I caught him by
the back of the collar and dragged him down the hallway. He yelped and struggled against me. His flailing
sent flairs of pain through me, and I was ready to put a
bullet in him when he aimed a kick at Frank.

The poodle leapt back before Arnold's boot made
contact. I stopped and twisted my fist into his collar
until his air was cut off. I could hear his choking gur-
gles. "I can snap your ankle, too, if you try that again,"
I warned.

He went limp, and I loosened my grip on his collar. I dragged his dead weight down the hallway. Once inside the break room, I flipped the light on and let go of him so suddenly his head bounced against the floor with a thump.

Frank padded into the room. When I pulled a chair close to Arnold's prone form, the poodle sat beside me. "Sit up," I barked at the man.

He pushed himself carefully upright and leaned back against the wall. His face was devoid of color, and sweat lined his brow and upper lip. He cradled his broken wrist against his stomach. His gaze darted to the gun at my hip. "Either shoot me or arrest me," he said, voice tight with pain and fear.

"I'm not going to do either," I said. "I'm taking a page from your buddy Jake's book. I'm blackmailing you." His eyes widened, but I continued before he could speak. "You lied about a lot of things, but you didn't lie about your wife being ill."

"Leave her out of this," he whispered.

"Elaine is her name, isn't it?" I asked, and he swallowed. "She was diagnosed with ALS thirty years ago. That's a long time for someone to live with Lou Gehrig's. It's a cruel disease." His eyes grew damp, and I knew it had nothing to do with the pain in his arm. "Let me tell you how this is going to go down. When I leave here, you are going to clean up. Go to the hospital to have your wrist taken care of. Then tomorrow, call the police. When they arrive, you're going to tell them that Larson killed Jake Martin and then ordered you to get rid of the body. And you're going to take that story all the way to court."

"That will never work," he sputtered.

"You're going to make it work. You'll do a little time yourself for obstruction, but you're going to do it, and you are going to stick to the story that Larson killed Martin." I leaned forward, and he flinched back from me. "Because if you don't, all that money you've put into Elaine's care, into making sure she's comfortable and can continue to be so for as long as she has left, is going to disappear." I had not thought it possible, but his face paled further. "If you don't, she's going to be put in a musty old folk's home with caregivers who don't give a rat's ass about her and who will let her rot away in a corner. Bed sores will eat through her flesh straight to the bone. She'll lie in her own piss and shit. She'll drown in the fluid that builds up in her lungs. And no one will sit by her bed and hold her hand and tell her how lovely and loved she is." His chin trembled, and I softened my voice. "I know that's not what you want for her, Arnold."

"Go fuck yourself." A fine tremor worked its way through him, though. After a long moment, he looked up and met my gaze. "I'll do whatever you want me to do," he whispered. "Whatever you want. For Elaine."

I patted his shoulder with more force than was necessary. "I'm glad we understand one another." I called Frank to my side. "I'll leave you to your confession. Keep your story straight. Elaine is depending on you."

"You're a cruel son of a bitch," Arnold whispered, a tremor shaking his voice and a tear finding a path down his face.

I stopped in the doorway and turned back to him. "You're not the first to think so, and I'm certain you won't be the last."

THIRTY-SIX

FAYE

"I CAN COME with you," Evelyn said.

For a moment, I considered saying yes. I had lived a life on the run before, though, and knew the toll it took.

"I don't have another ID for you," I said. "And when everything comes out, you'll be accused of being an accessory."

She blew out a breath and began refolding the stack of sweaters I placed on the bed and packing them in the duffel bag. "I was one."

A rug hid the bloodstain that we had not quite been able to remove completely from the hardwood floors.

She said she did not need the details, but I explained everything to her, the papers I had drawn up, and the history that made this necessary. I remained quiet as I loaded the pistols and ammunition into the gun case.

She caught my hand, and I paused. "I'm sorry," she said softly. "I promise, if you are found one day, I will take care of Sam."

It was the one request I made of her. "Thank you. I'll miss you," I told her, and her eyes welled with tears. Mine burned in response.

We went back to packing. I kept it to the basics. Weapons and clothing. Sam had several more bags than I did, because I could not bear to make him leave more behind. We walked outside, depositing everything in the drive.

Sam clung to Evelyn when she knelt to hug him. She let out a trilling whistle, which he mimicked, and when she drew back, her face was damp. She held up her hand. "High five, bud."

For the first time, he did not just place his palm against hers but drew back and cracked their hands together. She laughed and ruffled his hair as she straightened.

She hugged me for a long time, with her arms wrapped tightly around me. I closed my eyes and imprinted the moment on my memory. When she finally drew back, she plucked her glasses off and polished them on the hem of her blouse.

"This time, I think you should go with blonde," she said. "That color would suit you better than the black."

My chuckle was waterlogged. "Be well, Evelyn."

She turned and retreated toward the inn. "I'm not telling you both goodbye," she called over her shoulder. "And I'm not going to watch you leave."

I watched her leave, though. I waited until she disappeared inside before I turned and began loading our bags in her car. She signed the title over to me, and I gave her cash to get another vehicle.

"He hasn't been reported missing yet."

I froze at the sound of his voice, heart sinking into my stomach. I swallowed and placed a hand on Sam's head. When he glanced up at me, I nodded toward the side yard. "Go play over there for just a few minutes."

He could sense the tension humming through me, and he clung to my hand.

Hector moved slowly down the drive, Frank trotting at his side. In the crook of his arm, Hector carried a little red bundle of fur.

When he reached us, he offered the puppy to Sam. The little boy's face lit when Hector placed the puppy in his arms and the slim blue leash attached to the puppy's collar in his hand. "You'd be doing me a favor if you took this guy for a walk."

Sam glanced up at me, torn by excitement over the small, wriggling bundle he held so gently and carefully.

I forced a smile. "Go ahead."

When boy and dog were out of earshot, I looked up and met Hector's shrewd gaze. "I don't know what you're talking about," I said carefully.

Hector studied me, his gaze lingering on the swollen, bruised side of my face. He looked as battered as I felt. His nose was broken, the swelling and bruising spreading out around his eyes. He held himself gingerly, as if even standing and breathing were a painful experience.

He was silent for a long moment, and his gaze moved from my face to focus on Sam and the puppy. "One thing I've learned about the law in the last thirty years is that it isn't fair and it isn't just. Not always. Not even most of the time. The men and women standing behind the law, the ones securing the blindfold and loading the scales. They determine whether justice is served or not." He turned back to me. "Would you like some company?" he asked. When my brows went up in surprise, he tipped his chin toward the boy and dog. "The road is a lonely place." He said it as if he knew from experience.

"I can't take your dog."

Hector rested his hand on Frank's head where the poodle sat beside him. "I know a poodle breeder in the area. I contacted her the other day to see if she had any puppies available. That little guy was the last of the litter. I didn't get him for me or Frank, though."

I struggled to wrap my mind around what he was telling me. "You...bought Sam a puppy?"

He looked away, and I thought he might be embarrassed. "I know when I was a boy, there was nothing I wanted more than a dog of my own."

"I..." I was not certain what to say. A peal of laughter drew my attention to Sam, and my heart crept into my throat. He knelt on the ground with the standard poodle puppy bouncing up and down in front of him trying to lick his face. It was the first laugh I had heard from him in five years, and the knot in my throat was difficult to swallow around. "Thank you," I said around the lump in my throat.

When I glanced at him, I found him watching Sam and the puppy with a faraway look in his eyes. Sensing my gaze on him, he turned to me.

"I would do anything to keep him safe," I whispered.

"I think you've proven that," he said without a trace of irony in his voice.

"With Kevin..." I swallowed. "It was more than just physical abuse. He would have crushed Sam."

"If she knew, she would be relieved that you took him and spared him that."

My gaze flew to Hector's. "How long have you known?"

"That Sam is not your son? Since I ran your fingerprints and found the case report on Mary Gibson's murder."

The instinct to run was almost overwhelming. My

heart galloped away from me, and I struggled to slow my breathing.

"Do you need to sit down?" he asked when I bent double and braced my hands on my knees.

I shook my head, but I could not form any words yet. I closed my eyes and sucked in a breath through my constricted throat. There was a nudge against my legs and then a cold, damp nose pressed against my cheek.

I blinked and met Frank's dark gaze. The poodle stared into my face with such a canine look of concern that I could not help but smile. I straightened, and he moved to press his head against my leg. I stroked his ears and looked to Hector.

"I didn't kill her. I..." My voice broke, and I cleared my throat before continuing. "I loved her. She meant everything to me."

"Did Hastings know?"

"About our relationship?" I nodded. "I knew things would be different. I didn't expect things to continue like they had been between us. But I gradually heard from her less and less until I realized it had been months since I had seen her or received even so much as a text from her." I closed my eyes and remembered my heartache and my resentment. "I should have been more concerned, but I was busy with my bakery, and it was painful, losing her. I thought some distance would help. I just... I didn't realize what the distance signified on her side."

"How did you find out?" he asked.

"She came to me."

I swallowed, remembering the knock on my door in the middle of the night, recalling the emptiness in her eyes. She had been so silent and fragile. She was soaked to the skin from the storm raging outside, chilled and shaking. When I led her into the bathroom and helped her take her clothes off as the shower heated, I saw two bruises. One was in the shape of a hand print around her upper arm, the other a set shaped like fingers on her thighs.

"He's usually careful not to leave bruises," she said, voice so hollow and dead it terrified me.

I had also seen the burgeoning swell of her stomach.

"Stay here with me," I told her. "I'll help you."

She placed her hand against my cheek and smiled at me with such sadness it broke my heart. "There's no help for me. Not with him."

And it was true. Within several hours, there was another knock on my door. When I met her gaze, I saw the terror in her eyes.

"I shouldn't have come," she whispered. "He'll hurt you to get to me."

"Don't go back with him," I begged. "Let me call the police. Surely they can—"

"I've tried the police," she said, and then she crossed to the door.

He still had the same unwavering gaze I remembered from when I first saw him in the club. But now instead of interpreting it as confidence, I saw it for what it was. Arrogance and cruelty.

He gripped the back of her neck, and I saw her flinch, but his voice was all soft charm. "Darling," he murmured, "I've been so worried about you. It's time for you to come home."

I stood, but her eyes flashed to mine in warning. Her shoulders bowed and her head dipped, and I wanted to kill him. But instead, I let him lead away the person I cared about most in the world.

I did not see her again until after she had Sam. She showed up in the middle of the night again with just the clothes on her back and the baby in her arms. She and Sam stayed for three days before Kevin arrived.

It was the same pattern for the next three years until the day she arrived with panic written into every line of her body. Sam's arm was in a cast.

He was quieter than usual, his laughter and toddler chatter subdued as I led him into the bedroom I set up for him. I left him with the toys I collected for him and joined Mary in the hallway.

"We can't go back," she whispered. She placed her hand on her slightly curved stomach. "And I can't have this baby."

"Then you don't have to," I promised her.

I took her to the clinic and sat in the lobby with Sam sleeping in my lap while she had the abortion. I left my assistant in charge of the bakery, and we moved to a different part of the city every month. I thought it was an easy city to hide in. We managed it for five months. But his connections were too vast, and I had underestimated how ruthless and determined he would be to find them.

Mary had not, though. I frequently awakened to find her absent from my bed. When I went to find her, she was always inevitably sitting guarding the front door with the pistol I purchased balanced carefully on her knee. I knelt at her side and rested my cheek against her thigh.

"Come back to bed," I said softly. "You and Sam are safe."

"I'll just keep watch a little longer," she would always respond. "Just to make sure."

She was not the Mary I had fallen in love with, though I loved her still. She was no longer bright and effervescent. Her confidence had been stripped away, and that spark that always clung to her had been snuffed out.

I could not fix this Mary. The pieces of her had not been broken. They had been shattered and ground underfoot. I could only sweep those sharp, slivered fragments into a pile and cradle them in my hands. But even that was not enough.

When I heard the knocking on my front door, I assumed it was the concierge delivering the food I ordered. But then I heard the sharp rise in Mary's voice and the sharp crack of my front door being kicked in. The screams came after that.

I snatched Sam out of the bathtub and stood paralyzed by fear for an instant. His naked, soapy body felt so fragile in my arms. He should have cried. Another child would have. But he had been through this too many times already in his short life. He was frozen against me, eyes wide and unblinking, like a small wild creature staying impossibly still to avoid being seen by a predator.

All the while, Mary screamed. The sound of furniture being broken and glass shattering punctuated the screams. The sound of blows connecting with flesh interrupted her cries. I clutched Sam to me and ran into my bedroom, closing it as silently as I could manage and locking it behind me. I raced to the window and my hand fumbled at the lock. As I yanked it open, Mary suddenly went silent, and after a moment, I heard him calling my name.

I bit my lip so hard it bled. I would not be quick enough on the fire escape, and I couldn't risk falling with Sam. Heavy footsteps seemed to thunder through the penthouse.

I left the window open and raced to my bed, dropping to my knees just as the doorknob rattled. A whimper escaped Sam, and I pressed my hand over his mouth as I lay down and slid us under the bed.

"Shh, baby," I murmured right in his ear. My voice shook. "Shh. We have to be quiet. Don't make a sound."

I clung to him. We both flinched when my bedroom door burst open and cracked against the wall. I cupped my other hand over my own mouth to keep myself from screaming and closed my eyes tightly.

I left Sam hiding under the bed when Kevin finally left that day. The silence was so loud it seemed to echo. I crept down the hallway, dread building inside me. The penthouse had an open floor plan. As soon as I reached the end of the hallway, I saw her.

A whimper was the only thing that escaped me as I crossed to her. I was not certain how my legs carried me that far. She lay sprawled on her back, legs and arms bent at angles that reminded me of a broken doll. Her face was covered by a throw pillow from the sofa.

I fell to my knees beside her, and my hands shook as I pushed the pillow aside. A moan ripped from me at the sight of her wide, sightless, bloodshot eyes.

He had hurt her before holding the pillow over her nose and mouth and suffocating her. Her face was already bruised and swollen. Blood was smeared across her face from a split lip, and he had shoved the pillow over her face so forcefully, he broke her nose.

I rocked back and forth, trying to contain the storm

of grief welling within me. I needed to get Sam and get out of here, but I could not force myself to move from her side. I picked up her limp hand and pressed it against my cheek, choking on the sobs I struggled to keep at bay. I pressed my lips to her palm before placing her hand gently back on the floor and leaning over her to close her eyes.

She died frightened and in pain. The knowledge threatened to crush me. I would have remained by her side, but movement from the corner of my eye startled me violently.

Sam stood at the end of the hallway, eyes wide and unblinking. Galvanized, I scrambled to my feet and rushed to him. I lifted him into my arms and pressed his face into my throat.

"Don't look, baby. Don't look," I whispered brokenly.

We fled down the fire escape. I could not be certain he was truly gone and was not lying in wait. It had not occurred to me how he would twist and warp the story until I saw the news feature a day later. He had ensured there was no connection to him at all. It was a story of a lover's quarrel ending in murder. I killed my girlfriend in a jealous rage and kidnapped her son.

"She came to me for help," I said to Hector. "But I couldn't keep her safe." My fingers were buried in Frank's hair, and I glanced up to find Hector studying me.

"You've kept her son safe," he said. Something within me wilted in relief at hearing that affirmation. "And now Hastings won't be able to hurt anyone else."

I said nothing.

He did not seem to need confirmation, though. "I

looked into the case. There is a lot of evidence planted against you for her murder."

It was nothing I had not suspected. I hesitated. At the end of the day, he was still a police officer. But it was as I told him the day I went to him for help: I did not think law and order were high on his list of priorities. "If I were to turn myself in and go to trial, would I be convicted?"

He rubbed his jaw. "Yes," he said reluctantly. "I think you would be, from what I've read of the police reports. And now with Hastings... It wouldn't be good."

The keys to Evelyn's car were clenched so tightly in my hand that the metal was biting into my palm. I forced my grip to relax. "I thought as much. It's why I've never tried to come forward before." A thought occurred to me. "What's going to happen to Senator Larson?"

Some indecipherable expression moved across his face. "He's going to go away for murder. He killed a taxidermist who wanted in on his operation."

"Will that close down the poaching?"

"For here and now? Yes. It's not enough for these species, but it's a start."

We stood together silently watching boy and dog play together before Hector asked, "Where will you go?"

I made a noncommittal sound.

"You have a passport to let you cross the border? In a name other than Faye Anders, if Hastings's disappearance gets out before you get there?" he asked.

"Yes," I admitted.

He met my gaze. "Alaska is an easy place to disappear."

I understood what he was telling me. I took a long moment to study him. There was no softness to the man.

His face was lined, his eyes hard. I was not certain I had ever seen him smile.

"I hope you find out what happened to your wife and daughter."

The hard edges eased for a moment. "You and your boy better get going."

"I drew up the paperwork," I said. "The inn is yours, if you want it."

His eyebrows went up. "Why would you do that? Give it to Evelyn."

"I tried," I admitted. "She doesn't want it, though she would like to continue living here. And I did it because you don't have a home right now, and that is partially my fault."

His expression was so bemused I almost smiled. "What would I do with an inn?"

"That's for you to figure out." I turned. "Sam," I called, and the young boy scooped the puppy up in his arms and joined us. His lips trembled in a sad semblance of a smile as he kissed the little red ball of fur's head and then offered the puppy to Hector.

For the first time, I saw Hector's mouth curve as he gazed down at Sam, though his was a sad semblance of a smile as well. "I'd like for you to look out for this little guy. That pup needs a boy, and he's picked you."

Sam's gaze flew to mine. I nodded. He had to tilt his head back to meet Hector's gaze, and they stared at one another for a long moment.

"I'll take good care of him," Sam said, his voice hoarse and soft. It made my eyes burn to hear it.

"I know you will," Hector said. He reached out and rubbed the puppy's head, his hand dwarfing the small dog, before he glanced at me and nodded. He called Frank to his side, and then turned around and walked away.

Sam moved to take my hand.

"You know I love you, don't you?" I asked. He looked up at me and smiled before nodding.

I stowed our bags in the hatchback as Sam climbed into the backseat with the puppy cradled in his arms. I hesitated before closing the door, but I could see no evidence of what had previously been stowed in the cargo space.

I climbed behind the wheel and glanced in the rear-view mirror as I turned the ignition, adjusting the mirror so I could see boy and dog. Both were smiling at one another.

"Are you ready?" I asked, forcing lightness into my voice for his sake. "You'll have to think of a good name for the puppy."

Sam met my gaze in the mirror and started to nod before he stopped himself. "Yes," he said. "I'm ready."

I drove north.

EPILOGUE

THREE MONTHS LATER

"DAMMIT, COCOA!" THE woman shoved her sockless feet into her boots and wrapped her robe tighter around her. "Come back here, girl!"

But the chocolate Labrador retriever was gone, tearing into the tree line with a scent up her nose and wanderlust in her heart.

The woman grabbed a flashlight and her rifle and started out after the dog.

It took thirty minutes of searching the woods before there was a response to the woman's whistles and calls. A bark sounded in the distance. Moments later, the Labrador crashed through the underbrush back to her owner's side.

"What do you have?" she asked, but the dog raced ahead of her through the woods toward home.

The woman sighed and followed. When they reached their back porch, she commanded the dog to drop her prize. The Lab obeyed reluctantly, and her find bounced on the wood deck, gave a slight, meandering roll, and came to rest against the foot of one of the Adirondacks.

The woman dropped her flashlight.

The dog moved to grab her find from the forest, but the woman caught her collar. "Leave it," she said sharply, and ushered the dog inside. She hurried to find her cell phone.

And on the deck, the narrow beam of the flashlight lit the hollow eye sockets of the skull.

* * * * *

ABOUT THE AUTHOR

MEGHAN HOLLOWAY FOUND her first Nancy Drew mystery in a sun-dappled attic at the age of eight and subsequently fell in love with the grip and tautness of a well-told mystery. She flew an airplane before she learned how to drive a car, did her undergrad work in Creative Writing in the sweltering south, and finished a Masters of Library and Information Science in the blustery north. She spent a summer and fall in Maine picking peaches and apples, traveled the world for a few years, and did a stint fighting crime in the records section of a police department. She now lives in the foothills of the Appalachians with her standard poodle and spends her days as a scientist with the requisite glasses but minus the lab coat. She is the author of *Hiding Place*, *Hunting Ground*, and *Once More Unto the Breach*, all available from Polis Books.

Follow her at @AMeghanHolloway.